Text copyright © 2020 Pam Rhodes
This edition copyright © 2020 Lion Hudson IP Limited

The right of Pam Rhodes to be identified as the author of this work
has been asserted by her in accordance with the Copyright, Designs
and Patents Act 1988.

Published by
Lion Hudson, part of SPCK Group
Prama House,
267 Banbury Road, Oxford OX2 7HT, England
www.lionhudson.com

ISBN 978 1 78264 285 5
e-ISBN 978 1 78264 286 2

First edition 2020

Acknowledgments
Song lyrics on p. 234 from the The Scouts, reproduced by permission.

A catalogue record for this book is available from the British Library

Printed and bound in the United Kingdom, December 2021, LH57

"Brilliant, witty, and full of down-to-earth humour. Springtime at Hope Hall is the perfect 'Church Hall' anecdotal read. It brings back fond personal memories of my time in such halls, and it's a funny reminder of how similar we all are as people... similar, yet quirkily different. Enjoy!"
JB Gill, TV presenter

"Once again Pam Rhodes has created a community that you want to know more about, all centred around the activities of those who use the town hub, Hope Hall. All human life is there and is vividly brought to life as we follow the stories of people who hire it – from dance groups to drop-ins, from food banks to faith groups. We meet Kath, Maggie, Ray and the many others whose lives are connected through the hall, and see the importance it plays in their lives. Having been involved with many halls over the years, this book totally captures the different groups who 'own it' for an hour or two each week... A delightful read."
Revd Cindy Kent MBE, broadcaster

D0995875

By the same author

With Hymns and Hearts and Voices
Fisher of Men
Casting the Net
If You Follow Me
Saints and Sailors

Springtime at Hope Hall

PAM RHODES

LION FICTION

To everyone who has a favourite local hall in which they've danced, sung, played, learned, or just had fun

Chapter 1

"Mind your backs! Coffee and cakes coming up!"

Maggie negotiated her way up the last few stairs taking her to the balcony lounge where the others were waiting. Kath hastily pulled a chair out of the way so the tray could be placed straight onto the coffee table.

"Oh no," Kath sighed. "How could you? You know that I can't resist your chocolate muffins. How am I ever going to get rid of my Christmas spare tyre if you keep baking my favourite cakes and forcing me to eat them?"

Maggie grinned. "Well, I'm sure someone here will manage to eat yours if you really don't want it, especially as these muffins have just come out of the oven and the chocolate inside will still be warm and runny."

Tutting to herself, Kath grabbed a cake, sighing happily as she sank her teeth into the soft sponge. One by one, cakes and coffees were taken as the group took their places on the comfortably faded settees and armchairs arranged around the table.

"Don't tell my wife about this," said Trevor, who'd been the accountant at Hope Hall for nearly twenty years. "It's this diabetes thing. I haven't actually got it, but ever since the doctor said my sugar count is rising, Mary's become a real dragon. No sugar in my tea, no biscuits anywhere in the house. She didn't even let me have brandy butter and rum sauce on my Christmas pudding. Do you think I could report her for husband abuse?"

"Take her back a cake," suggested Maggie. "Tell her it's the one you didn't eat, but saved for her."

"That's the problem with forty years of happy marriage," replied Trevor. "She'd see straight through it. Mary knows me better than I know myself."

Kath noticed that Ray, who was sitting to one side of Trevor, had stopped eating his cake and lowered his face towards the floor. Her voice was soft as she spoke to him.

"How is Sara, Ray?"

His face was drawn with sadness as he looked up at her. "I had to call the doctor out twice over Christmas. He thinks she should go into a nursing home – but that's not what she wants. I made her a promise."

Kath nodded with understanding. "And does the doctor think she needs treatment you can't give her at home?"

"They won't give her love in hospital, will they? She's so weak now, I dread the thought of moving her."

Shocked at the bleakness in her old friend's face, which seemed to have aged a decade over the months of his wife's illness, Maggie reached out to cover Ray's hand.

"Could that care come to her? What about those specialist cancer nurses you hear of?"

Ray wearily shrugged his shoulders. "No one can look after her like I do."

"Of course not," agreed Kath, taking her time before speaking again. "Have you had any contact with the hospice?"

Determination tightened Ray's features. "We don't need that. Sara says that's the place you go to die, and she's not thinking of dying any time soon."

"Hospices aren't only about dying. They're mainly about trying to live every minute of your life without pain, with peace of mind."

"She's not going in there, and that's that."

Kath took a sip of her coffee, keeping her tone casual when she spoke again. "Someone was telling me about that new service, Hospice at Home, that's started up. Apparently, they've taken on a team of specialist nurses who are there right round the clock. They can drop in to check on things every day, just to make sure that the patient always has the right pain control and medical help. It must be so reassuring for the carer to have support when the person they love dearly is going through a tough patch. I can only imagine how lonely an experience that must be. It would be good to know there's someone you can call at any time who really understands what you're both going through."

Ray's shoulders dropped. "It's the night time that's worse. She never sleeps well, but she gets really frustrated when it's dark, because she thinks she ought to be asleep. The pain wakes her up, and then I don't know what to do for the best. She's crying out in agony and I'm at a loss to know how to help her…"

"You can't do this alone, Ray," said Maggie. "And the people at the hospice will understand that she wants to be at home."

"Will they?"

"Would you let me have a word with them?" offered Kath. "Perhaps later this week when I pop in to see Sara, one of the hospice nurses could come with me to talk things through with you both?"

Ray considered the question in silence before finally nodding agreement.

Maggie squeezed his hand. "Now, you'd better polish off that cake of yours before Kath finishes it for you!"

Brushing off the teasing, Kath leaned down to draw her laptop out of her flat leather bag, then sat back up again, running her fingers through her short dark hair, which immediately snapped back into immaculate shape.

"Right, down to business! The start of another year here at Hope Hall – and what a special year this will be. Our grand old lady is about to celebrate her one hundredth birthday and we need to mark the occasion in style."

"Nineteen-twenties style, do you mean?" asked Trevor.

"That could be fun. We'll have to think about how best to do that, because we can celebrate in different ways throughout the whole year. The date when the actual foundation stone of the building was laid was in August 1920, and that obviously deserves some sort of special ceremony in August this year – but I think our Easter Monday Fayre could also have an anniversary feel to it. Don't you?"

"What about the groups and clubs that regularly use our facilities now? Do you think they might like to get involved?"

"I hope so. I've sent out information to them all, and I'll chase that up now we're into the New Year."

"Have all those groups signed up again for this year?" asked Trevor.

Kath unfolded an impressive paper chart, which she spread out on the table between them.

"Most of the old, and a few newcomers too," she said, using her ballpoint pen to point out various bookings. "The playgroup will continue to have their regular booking in the old school hall between eight-thirty and one every weekday morning, and the Call-in Café will be open as usual in the foyer and up here in the balcony lounge from eleven to two each day – providing that's still okay with you, Maggie, as you're the one in charge of catering for both."

"That's fine," agreed Maggie. "And I'll do tea, sandwiches and cakes on Wednesday afternoons for the Knit and Natter Club at this end of the main hall, and the Down Memory Lane group at the end near the stage at the same period between two and three-thirty. Most of those ladies like to pop between both activities anyway, so it's nice when they all have tea together."

"And I'm assuming you're all right to carry on providing the meal for the Grown-ups' Lunch every Tuesday too?" continued Kath.

Maggie chuckled. "I think there'd be a riot if we didn't! The numbers for that just keep going up and up. It's the highlight of the week for so many who might otherwise not get out at all for days on end."

"Will Good Neighbours still be organizing all the travel arrangements for those who don't live near enough to walk?" Trevor directed his question at Kath.

"Yes, Good Neighbours is really growing. We're lucky to have a group of volunteers like that in our community. Oh, Trevor, tell them about the grant we've been awarded!"

"Two grants, actually: our usual allowance from the local council, and then, out of the blue, a donation of £1,000 from the Carlisle Family Trust Fund that we sent an application to a few months back. We didn't think we were going to hear anything from them, but apparently part of their remit is to support projects that make life easier for the elderly and infirm in the area, and we fitted the bill perfectly!"

"What about the line dancers?" asked Ray. "Are they coming back again? Because I usually have to make sure the main hall is clear and the PA system is set up for them on Wednesday nights. The place needs closing up after ten when they leave too."

"Yes, they're all booked in – and we're going to continue with our Open Dance nights on the last Friday of each month too. Those evenings aren't scheduled to finish until eleven, so I guess it's sometimes midnight before you can lock up after them."

"Often later than that," nodded Ray. "They always have such a good atmosphere, those dance nights – perhaps because they just feature a rota of two or three local bands who are well known in the area with a lot of their own fans who come along every time – and never want the evening to end!"

"It's a bit like that for the Rainbows, Beavers, Scouts and Guides," said Trevor. "It's a while since I've been a Scoutmaster, but I still like to pop in every now and then on Monday and Tuesday evenings and see how they're getting on. They're often so engrossed in their projects and activities that home time comes round far too soon."

"Any more day-time bookings I might have to cater for?" asked Maggie.

"Well, none needing anything that the Call-in Café can't provide or just prepare when it's open from eleven to two every weekday. And on Mondays we have to make sure the kitchen is clear and the tables in the foyer cleaned up in good time for the St Mark's Food Bank team. They open at two-thirty, but always arrive half an hour earlier than that, because they've got a lot to set up."

"Did you say there might be some new groups this year?"

Kath looked down at her notes. "I've had an enquiry from a dancing teacher called Della Lucas. Does anyone know her?"

"Isn't she Barbara Lucas's girl?" asked Maggie. "You know – the dancing teacher who used to hold her classes at the Congregational church hall. I think Della is her daughter; the one who's been sailing around the world doing dance shows on cruise ships."

"Not any more, it seems," replied Kath. "She's back home, and courting a lad she knew from school. Her mum says they're planning to get married, so she's putting down her roots back here again."

"What kind of dancing does she have in mind?"

"I'm not sure yet. She's coming in next week to talk things through. I'll report back to you all then."

"I hope it's ballroom dancing," mused Trevor. "Mary and I used to be quite good at that."

"Just not modern jive, if it's all right with you." Maggie's comment was quietly spoken, as if to herself.

Kath looked at her friend with understanding. "Point taken, Maggie. Mind you, I think those modern jive evenings are better suited to where they're usually held at the community centre on the new estate. All that energetic jiving is a bit too lively for the old bones of Hope Hall."

"Oh, I don't know," retorted Maggie. "Dave's got old bones and should have slipped gently into maturity by playing carpet bowls or joining a whist club. But the music they play at that modern jive club brought out the teenager in him. And if it weren't for that young floozy throwing herself at him—"

"He'd be acting his age, and still being looked after with love and care by his devoted wife of twenty-five years," finished Kath.

"His loss," pronounced Trevor. "He's a very silly man, your Dave. You're worth so much more than that."

"I ought to go." Ray was looking anxiously at his watch. "I don't like to leave Sara too long."

"Oh yes, of course," was Kath's instant reply. "But Ray, can we take the burden of responsibility off your shoulders a little, while Sara is needing so much of your time? You've been caretaker here for over a decade—"

"Twelve years."

"Twelve years," agreed Kath. "And we wouldn't have it any other way, because this old building is in wonderful shape thanks to your skill and care. But Sara must be your first priority. So would it be useful if we provided some help with parts of the work that you could oversee rather than have to undertake yourself – just for a while?"

Ray stiffened. "A cleaner perhaps? Someone who could do those night-time lock-ups for you? At the moment, you're on call here from morning till night. We've come to rely on you completely, but you can rely on us too. Just tell us if there's anything we can do to help you."

"I need this. It's not just the money. This is my job. I take pride in it."

"We can all see that," smiled Kath. "And we need you. We never worry about a thing as long as you're in charge of all the practical requirements of this place. No, I'm just thinking about whether an extra pair of hands would be useful right now. You'd still be in charge, in control of everything, but perhaps someone else could do the setting up and cleaning after those evening events? A temporary post, of course, until you are able to take over the reins completely again."

"Who?" Ray's expression was hard for Kath to read. She wondered whether he was irritated or relieved.

"We'd be guided by you. Who would you suggest?"

He sucked in breath between his teeth as he considered the question for long seconds of silence.

"A cleaner," he said at last. "A cleaner might be good. Someone who does just what I tell them – nothing more and nothing less."

"Right!" There was a general murmur of agreement around the table.

"Does anyone spring to mind?"

Kath's question remained unanswered during the chatter that followed.

"Let's put an advert on the Call-in Café noticeboard," suggested Maggie. "I'm sure we'll find someone who'd be interested."

"The right person," insisted Ray. "I need to choose."

"You can help me write the advert," agreed Kath, "and you'll be in charge at every stage."

Ray got up abruptly, pulling on his anorak as he headed for the door. "Bye then."

And as he set off down the stairs with their best wishes ringing in his ears, Ray had to watch his step because of the sudden mist that clouded his eyes.

When Kath let herself back into the flat, Prudence was immediately there, wrapping herself possessively round her owner's legs. Smiling, Kath picked Pru up, burying her nose in the long, grey fur as she flicked the switch on the kettle, then grabbed a sachet of food to fill the cat bowl. Purring loudly, Pru ate as if she'd not been fed for weeks and, once finished, turned to the fresh bowl of cat milk that Kath had placed beside her.

Carrying her cup of Earl Grey tea back into the study, Kath opened the laptop to check her emails. Among the long list of adverts and daily sales messages, there was a chatty update from her sister Jane in Australia, and news of a special offer from the new gym that had recently opened in town. Then her eye was caught by the name of the London hospital at which she had spent most of her working career, finally rising to the rank of Senior Administration Manager. Clicking open the email, she found it was an invitation to an anniversary reunion of colleagues who had worked together at the hospital ten years earlier. She smiled at the thought of all the old friends who might be there, then checked her diary. It was some way ahead, not until the middle of February.

Kath sighed at the challenge presented by this invitation. She hated the thought of travelling home from London too late at night. Looking again, she saw that they were asked to gather in the hospital library for drinks from five o'clock onwards. Perhaps that could work, providing she could get back to Waterloo Station before ten. The nine-fifty train would be just perfect.

It was odd how vulnerable she felt nowadays at the very thought of having to make her way across the capital city. After all, she'd spent twenty-five years in London, always fearless and confident in the frantic bustle of life there. Now that she was back in her home town near the south coast, her days were calmer and her surroundings quietly reassuring in their nearness and familiarity. Travelling alone on the underground, with strange faces around her, was something she'd now prefer to avoid.

Am I getting old? she thought, then immediately dismissed that notion as she bashed out a reply saying she'd love to join everyone at the reunion. Her finger hovered over the Send key, but in the end didn't actually press it. *Later*, she thought. *After all, it's not happening for a while. I'll think it over for a week or two, then reply later.*

It was hard to believe that it was four years now since she'd left the hospital. She'd loved her work there, knowing that her quick mind and logical thinking brought organization and progress into her section of hospital life, which could so easily descend into chaos. On her watch, timetables worked, the staff's concerns were heard, their personal needs acknowledged and the importance of excellent patient care remained supreme. If she'd stayed on, in time she might well have been in line for a place on the Board. How different and challenging her life would be now!

But her mother's illness had stopped her career prospects in their tracks. With her sister Jane happily settled with her family in Australia, there was no one else who could step in when her mum's diagnosis was confirmed as Parkinson's disease.

And so, just days after her forty-fifth birthday, with a sense of resignation that matched the heaviness of her heart, Kath handed in her notice from the job she loved, and moved back to the house she'd grown up in to take on the role of full-time carer for her mother. For the following two years, she watched as the woman she loved, and to whom she owed so much, struggled with the cruel condition that robbed her not just of dexterity and movement but, most tragically, the dignity that had always been her hallmark.

This was particularly unbearable for her mother, who had always been such a smart, active woman, involved in local politics in her later years because she believed the concerns and views of her neighbours needed to be represented with energy and logic. She'd always had deep reservoirs of both, juggling the demands of being a headteacher with bringing up her two daughters and supporting her husband in his career as a respected solicitor in the town. There was no one Kath had ever admired more than her mother, and pity overwhelmed her as she saw her mum crushed at the thought of what lay ahead after such a devastating diagnosis.

The loss of her dad a few years earlier had been bad enough, but the gradual deterioration she saw in both the body and mind of her mother as the condition progressed was, at times, more than Kath could bear. She found herself drawing on the professional manner she had acquired during her years of hospital management, remaining positive, loving and reassuringly practical as her mum's health slipped away.

And so it was that, when her mother died two years later, Kath found herself at the age of forty-seven, living alone in the family home, uncertain for the first time in her life as she pondered what her future might be. Should she consider moving back to London to take up the kind of executive management role she'd previously enjoyed so much? It didn't take her long to realize how alien that world would now feel to her. During those two years of being a full-time carer, as Kath's world had become smaller and more isolated, she sensed her confidence slipping away too, as surely as the days and weeks on the calendar.

For a while, she spent her time sorting out her parents' affairs, cushioned by the substantial inheritance that had come her way, which ensured that her lifestyle could remain very comfortable indeed. With her sister's agreement, she sold the family home and bought a spacious second floor apartment in the small, exclusive development with its parkland views and, on a good day, just a glimmer of the sea down on the coast sparkling far off on the horizon.

The opportunity to take over the role of administrator at Hope Hall came up just at the point when she knew she needed a new project to occupy both her time and her brain, which had stagnated into uncharacteristic lethargy during her mother's illness. It was the new vicar's wife, Ellie, who'd mentioned the opening to her when their paths crossed during their early morning runs around the park next to which St Mark's Church stood opposite her own apartment block.

Kath remembered Hope Hall from long ago, when she was growing up in the town. She'd gone to Brownies there, and youth club some years later. She'd had her first kiss around the back of that hall when she was fifteen years old. She'd fancied Graham Sutton for ages before he'd finally noticed her, and that kiss was a rite of passage she would never forget. She soon forgot Graham Sutton though. It turned out that his interests were limited to football and drinking, usually both at the same time. His kisses were nice, but his company bored her. When she dumped him three months later, he hardly noticed and she didn't care.

That the post was hers was a foregone conclusion five minutes after the interview started. Kath's obvious management skills and marketing experience, combined with her friendly but firm attitude – which was necessary given the various groups using the hall – made her the perfect choice. Kath's parents had been well known and liked in the town, with their commitment and expertise in so many areas of community life. Just the fact that she was their daughter was probably enough to tip the scales. This combined with the fact that, because she'd been left so comfortably well off after her mother's death, she was able to astonish the committee by agreeing to accept a very modest salary, far below her experience and qualifications. They practically bit her hand off in their enthusiasm to see her sign the contract.

On her first day in her new role, an image of Graham Sutton flashed unexpectedly into her mind as she put the key in the brightly painted, original wooden doors at the front of the building, which faced out over a small walled garden towards the road. She remembered coming through that entrance with Graham during her youth club days. She recalled how, at that time, the door led straight into the hall, with its high ceilings drawing the eye towards the carved arches that stretched in a series of dark brown arcs across the room right down to the stage at the other end. She smiled as she remembered the old red velvet curtains that had hung across the stage for years, faded and full of dust. They had been replaced by heavy, golden drapes to match the walls, which were painted in a fresh, sandy colour. This toned perfectly with the arched beams, which had been stripped back to the original pine before being coated with a honey-coloured varnish.

The entrance had changed too. Now, instead of stepping straight into the hall from that main front entrance, you found yourself in a wide, welcoming foyer, with a staircase immediately on the left, opposite a row of cloakrooms with toilets, including a disabled facility, lining the other side. The door beyond the staircase led into a well-equipped kitchen, with one hatch facing the foyer and another, including a bar area, opening directly into the hall. Scattered across the foyer were several round tables covered in pretty, red and white gingham cloths made of a material that was easy to wipe with a damp cloth. The foyer was set up to welcome locals to the Call-in Café from eleven till two on any weekday, for hot drinks, freshly made snacks and Maggie's legendary cakes. The whole area, including the new wooden partition with its elegantly etched clear glass in large double doors that opened on to the main body of the hall, had all been added after a period of enthusiastic and very successful fund-raising less than five years earlier.

That rebuilding programme had also created one of the most popular areas in the hall: the balcony lounge. The huge, airy space had been created at first-floor level across the whole of the front wall of the hall, which brought it directly in line with the beautiful semi-circular windows that had been peering down on either side of the main front door ever since Hope Hall had been built a hundred years earlier. Kath had always thought those windows looked like wide-open eyes above the pursed-lip shape of the entrance door. Others must have thought that too, because for as long as she could remember, those front doors had always been painted bright red, so the whole effect was that the front of Hope Hall looked like a warm, smiling face.

The stairs just inside the front door wound their way up to the balcony, with its huge windows shedding bright sunlight across the dusky pink walls and homely furnishings. This was where visitors often enjoyed their coffee and cakes. It was also where, throughout every day, secrets were hesitantly revealed, comfort was given and worries were unburdened – about emotions and fears, family and work, friendship and loneliness, money and loss. This was a place where it was okay to cry and prayer felt natural – where there was warmth, welcome and huge soft cushions to sink into.

The refurbishment programme had also added a whole new building to the growing Hope Hall complex. The old primary school that had been established for local children during Victoria's reign had been standing on that site for forty years before Hope Hall was built alongside it in 1920 as a memorial to all who'd lost their lives in the First World War. Now, with the construction of a new connecting corridor, it was possible to walk straight out of a side door of Hope Hall into the old school building, where new washroom facilities had been installed, and former classrooms had been converted into meeting rooms of various sizes. Kath's office was on the ground floor just inside the school building, and the hall, which must have seen hundreds of school assemblies down the years, had become the colourful and well-equipped home of the playgroup that met there every weekday morning.

Kath snapped her laptop shut, and thought about the meeting of the Hope Hall committee she'd just left. They'd needed to get together to prepare themselves for the start of another year of activities, and although she would later write up a formal record of what they'd covered, these occasions always became a relaxed gathering of old friends who were used to working well together. It was 2nd January and the hall wasn't due to reopen until after the weekend, on 5th January. Normal service would soon be resumed – thank goodness!

That meant Christmas was over and done with for yet another year. Ever since her mum died, Kath had found Christmas poignantly painful. She remembered so many happy family Christmas Days in their old home. Now, Jane lived on the other side of the world, their parents were gone and their home belonged to a completely different family. The only relatives Kath now had in the country were cousins in Yorkshire, whom she barely knew. She'd received several invitations from kind local friends wanting her to spend Christmas Day with them, but she was too embarrassed to accept, feeling she'd be like a spinster aunt who had to be endured because it was the polite thing to invite her along. She delicately refused all invitations, saying she already had plans for Christmas, then booked Pru into the cattery and herself into a large impersonal hotel an hour's drive away. She didn't leave her room for two days, ordering Christmas dinner on room service, which she followed with the goodies she'd brought herself: several bags of salted cashew nuts, a large tube of Smarties, and a big box of Turkish Delight that she poured over a huge fruit salad so that she could fool herself she was still eating healthily. She cried over carols from Kings, chuckled at the reruns of classic old comedy shows, and watched back-to-back movies, usually nodding off to sleep before ever finding out "who-dunnit".

And now it was back to business. With a sigh of relief, Kath leaned down to stroke Pru, who was luxuriously stretched out on the settee, then headed towards the ensuite attached to her bedroom to take a shower.

"Nanny!"

Bobbie stretched out his arms towards Maggie as he pelted towards her, a two-year-old bundle of love and excitement. Hastily grabbing a tea towel to wipe the flour off her hands, Maggie scooped him up into her arms, covering his face with kisses, which made him squirm and giggle.

Her daughter Steph followed behind, carrying a couple of carrier bags bulging with supermarket shopping.

"Hi, Mum. I think I got everything. They didn't have any blueberries, so I've brought red grapes instead."

Maggie grinned at the thought of grapes being substituted for blueberries in her muffins, but knew that at home both Steph and

Bobbie ate red grapes as if they were sweets. They'd work their way through this bunch long before the two of them left.

"These can be sultana and apple muffins instead then." She smiled at Bobbie. "Would you like one later?"

Nodding enthusiastically, Bobbie wriggled until he was back down on the floor, where Steph helped him off with his coat before he dashed off towards the overflowing toy box in Maggie's front room.

"Smells nice in here. Is that a ginger cake?"

"Six of them. I thought I'd get ahead while I've got time this week. I can freeze a lot of cakes and puddings so I'm not caught short when there's a rush on."

"Fancy a cuppa?"

"Oh, yes please."

Steph filled the kettle before reaching up to take down two brightly coloured mugs from the cupboard. Mum liked her tea strong and dark. Steph preferred hers milky with two sugars. Just in time, she remembered her New Year resolution to start using sweeteners. Grimacing, she dropped two tiny pellets into her mug from the pack Maggie always kept next to the sugar jar. It wouldn't taste the same. Steph was already wondering how long her good intentions would last.

"Dad called last night." Steph's voice was hesitant as she spoke.

Without reply, Maggie picked up the dishcloth and rubbed purposefully across the work surface.

"He wants to meet up."

"And? Are you going to?"

"Well, you know I don't want to. I've told him that, but he just keeps asking."

Peering closely at a tiny speck of stain on the surface, Maggie seemed too preoccupied with furious scrubbing to answer.

"He says he wants to explain."

Still no comment from Maggie.

"And he'd like me to meet her."

The dishcloth thudded into the washing-up bowl as Maggie threw it across the room with perfect aim. Just as suddenly, the anger seemed to drain out of her and she slumped back against the work surface.

"Come on," said Steph, drawing Maggie close. "You go and get comfy, and I'll bring the tea through."

Hand in hand on the sofa, they sat in silence for several minutes, their tea untouched as they watched Bobbie pushing a fire engine around the carpet.

"He's just an idiot, Mum. I'm so angry with him."

"There's no fool like an old fool."

"I bet he'll want to come back once he's got tired of babysitting a girl who's half his age."

"Half my age too."

"This isn't about you, Mum. It's all about him."

"Look, when the man you've been married to for more than twenty-five years takes off with a twenty-eight-year-old bimbo who wears dangly earrings, tight leggings, false nails an inch long and huge, long eyelashes that are so thick they cause a draught whenever she blinks, *of course* he's comparing her to his dowdy, cuddly, mother-of-two, built-for-comfort wife. I mean, just look at her: size twelve and five foot seven in her bare feet. Then look at me: three inches shorter and three dress sizes bigger! Her hair is long, thick and shiny. Mine is mousy brown, so fine that when the wind blows it looks as if I've put my finger in a socket, and goes lank whenever I get near steaming cooking pots, which isn't a good look for someone who's in charge of a kitchen. She's everything I'm not!"

"But just look at him!" retorted Steph. "Fifty-one last birthday, works for British Gas! He's hardly heart-throb material for someone her age, is he? Just wait until she's fed up with his smelly socks dropped all over the bedroom floor, when she's had enough of that bellowing snoring of his, and his constant moaning about all his bosses at work being idiots. She'll be kicking him out in no time."

Maggie's face clouded as she considered this.

"Would you take him back?" Steph asked at last.

"He hasn't asked."

"He will."

"No, I wouldn't. At least, I hope not."

"Well, you can only feel what you feel at the time, Mum – but as much as I hate the whole idea that you and Dad have broken up, I know how badly this has hurt you."

"He's not the man I married. The Dave I remember was kind and loyal."

"And the man he's become is selfish and vain. I mean, if it were just a mid-life crisis, we'd understand that whole fitness thing he got into, but going to a jiving class where everyone else is half his age? When did he last jive? When he was a spotty teenager! He's behaving like a big spoilt kid!"

In spite of herself, Maggie smiled. "When did you get to be so sensible and grown up?"

Steph squeezed her mum's hand. "I've had a good teacher – the best wife and mother any family could ever have."

Bobbie abandoned the fire engine and went back to the box to pull out a bright yellow digger truck.

"The thing that really gets me," continued Steph, "is that her little boy is only a year older than Bobbie. And that girl of hers can't be much more than five, because I know she started school back in September. He's swapped his own grandson and a family who loved him for a single mother bringing up two children who are nothing to do with him."

The lights and noises from the digger truck weren't working. Boiling with frustration, Bobbie brought it over to his mummy to switch them on. As Steph handed it back to him, Maggie asked, "So, *are* you going to see him?"

"There's part of me that really wants to. I'd like to talk some sense into him. I want to remind him he's my dad and Bobbie's grandpa. I'd actually like to box his ears for the way he's hurt you!"

Maggie picked at a piece of cake mix that was stuck to her apron. "Darren's reaction surprised me, but of course he's always idolized his dad."

"That brother of mine is a traitor!" snapped Steph. "Going round for drinks on Christmas Eve, playing happy families! How could he?"

"He said it was very civilized. That's the word he used."

"He's a rugby player and a computer game addict. He's got no idea what civilized is!"

Maggie couldn't help but grin as she replied, "Well, I suppose in his own way he was trying to sort things out – move on to the next stage, whatever that is."

"That didn't work then, did it? Darren's the same age as her. Will she be fancying him next – or is she only interested in a sugar daddy? And talking of money, how are you doing, without Dad paying the bills?"

Maggie sighed. "I've been transferring money from our savings account to make sure the direct debits and standing orders are all paid. That won't last long though."

"Right, that settles it!" decided Steph. "I'm going to ring him this evening and arrange to meet up with him somewhere completely neutral. It's time that father of mine was told a few home truths."

Chapter 2

The advert looking for a cleaner was pinned up on the Call-in Café noticeboard before the doors opened on the first day of the new Hope Hall year. By the time Maggie shut up shop on coffees and snacks three hours later, she'd already had two enquiries. One was from a pensioner who was in the habit of nodding off whenever she was left alone in a seat for more than ten minutes, and the other came from a young mum with three children under the age of five. She looked constantly harassed and probably didn't have a spare minute to call her own. It didn't take much to see that a few extra pounds a week to spend on her children would come in handy, but Maggie didn't feel that a woman who already had such a lot on her plate would be quite right to help out Ray when his own peace of mind and ability to cope were so fragile.

It was the following day, when more than thirty members of the Grown-ups' Lunch Club came in for their Tuesday treat that the subject of the job vacancy came up again.

As usual, Kath had organized volunteer drivers for all the members who needed transport to bring them to Hope Hall, and then take them back home again later. The Good Neighbours scheme was an arrangement through which volunteers were able to offer help to those who needed it in a variety of ways. Mostly, that help was essential and practical, but the scheme also catered for more frivolous activities, like outings or entertainment – the kind of small luxuries that added the occasional sparkle to an elderly or housebound person's life. A small fee would be given directly to the volunteer driver by whoever had booked them, and the rate decreased if the car was shared. That meant that often a small group would decide to book transport to the out-of-town supermarket, or the nearest big town with a good shopping centre. For those who lived alone, often without family members on hand to break the long hours of solitude behind their own front doors, the opportunity to travel, laugh and share time together was a real treat.

Other jobs could be ordered through Good Neighbours too. Kath had the contact details of plumbers, handymen, carers, chiropodists, cooks and childminders – all of them local, and good-hearted enough to want to share their skills with those in the community who needed help with things that they simply couldn't do or afford themselves. Charges were always kept low, and if someone genuinely couldn't afford the service they required, Kath could tactfully waive the fee. It had soon become clear, though, that for most of these pensioners, however tight their budget, there was dignity to be found in "paying your way". It was a scheme that worked for everyone.

Maggie heard Shirley Wells before she saw her.

"Blanche!" Her voice was like a foghorn as it pierced the air from the serving hatch where she was standing, right across to the other side of the foyer, where a tiny lady in a grey coat and headscarf was about to disappear into the Ladies.

"Sorry. She's stone deaf!" apologized the caller, before yelling again. "Blanche, do you want a sandwich *and* a chocolate cake, or just the cake?"

A helpful lady also in the queue for the Ladies stopped the unsuspecting Blanche and turned her round to look towards Shirley while repeating the message loudly and clearly into her hearing aid.

"She says do you want sandwich *and* a cake, or just a cake?"

"What sort of sandwich?" asked Blanche.

"What sort of sandwich?" the helpful friend shouted over to Shirley.

Shrugging her shoulders with a huff, Shirley turned back towards the counter to ask Maggie what was available.

"Cheese, ham on the bone, egg mayonnaise, roast beef, prawn salad, sausage and brown sauce, tuna and cucumber…"

Shirley held up her hand to stop Maggie in full flow. Turning towards Blanche, she bellowed across the hall, "Strawberry jam. Your favourite!"

Once again, that message was relayed by the helpful friend.

Blanche's face lit up at the news. "*Two* sandwiches *and* a piece of chocolate cake, please!"

"You know her well then, do you?" observed Maggie.

"I'm her carer. Well, not officially, but she's my neighbour and she's always been good to me, and she hasn't got any family worth having now, so I keep an eye on her."

"Does she live alone?"

"Her husband died years ago, and that good-for-nothing son of hers hasn't been near her since the funeral, when he realized there wouldn't be any money coming his way. I just make sure she has a good meal every day, and that her house is neat and tidy. It was always that way when I went to visit her as a kid, and she can't do housework herself now. I'm a bit OCD about tidiness, if the truth be known. Horrible habit to have. I drive everybody crackers making sure everything is clean and put away. I just know, though, that it would upset her if her house was left in a pickle, so I do it for her."

"What do your own family think of that?"

"Aww, they're all big and ugly enough to look after themselves now. After all these years, I've got my husband, Mick, well trained in chores around the house, and he's at work all hours anyway. We've got two boys and a girl. My eldest son lives in Bristol, so he's a couple of hours' drive away. His younger brother is living with his girlfriend on the other side of town, and my daughter got married last year to a police sergeant. They moved up to Yorkshire four months ago."

"You're not working then?"

"No. I'd like to, now I've got a bit more time on my hands, but who'd have me? I haven't got any qualifications worth having, and I can't stand idiots. Who wants a woman with an OCD tidiness fetish and a very big mouth?"

"Funny you should say that," replied Maggie, pointing towards the noticeboard.

The interview was organized for two days later. Kath and Ray were waiting in one of the school meeting rooms when Maggie shepherded Shirley in to meet them. Kath was immediately struck by Shirley's choice of interview outfit. She was wearing very high stiletto heels, tight black trousers and a low-necked blouse in exactly the same shade as her bright red lipstick.

Her answers were confident and disarmingly honest, even though they weren't relaying information likely to persuade her interviewers that she was right for the job. No, she'd never worked as a cleaner before. No, she couldn't provide work references, because she hadn't been employed outside the home at all while bringing up her family. Yes, she was always good at getting on with people, as long as they weren't idiots who obviously should know better. Yes, she could work whenever required – providing it didn't get in the way of her routine of looking after her elderly neighbour – and she'd prefer if it wasn't on Monday nights, when she played darts in the local pub team, or Tuesdays, when her son and his partner always came for tea. However, her eyes lit up with enthusiasm as she answered Ray's questions about cleaning techniques, product choices and her knowledge of hygienic practices, especially in kitchen areas.

Finally, Shirley was asked to wait outside for a few minutes while the committee considered her application. It didn't take years of management experience for Kath to decide immediately that Shirley plainly wasn't right for the job, and Maggie was inclined to agree – until Ray came up with another suggestion.

"You can't do that!" was Kath's instant reaction. "That's unprofessional – and unethical too."

Without a word, Ray went to call Shirley back in, as Kath and Maggie looked on in alarm.

"I'd like to have a cup of tea in your home right now, Mrs Wells. Would that be agreeable to you?"

If the question surprised her, Shirley recovered quickly. "Fine. English Breakfast okay?"

A hint of a smile touched Ray's lips. "And just one more question, Mrs Wells. What would you wear if you got the role of cleaner here?"

There was a definite twinkle in her eye as Shirley replied, "Well, not this – obviously! This is my interview outfit, because this is an interview. My cleaning kit has rubber gloves at the top of the list. I wouldn't dream of scrubbing without my Marigolds…"

Maggie coughed to hide a chuckle.

"Right, are you all coming – or just him?"

"I can't, I'm afraid," said Kath. "I have a potential client who wants to start a dancing class here coming in at ten."

"I wouldn't miss this for the world," grinned Maggie over her shoulder as she scuttled down the corridor after Ray and Shirley.

Ten minutes later, the two of them followed Shirley through a small front garden with its lawn surrounded by neat rows of shrubs. She strode on ahead to put the key in the door, standing back to usher them in. A fresh aroma of lemons hung in the air as they walked through the hallway with its light moss-green walls covered in family photos that seemed to date back for several generations. In the lounge, a floral sofa and two comfy matching armchairs, on which there were various shapes and sizes of fat cushions, had been strategically positioned around a glass-topped coffee table. On its surface several coasters had been placed in an exact semi-circle around a large pottery bowl that looked as if it might be a memento from a holiday in Spain. Everything sparkled and shone: the glass table, the windows, the huge bevelled mirror above the spotless coal fireplace. The lounge led directly into a dining room with French doors that opened out on to a beautifully kept back garden, with its wooden shed painted in a jaunty turquoise that looked like the colour of the sea on a postcard from a Mediterranean island.

Ray didn't stop to admire the back garden, as Maggie did. It was plainly the kitchen that he wanted to see.

"May I?" he asked Shirley, as she appeared in the doorway.

"Be my guest."

He bent down to open several cupboards underneath the marble-topped work surface. Rows of saucepans, serving dishes and jugs appeared, all stacked in size order. The cupboards at eye level revealed tumblers and wine glasses arranged with military precision, and rows of tins, jars and packages lined up, Maggie suspected, in strict alphabetical order.

Ray inspected the sink and draining board, wiping his finger over the shining surface. Then he leaned down to peer closely at the ceramic hob. Finally, he turned to Shirley.

"You'll do," he said. "You'll do very nicely. When can you start?"

Shirley eyed him thoughtfully. "I know you're the boss, but I have my own way of doing things and if I think my way's better than yours, I'll tell you."

"And I'll agree if you're right – but I'm no pushover. I believe in high standards."

"Then you'll do nicely for me too!"

Ray nodded agreement, his smile broader now. "So, what do you have to do to get a cup of tea around here?"

"Well, there I was, sailing around the Caribbean on a grand cruise ship, and it suddenly struck me. I missed home. I missed Steve. So, when he sent me that text saying he'd been thinking about us getting married, I just knew what I needed to do. I mean, I love dancing professionally – of course I do, it's all very glamorous – but I feel as if I'm through with that now. I'm ready to settle back here with Steve. He's my future. This is where we'll bring up our little family. But I can't give up dancing completely. I went to dance college in London for three years, you know. I got all my teaching qualifications then, and I've never used them. Well, it's time I did. I've made up my mind. I'm going to start my own dance classes."

Della Lucas's knees were practically touching Kath's in her enthusiasm to explain her feelings and her plans.

"You may know my mum Barbara. She ran the big dancing school in the town for years, although she's retired now."

Kath smiled. "Of course. She held classes at the Congregational church hall for a long time, didn't she? Her pupils put on their Christmas show here a couple of years ago. The children were excellent."

"Yes, Mum's always been great with putting together productions of any sort, and I'm hoping some of her skills have rubbed off on me."

"So, how can we help you?"

"I'd like to run my classes here."

"What sort of space and facilities would you need?"

"The main hall would be good. I used to do ballet displays in this hall myself when I was little. I was only three when I started, and they all spoilt me because I was the youngest in the class. Everyone said I was so cute. I've not stopped dancing since."

"So, is that what you have in mind? A ballet class?"

"No. I don't think the kids want that nowadays. Street dancing, body popping, break dancing – that's what they're into now."

Kath laughed. "Just those names sound terrifying. Can you do all that?"

"Well, to be honest, it's not really my thing, but my body is my work instrument, highly tuned and fully flexible, so I can do anything I like with it. Whatever the dance is, I can definitely teach

31

it, because I'll adapt the moves to suit the kids I'm working with. No worries."

"What age group would you be aiming at, and how many would you envisage attending the class?"

Della shrugged. "Oh, the kids will flock to learn this stuff. Teenagers mostly – up to about fourteen or fifteen years old, I suppose – but I'd like to start them younger, perhaps from about ten onwards? So, for that street dance class, if I get the age group right, I reckon I'd get at least twenty coming regularly, but it could easily end up being twice that number."

Kath nodded. "And the other classes?"

"Well, I've always loved tap dancing, and that's really coming back into fashion now. So I plan to start a tap class – great for fitness, great for rhythm, great for kids, because it's so easy to learn the basics —"

"I worry that it wouldn't be quite so great for our wooden floor that cost a fortune just five years ago," interjected Kath.

"No problem at all," replied Della, her lips pursing like Betty Boop's. "Your floor will do perfectly for tap dancing."

"But will tap dancing be perfect for our floor – especially if the hall is full of children who are absolute beginners wearing heeled shoes fitted with metal plates on the sole?"

Della stiffened. "I teach my pupils to tap properly. If they do as they're told, there will be no scuffing at all."

"And if they *don't* do as they're told? If there's even the slightest chance of damage to our hall surface, I'm afraid that particular class is out of the question."

"My dancers will *not* scuff that floor."

"Then you must understand that there needs to be a clause in any contract we enter into with you, making it clear that you will have to take full personal responsibility for damage caused that way, or any other, as a result of your classes. Are you prepared for that?"

"Fine!" retorted Della, glaring directly into Kath's eyes. "I'm a professional and I will run these classes to professional standards, whatever the age of my pupils. I'm only interested in teaching people who really want to be there, whatever kind of dance is involved. If they muck around, don't listen or think it's okay to do their own thing, they'll soon realize I won't be doing with that. They'll be out on their ear!"

Kath found herself smiling at the young woman's confidence, which was very reassuring. Sensing victory, Della sat back in her chair as the atmosphere relaxed.

"So just the two classes then?"

"Well, maybe not. I'm worried about my nan."

"Oh?" Kath was taken aback by the sudden change of subject and wondered where the conversation was going.

"She used to be a bundle of energy, running her own shop, always cleaning, cooking, walking everywhere. I could never keep up with her when I was little."

"Really?" replied Kath, wondering where this was leading.

"But she's stiff as a board now. She groans every time she stands up and is always complaining that her neck hurts, or her back or feet."

"I see," said Kath, who didn't really see at all.

"The thing is, our bodies are like cars. They need the right maintenance. Nan's not maintained her body, and her mind's not in good shape either. Since Pops died last year, she doesn't go out much. She watches telly all the time, and she's started talking about having a chairlift put on her stairs, would you believe! She's obviously going about things completely the wrong way – anyone can see that. So, I've made a decision. I'm going to save her from herself."

"She could well be suffering from depression after the loss of her husband – and is possibly very tired after the busy life she's had. How old is she?"

"Really old. She was sixty last year."

Given that her fiftieth birthday wasn't far off, Kath bristled. "Oh, I think there may be hope for her yet—"

"There will be if she gets the right exercise. And that got me thinking. There are lots of old people out there who aren't looking after themselves properly, so I'd like to run an exercise class for oldies."

"They may not like being called that."

"Oh, I'll think of a name – that's just a detail. But what I'm planning is a class that's split into two. The first part would be armchair exercise, for people who can't stand for long or who are a bit shaky on their pins, and then I'll move on to more mobile dance moves that will just get them going. Lots of old songs they can sing along to, a bit of old-time dancing thrown in, but plenty of good, healthy moves too. It will be like zumba for the aged."

Kath put her hand up to her mouth, hoping to hide the way her lips were twitching with amusement.

"Well, that's certainly an interesting idea, but you *will* have to work on that title. I reckon both those suggestions could go down very well, though. A lot of people of fifty and above come here for a variety of activities throughout the week. I can think of quite a few who might be interested in a class of that sort."

"That's settled then. What else do you need to know?"

"Do you see these three classes being run in one long session, or would you want to spread them throughout the week?"

"All in one session on a weekday evening would work best for me. Supposing I start at four o'clock, then I'd run those classes for grannies until about five. After that, there would be a bit of a break while the groups change over before I start the tap class from five-fifteen until six-fifteen. Then I'd have another break of fifteen minutes before the street dancing class gets underway at six-thirty until seven-forty-five. A quarter of an hour for clearing up, and we'll be out by eight. How does that sound?"

"It sounds as if you have certainly put a lot of thought into all this. We'll need to talk in detail about fees, insurance and any particular facilities you need us to provide—"

"I'd like a piano for the first two classes. There's one in the hall already, isn't there?"

Kath nodded.

"I'll bring along my music system for everything else."

"Will you need changing rooms?"

Della frowned as she considered the question. "Probably not. Most people will come dressed in dance gear or loose clothes. They might like to buy drinks, if they're on offer."

"Opening the bar, even just for soft drinks, would be an extra expense – but there's a very good coffee machine in the foyer, and a cold drinks dispenser too. On the other hand, it may be easiest if you just ask them to bring along with them whatever soft drinks they'd like."

"What night then? Have you got an evening free?"

"How about Thursdays from four till eight?"

"Perfect!"

"Well, I'll discuss your proposals with the committee and come back to you within a day or two."

Della clapped her hands together like an excited child, before springing up with the speed of a gazelle. "It will be great. I promise you, it will!"

And practically pirouetting out of Kath's office, she disappeared from view.

Jen snatched up the phone the moment she saw Carol's name on the screen.

"Where have you been? It's bedlam here. You know I can't open up the playgroup on my own. There's a queue of mums and kids standing on the doorstep."

"It's the car again!" wailed Carol at the other end of the line. "It conked out in the middle of that big roundabout near the station. Everyone was hooting at me and shouting out of their windows – and I've got Little Joe in the back. A lorry driver and his mate got out and helped me push it down a side street, but I don't know what to do."

Jen could hear the utter despair in her friend's voice.

"Have you called Phil?"

"A fat lot of good that would do. If he won't listen at home when I tell him what a wreck my car is, he's not going to listen while he's in the office, is he? He's far too *busy* for that!"

"Breakdown cover?"

"If I had it, I'd be ringing them instead of you."

Jen looked up with relief to see that the two other playgroup assistants, Fleur and Marie, had just arrived, ushering excited children and exasperated parents into the school hall along with them.

"Tell me exactly where you are, and I'll ring Rob. He'll be at the garage by now. He'll sort something out."

"Tell him I'm parked in that small layby outside the newsagents in Station Road. Can you hear Little Joe screaming in the back? He's hungry and doesn't know what's going on. Honestly, Jen, I know how he feels. I could just bawl my eyes out right now."

"I know, love. That car of yours has got to go. Look, stay put and don't worry. Rob won't let you down, whatever he's doing. He'll be there before you know it."

True to her word, a mechanic's truck pulled alongside Carol's car ten minutes later. Carol heaved a sigh of relief as the familiar figure of Rob climbed out and walked towards her car. They had all been friends since they were teenagers. The boys had played in the same football team, and it was at a post-match party when they were all sixteen that Carol and her best friend Jen had met Rob and his best mate Phil. They'd hit it off immediately as friends, falling naturally into couples who had stayed together ever since. Several years later when Rob and Jen were the first to tie the knot, Phil was best man and Carol the maid of honour. The roles were reversed the next year when Phil and Carol followed them up the aisle.

Whereas Jen was blonde and petite, Rob was tall and dark, with broad shoulders and huge hands that worked with surprising dexterity and skill as he checked one part of Carol's car engine after another.

"Try turning it over now," he shouted from under the bonnet.

The car started first time. Carol let out a long sigh of relief as she slumped back in the seat, sitting up again abruptly when Rob's face peered through the side window. He glanced over to where Little Joe had now thankfully fallen into exhausted slumber, having shrieked for most of the last half-hour.

"Tell that stupid husband of yours that this old rust bucket has got to go. You're not safe driving it, especially not with Little Joe in the back."

"Oh Rob, you know what he's like. We've got a lot of bills at the moment. Phil won't see this as a priority."

"You mean he's an old skinflint! You need a new car, Carol. Tell him!"

"Honestly, we haven't got the money to spare right now."

Rob went silent for a while as he considered the options.

"Well, you know I'm always keeping an eye out for good used cars that I can sell on. I can sort you out a run-around that's safe and reliable and doesn't cost a fortune. You know I'd see you right."

"Oh, that would be great, but the money's just not there..."

He thumped the roof of the car with the palm of his hand. "Well, Phil's got his shiny new company car, hasn't he, so he's okay. He's being selfish, Carol, and it's not right. This old banger is dangerous."

His expression suddenly softened as he realized she was near to tears.

"Look, use the car now, but if you can possibly manage without it for a day, drop it into the garage later this week, and I'll do whatever I can to check the basics and keep it running for you."

"Thank you so much, Rob. You're a life-saver. And I will tell Phil what you said."

"I'll tell him myself. I'll give him a piece of my mind, the old miser!" And with a quick peck on Carol's cheek, Rob waved over his shoulder as he headed back to the truck.

Minutes later, Carol turned into the car park at the back of the old school building. She lifted out her son and her huge bag that seemed to contain everything in the world she ever needed, then hurried into the hall, where the playgroup was in full swing, just as it was on any weekday morning. Hanging their coats up, she changed Little Joe into his soft play shoes before leading him in to join another two-year-old boy who was in the sand pit. The toddlers eyed each other with suspicion before Little Joe launched himself into the pit with a screech of delight.

Jen looked up and mouthed the word "okay?" from the table at which she was sitting with three older girls, all of them engrossed in sorting out paints, crayons and glitter glue for the art masterpieces they were about to start. Carol nodded and with a thumbs-up hurried towards the snack corner, knowing she was already way behind in preparing for the early morning break, which should have started ten minutes earlier. Nimbly she sliced up fresh fruit and vegetable sticks, then buttered and filled finger-shaped brown bread sandwiches, which she placed alongside the small, square oatmeal biscuits that she'd made at home the evening before.

Carol felt as if she didn't stop for breath for the rest of the morning, but then playgroup was always like that. With twenty children under the age of four in their care, there was never a dull moment. Time sped by, with toilet visits, tantrums and tears, along with the spills, stories, falls and giggles that claimed every second of her time until the final mum arrived, several minutes later than she should, to collect her darling offspring. Clearing up at the end of each morning was a work of art that the playgroup team had mastered to perfection. Fleur and Marie were both out of the door within ten minutes of the finish time, leaving Jen to flop down in a chair as Carol placed a cup of coffee in her hand.

Several sips and two chocolate biscuits later, Jen glanced over at Carol, who had Little Joe on her lap as she tried to drink her coffee.

"What's up with the car then? Did Rob say it needed to be put out of its misery?"

In spite of her exhaustion, Carol grinned. "Yes, but he was great. He got it working again in no time. It is on its last legs, though."

"What did Phil say?"

"Nothing. I couldn't get through to him. He was in a meeting."

"But he's rung back?"

Carol fumbled around in the bottom of her voluminous bag to pull out her mobile. Pushing a few buttons in quick succession, she stared at the screen. "Nope. No call from him."

Jen shook her head in disbelief. "You had Little Joe in the car – his son! There could have been an accident with you in that old banger, stuck there like a sitting target on that great big roundabout. And it was rush hour, for heaven's sake. It's always a nightmare then. He *should* have got back to you."

Carol plainly agreed, but took another sip of coffee rather than reply.

"How are you two?" Jen asked, in a casual tone of voice. "Getting on okay?"

"Sort of," shrugged Carol.

Jen looked sharply at her. "What does that mean?"

"Oh, you know Phil. He's always been the same. He's not a man to show much emotion."

Jen grunted. "Except for that precious old bike of his."

Carol grinned. "That precious *vintage* bike of his, you mean."

"It's a pile of old scrap metal—"

"It's a rare specimen that needs a bit of TLC."

"It's you that needs the TLC," huffed Jen. "How many hours

each week does he spend on that bloomin' bike? How about his wife and son? They need a bit of attention too."

Carol shrugged. "We're okay. Marriage is like that, isn't it? Ups and downs."

Jen took a gulp of coffee and said nothing. The silence between them spoke volumes. Suddenly, Jen reached across and squeezed her friend's arm.

"Come on then. My feet hurt and I need to get home. See you tomorrow – even if you and Little Joe arrive perched on your pedal bike."

Shirley started work at Hope Hall two weeks into January. Ray came in that morning to introduce her to the cleaning cupboard, the equipment and the key people she needed to know.

By the end of her second day, there were fresh flowers in pretty jugs in each of the cloakroom areas, and in every cubicle the last sheet of toilet paper was folded into a neat triangle as if in a hotel suite. Taps shone, floors gleamed with polish and there was a new notice alongside the basins, which read:

Please leave this room as you would wish to find it.

By order of THE MANAGEMENT

The following week, she spring-cleaned the kitchen, turning out the huge old store cupboard that had depths to it that no one had dared to plunder for as long as anyone could remember. Fearlessly, Shirley waded in, pulling out old cardboard boxes and plastic containers, and then scrubbing the walls to within an inch of the brickwork before putting only half of the original contents neatly back inside again. Maggie said that Shirley had unearthed tins, packets and bits of cooking equipment that hadn't seen the light of day for years, some of them dating back to an era long before Maggie had come in with her own modern set of utensils and preferences.

The two women hit it off straight away. Everyone knew when Shirley was in the building – sometimes for all the wrong reasons, as her distinctive cackle of laughter could be heard corridors away, wherever she was. She bellowed across the yard at one of the playgroup mums as both she, and her two young children, casually threw sweet papers onto the ground. She directed an outburst of colourful language at a delivery man who tried to leave the wrong parcel with them when she could see the right one still sitting in the van. She brushed every tiny crumb off the tables at the Call-in Café, told raucous stories to giggling groups of elderly lady members of the Grown-ups' Lunch Club, and over the weekend had washed and ironed all the curtains in the building (except the huge stage drapes, which she told Ray she was planning to steam clean in situ) so that they were back on the rails, radiantly fresh and smelling of lemons, by first thing on Monday morning.

For the first two weeks Ray popped in often, watching her work, giving a piece of advice here or a slight criticism there – but it wasn't long before he realized that Shirley had not only got everything he'd asked for in hand, but a good deal more besides. In one of their quieter moments, when the two of them had sat down to enjoy a cup of tea, Shirley asked Ray about his family. Before he knew it, he had told her about Sara, and the awful illness that was eating away at her health and her naturally sunny personality. With surprising sensitivity, Shirley understood. Kindly and firmly, she ushered Ray out of the building, saying that she'd be happy to drop in to do a bit of housework to help him out any time at all – "free of charge, I'm your friend".

Her kindness touched Ray. He had always kept his worries to himself, but he was discovering that there were several people at Hope Hall who quietly and thoughtfully let him know that their help was there if he and Sara needed it. Kath, in particular, was certainly proving to be a wonderful friend. As good as her word, she'd arrived at the house a few days after their conversation about the Hospice at Home nurses with a member of the team standing beside her. Sara and Ray began by listening politely, knowing for sure that their service wouldn't interest them at all. Half an hour and a cup of tea later, it was all arranged. A nurse would be calling in every day to monitor Sara and discuss her immediate needs. If Ray needed someone to sit with Sara when he had to be out during the day, or perhaps overnight if her pain was particularly troublesome, they could cover that time. This would mean that Ray could get his own much-needed rest. The kindly, practical, experienced approach of the whole hospice team took the couple by surprise. This was right. They both knew it as they held hands to tell Kath and the nurse that they would welcome any help available to them.

Ray's spirits were cheered even more as he saw how Sara flourished under the new arrangement. It was as if a burden of worry had been lifted from her shoulders, and he realized that *he* had probably been that burden. She loved him, and worried about the extra work her illness was creating for him. Knowing that the hospice team were as concerned about his welfare as hers, she relaxed into their care, sleeping more peacefully, eating with more enthusiasm and looking better than he'd seen her for a while.

It was an illusion though. He knew that she was fading. He could see the same knowledge in her eyes when she looked at him. He would simply put his arm around her thin shoulders and bury a kiss in her curls, sparse and thin now from the effects of age and illness.

"Love you to the moon and back," he'd murmur, and she'd smile up at him.

"Love you more."

And their lips would meet with all the sweet tenderness of a long lifetime of love and understanding.

Chapter 3

As soon as she got the go-ahead from the Hope Hall committee, Della went into overdrive promoting her new dance classes.

When Kath said she was planning to get a mention of the classes in the What's On section of the local free paper, and that a few basic posters around the foyer would probably help too, Della's expression was a picture.

"Thanks, but that's really not enough. We've got to get it out there. Social media's the way. Leave it all to me. I'll design the posters and give you the wording for the paper too. Right?"

"Right," agreed Kath, half relieved to have the job taken off her hands, half concerned about just *how* Della would describe her new ventures.

Two days later, with a flourish of excited achievement, Della laid the poster designs across Kath's desk. Kath glanced at the first one. The large lettering in the middle was surrounded by comical little cartoons of elderly people looking miserable, with mobile scooters and zimmer frames, or nursing sore backs, shoulders and feet.

Are you feeling your age? Stiff as a board?
Can't reach your toes? Come and get moving!
ARMCHAIR EXERCISE followed by DANCE SING-ALONG
for the OLD but BOLD!
THURSDAYS 4 p.m.
MAIN HALL

Kath chose her words carefully. "It's certainly eye-catching. You don't think people will be offended by being described as old?"

"They are old. That's the point. No, this poster is exactly right. It's what I want. Now, what do you think of this one?"

The next poster had pictures of shoes and musical notes dotted across it.

HAPPY FEET

Tap dancing for fun!

Beginners welcome!

5-year-olds and above

THURSDAYS 5.15 p.m.

MAIN HALL

Kath nodded approval. "That says it all. I should think that class will prove very popular."

Della beamed as she moved the last poster over to the top of the pile. "I thought you'd like that. You'd be a bit over the hill for signing up for *this* class though!"

HIP-HOPPERS

Have you the bottle for break dancing? How's your locking, waving, robotics, b-boying and dime stops?

STREET DANCING is the way!

10–14-year-olds

THURSDAYS 6.30–7.45 p.m.

MAIN HALL

"Well," said Kath, "that all seems like a different language to me. But let's get these *out there* and see how things go!"

"Hello, Steph."

She looked across at her dad, who had chosen one of the darkest alcoves in the pub to wait for her. She unwound the long red scarf from her neck and drew down the zip of her jacket as she walked across to him. He stood up as if unsure whether he should hug her. She didn't give him the chance, pulling up a chair on the opposite side of the table.

"How have you been?" he asked.

"As if you care. You left us, remember?"

Dave grimaced. "That's my girl. Straight to the point. No niceties."

She stared at him. "What did you expect?"

"I didn't know what to expect. You called me about meeting tonight. It's what I've wanted for a long time. I'm just glad you're here."

"Well, I'm not sure if I'm staying."

"Shall I get you a drink while you decide? A Diet Coke, right?"

As she watched him walk across to the bar, she realized how different he now looked from the dad she'd always known. He was wearing tight, dark blue jeans with a pale pink shirt. His hair was razor cut at the sides, but longer on top, where his natural curls had obviously been gelled into shape so that it looked as if a small, stiff busby was perched on his head. *Hang on,* she thought. *Dad's hair was going grey.* Not any more, it seemed. His locks were now a dark chestnut shade, which looked rather odd against his eyebrows, which still matched his original hair colour. But *they* looked different too! She peered at the mirror behind the bar, which reflected a clear, close-up image of his face as he ordered drinks from the bartender. The straggly long hairs she was used to seeing had been trimmed and his eyebrows flattened into unnaturally neat lines across his forehead. His face looked thinner – or was that just because of the hair cut? Perhaps not, because where was the pot belly she used to pat whenever she teased him about how paunchy he was getting? He looked lean, perhaps even on the thin side. How ridiculous! Getting fit was one thing. Trying to look as if he were twenty years younger than his actual age was nothing short of pathetic.

"I couldn't remember if you liked ice or not, so I got some anyway," he said as he placed the glass down in front of her.

I've been drinking nothing but Diet Coke for years now, she thought. Why would I expect my father to know if I like ice or not? He'd have to be interested in me to know that.

"Your mum always liked ice with her lime and lemonade," he added, as if for something to say. "How is she, your mum?"

Steph turned on him then. "Do you mean is she falling apart without you? No, Mum's too busy trying to keep everything together and sort out the mess you left behind when you walked out on her. Do you mean is she upset? Well, wouldn't you be if your husband repaid you for devoting twenty-five years of your life to looking after him by taking up with a money-grabbing single mother half his age? Is she missing you? Missing your rubbish everywhere, and having football on the telly morning, noon and night? Missing having your dinner cooked and ready on the table, and doing all the clearing and washing-up afterwards because you think, as the *man* of the household, you should be waited on hand and foot? No! What she does miss is the husband who owns half that house and knows how much it costs to run, and yet he's swanned off to pay someone else's bills without a thought to how she's going to cope all on her own."

"Once things are a bit more settled, I'll talk to Mum about those bills."

"Talk won't help. Money is what she needs. Take responsibility for your actions, Dad!"

"I can't stretch to paying anything at the moment. Mandy and I—"

Steph practically choked on the Coke she was drinking. "Mandy? What's she got to do with you paying bills that are in your name in your house that you share in partnership with your wife? Mandy can pay her own bills. Mum can't. Sort out your priorities, Dad!"

With a sharp intake of breath, he looked her straight in the eye. "Mandy is my priority."

Steph sat back in her seat, suddenly finding herself with nothing to say.

"I love her, Steph. This isn't just a fling. It's the real thing. I love her."

"You're ridiculous. A ridiculous old fool."

"I want to marry her."

"Just one small obstacle there. You're already married and you've made a mess of that. Do make sure Mandy knows what lousy marriage material you are!"

"I'm going to ask your mum for a divorce."

"Good. She's better off without you. You're not fit to lick her boots!"

"I'd like to see her – to explain."

"Don't bother. There's nothing you can say to her that's worth hearing."

"I know your mum, Steph. After all these years, I know her well. I need to speak to her myself, but I don't know how to suggest it. Could you ask her? Ask her if she'll see me?"

"Ask her yourself. Pick up the phone and talk to her. I'm not passing on grubby little messages for you."

"Darren came round at Christmas. He spent the evening with us. He got on really well with Mandy."

"Whoopee for him. He's never had any more sense than you. Like father, like son."

"He said he'd have a word with your mum."

"Why? Because you haven't got the nerve to speak to her yourself?"

His head dropped and there was silence for a while.

"For the first time in years I'm happy, Steph. Really happy."

"Good for you. How old are her children?"

"Belle is five. Marlin had his third birthday last weekend."

"Well, isn't that just the perfect new little family for you! It's been weeks since you had any time to spare for the kids in your own family. You remember Bobbie, the little boy who adores his grandpa? Do you even care that he doesn't understand any of this, and thinks you don't like him any more? Have you just turned your back on him and swapped him for someone else's kids you think are better?"

"Mandy and I wondered if Bobbie might like to come over and play some time?"

Steph huffed with disbelief. Then she zipped up her jacket, rewound the scarf at her neck and walked out of the door without a backward glance.

"Percy Wilson, if you don't stop your hearing aid whistling, or at least turn it down, I'm going to lose my rag!"

"What?" said Percy, turning round to look at Ida's furious face, his expression a picture of innocence, presumably because he wasn't sure whether she'd spoken to him or not.

"Oh, for heaven's sake! There's no point you wearing that hearing aid, because you never listen to a word that's said to you – and all we hear is the deafening squeak it makes. Why don't you go to the doctor's and get it changed?"

He looked puzzled as he tried to make out what she was saying. In exasperation, Ida turned back to the other ladies on her table, her face red with indignation.

"Are you all right, Percy?" asked Connie, who was sitting next to him on the table alongside Ida's.

He looked up at her in surprise.

"That squeak must be driving you mad. Can I help? Turn it down a bit, perhaps?"

He winked at her and touched his right index finger to his nose. "No need," he whispered. "I only have it this high when Ida's prowling around. I love the way it always winds her up. I'll turn it down again now, so you and I can have a nice quiet chat."

Connie stifled a giggle as Percy tipped his head nearer to hers.

"We've got history, that Ida and me. She's always been a Bossy Boots – and I should know! Grew up in the same street, we did: Stirling Road, around the corner near the shops. Believe it or not, I'm still in the same house today. Her mum and dad moved into the posh end of the street when the new houses went up in the fifties. Perhaps that's what gave her those airs and graces. She was a little madam then, and she's an even bigger madam now."

"I didn't realize you'd known each other so long."

Percy drew his chair closer until the two of them were in a conspiratorial huddle.

"Certainly we knew each other – almost in the biblical sense, if you know what I mean," he whispered, his eyes shining with mischief. "Well, I exaggerate. I kissed her once, and she definitely liked it. In fact, she was so enthusiastic, I suddenly caught that gleam her eye – you know, the look some would-be brides get when they're collecting bits and bobs for their bottom drawer? In the nick of time, I realized that she only needed one last item to make her marriage plans complete: a husband! I never kissed her again. I was off like a shot."

Connie spluttered with laughter just as their conversation was interrupted by Jess, one of a handful of volunteers from the local senior school who regularly did work experience by coming along to help with food preparation and serving at the Grown-ups' Lunch Club.

"Mind your arm, Percy, so that I don't spill the gravy all over you!"

"Extra mash?" he asked, peering at the plate.

"Of course," replied Jess. "And two Yorkshires as well, because I know they're your favourite."

"You're a good girl. Bring the mint sauce over too, would you? There's a love. Oh, and if that's apple pie we've got for pudding, I'm partial to lots of custard. Could you tell Maggie that? Tell her I'll give her a big hug later if she can put an extra dollop of custard my way."

"Percy, you *are* awful!" As she spoke, Connie reached out for the condiments and daintily tipped a small pyramid of salt onto one side of her plate.

"... but you *like* me!" he guffawed. "Who used to say that? Some comedian or other. Dick Emery, wasn't it? My memory is awful, but I'm pretty harmless really. It's all good fun."

"In the same house for all those years then?" Connie cut up a neat cube of carrot and dipped it first into the salt, then the gravy, before popping it into her mouth. "You were never tempted to move away – for work, perhaps, or because your wife wanted to live somewhere else?"

At first, she thought Percy hadn't heard her question as he concentrated on cutting himself a large chunk of Yorkshire pudding, which he appeared to swallow without chewing it at all.

"Margaret lived in our street too. She was the girl next door – well, except for my gran's house in between. She never had any interest in moving away, and neither did I, especially as we had her dad and my mum to look after as they got older. Her dad went on till he was ninety-five, and my mum was ninety-two when she passed away the year before him. We were both the youngest in our families, you see."

"That's the way it was then," Connie agreed, carefully carving her meat into perfectly equal mouthfuls. "We looked after our own, didn't we? I cared for my mum for several years too, until she went into hospital and never came out again."

"Margaret and I both had elder brothers and sisters," continued Percy, "but they disappeared as soon as they could. It wasn't that they didn't care, because my brother Frank idolized Mum – but deep

50

down he was glad he didn't have to stay around to look after her."

"Well, it was a bit different for me. When I married Eric, we did move away, because he got a job in Portsmouth in the dockyard there. He's a gem, my Eric. He arranged to move back without a harsh word when Mum needed our help. Well, he never really had a mum of his own, you see, after her house collapsed on top of her during the war. He lost his baby brother then too, and his dad was never the same when he came back from Burma. So my mum became his mum really. He was very good to her – and very good to me. A good father too. He's always been a gem, my Eric."

"Lost him, have you?"

She looked at him in surprise. "No, he's in the shed. He likes potting – and he's never liked dinners cooked by anyone but me. He's not a *club* sort of person really. I just like to get out a bit. I've left his dinner on a plate in the oven – pork chops today. He can have it when he's ready."

"Hey," interrupted Percy. "Just take a look over your shoulder at that table of Merry Widows. I don't think Ida's stopped talking since she sat down, but she's managed to keep shovelling down her dinner at the same time."

Sure enough, three of the ladies on the next table were tucking into their roast lamb dinners in silence as Ida held court.

"For the old but bold! That's what it says. Have you seen that new poster on the noticeboard? Well, I think it's a bloomin' cheek. I mean, who do they mean by that? It must be us, mustn't it? Who else do they think can't touch their toes, are as stiff as a board and must be feeling their age?"

"Well," said Flora, who was sitting opposite her, "that certainly describes me. I haven't seen my toes for years! Mind you, I've not seen the notice either. What's it about?"

"It's a dancing class," replied Betty, with her mouth so inconveniently full that she had to dab her lips to be sure she hadn't dribbled anything out as she spoke.

"Is it ballroom?" asked Doris. "I was good at that. Bert and I won a cup once for our quickstep."

"It says it's armchair exercise," said Betty. "I rather like the sound of that."

"Will they have a telly on so we can watch the soaps while we're at it," chuckled Flora. "It will feel like being in an armchair then."

"Ah, but then it says they're going to do sing-along dancing."

"What dances?" enquired Doris. "Quickstep, do you think? Even though Bert's passed on, I reckon I could still manage a cheeky little quickstep!"

"The more important question," interrupted Ida, her voice booming across the chatter, "is the music. I happen to know who's running that class, and I would suggest that her music choices are likely to be highly questionable."

"Who?" demanded Doris.

Laying her knife and fork deliberately down on her plate, Ida drew in breath as if she were about to start a momentous speech. Her announcement needed their full attention.

"Della Lucas!"

"Who?" Doris looked puzzled.

"Della Lucas!" repeated Flora. "I know her mum. You do too. You know – the dancing teacher. She's taken classes at the Congregational hall for years."

"Oh, you mean that girl of hers? The one who used to be in the paper so often for winning all those dancing cups?"

"I haven't heard anything about her for ages," mused Betty. "Where's she been?"

"On the high seas, apparently," stated Ida. "She's been gallivanting around the world to all sorts of unsavoury places. Apparently she's now had enough and is back home with Mum and planning to inflict her outlandish ideas and her music on us."

"Sounds great," enthused Doris. "I'm going along."

"Me too," agreed Flora.

"You'll do no such thing!" Ida sounded like a stern headmistress. "We will keep our dignity and decorum until we know a great deal more about what little Miss Lucas has in mind. Is she properly trained? Does she have the right medical knowledge, the appropriate attitude, the correct equipment?"

"It sounds like it just needs armchairs," ventured Doris. "And I don't mind modern music. My granddaughter records CDs for me with all the latest music she's into, and I have to say I rather like it."

"Well," continued Ida, glaring around the table at each of them, "you are free, of course, to make up your own minds, but remember, when it all goes horribly wrong, I told you from the start it would be a mistake."

"We can always just leave if we don't like it."

Ida turned her icy stare towards Doris. "How many times have I told you, Doris, that you are too hasty? You jump in without thinking, without any research or preparation at all."

"The last time you said that," retorted Doris, "was when I fancied watching that American TV series, and you told me it was immoral and I wouldn't like it at all. Well, I did, and I'm still loving it – so you were wrong!"

Ida sat back in her chair, her hands raised in a gesture of surrender. "All right, do it. Make a fool of yourselves. Just don't come whining to me when you realize I told you so."

"Pudding, ladies?" enquired Jess, who had suddenly appeared at Ida's elbow with a tray of apple pies. "Custard for everyone?"

Kath and Ellie always chose a quiet corner in the tiny café at the end of the High Street when they met for a catch-up. From the moment Kath met the wife of the new vicar who had arrived at St Mark's two years earlier, she and Ellie had hit it off. Perhaps it was because the two of them shared the experience of holding down a high-powered management job before life took a turn in bringing them to the same small town twenty miles north of Portsmouth.

While Kath's former career had been in hospital management, Ellie had been running a local authority social work team when she first met James. He was the complete opposite to all her previous partners, who had mostly been artistic, easy-going and full of theories about how to put the world right. James was an academic and actually quite shy, preferring the company of books to large crowds. Becoming a vicar was quite an unlikely career choice for him, but the intense sincerity in his face as he explained that he wasn't choosing a career but a vocation that called him to serve Christ through caring for the community around him, touched Ellie's heart and conscience as nothing ever had before.

"He was so endearing," she sighed to Kath that February morning as they sipped their coffee. "His hair needed a cut and draped over his eyes – have you seen how blue his eyes are, by the way? And he looked as if he'd got dressed in the dark with only a charity bag of second-hand clothes to choose from. Honestly, he was a completely fascinating, inspirational, wonderful mess of a man. I fell in love with him instantly, and although I have moments every day when I wonder if I should see a shrink to work out why on earth I ever thought marrying such a man was a good idea, I wouldn't change him for the world."

"You make a good team," agreed Kath. "He's a wonderful priest, completely mesmerizing in the pulpit. He comes out with all the detailed theology, and can quote just about any line from the Bible. But you're the one who organizes everything around him: the family, the house, his diary. He'd be lost without you. In fact, we all would."

"Well," laughed Ellie, "in spite of all the management skills I needed to run that department, I'm still at a loss when it comes to running a parish without offending anyone. It's a minefield. There are so many strong personalities in that church. I think James manages to skim over any problems by being so spiritual and downright *holy* that people don't like to bother him."

"They run and ask you instead."

"Got it in one. That's marriage for you."

"Ah well, I wouldn't know."

Ellie looked at her friend for a few moments. "Why not, Kath? How come you never married? You're bright, beautiful and one of the kindest people I know. There must have been men beating a path to your door to win you over."

"Not that I noticed." Kath paused as she stirred her coffee thoughtfully. "Maybe I was too organized. Perhaps a little set in my ways? One man even told me I was scary. That scared me quite a lot too…"

"No regrets? No near misses?"

Kath's eyes clouded a little as she remembered. "Two who were really special, both of them around for several years. One of them did ask me to marry him, but I realized in that instant that he was too self-centred to make a good husband or family man. I loved him dearly as a boyfriend, but he would have driven me to distraction as a lifelong partner. When I said no, he told me I'd broken his heart, and then he walked out of the door very dramatically. I never saw him again."

"And the other one?"

"Oh, he never asked me. If he had, I'd have said yes. He was the love of my life."

"So was it you who decided the relationship should end?"

"Me – and Mum really. She'd just had the diagnosis of Parkinson's, and I couldn't bear the thought of her going through that on her own. It was the right reason to leave, but the decision meant that our relationship had to stop. It would never have survived being long-distance. The worst thing was that he completely understood. I suppose I wanted him to realize in a flash that he couldn't live without me, and beg me to stay. But he didn't – so I left."

"His loss," said Ellie, covering Kath's hand with her own. "And why should this be the end of your story? You meet people all the time. You're a terrific person, attractive, caring and organized. You've no idea who may walk into Hope Hall one day and sweep you off your feet."

Kath chuckled. "There's a good line in toothy, bald-headed, elderly gents with a twinkle in their eye. I'll give you that. Not quite my type though."

"Well, don't give up. You know what they say – God works in mysterious ways…"

"I don't think I'm in the market for mystery. Taller than me, half a brain, a nice smile and his own teeth will do nicely. Oh, and a good sense of humour and the ability to rub the aches out of tired feet – that would go down well too."

"Do we need one of those cupcakes?" suggested Ellie, eyeing up the display cabinet. "Or a scone and cream, do you think?"

"Both, I reckon!"

It was over their cakes that Ellie let Kath in on the latest upheaval to ruffle feathers at the church.

"You know how highbrow James can be. Oh, he knows he's got to move with the times – modern songs, worship bands, and not a 'thee' or 'thou' in sight – and he does all that, of course, because he has to. His heart, though, is completely old school. He loves traditional hymns. He's brought in that regular Sunday service using the words from the Book of Common Prayer – and he adores choral music. He was a choirboy at Lichfield Cathedral for years, and he relished every minute. All the responses, the anthems, the Glorias – they're right up his street."

"But…" prompted Kath.

"But the congregation were very sad back in the summer to say goodbye to Maurice, our organist and choirmaster, who retired after playing at the church for more than three decades. We managed with deputy organists for a while, but it was very hit and miss, and we almost lost our choir over the months that followed, without someone to lead them."

"I can see what's coming," said Kath. "James chose Gregory Palmer as the new organist and choir leader—"

"And Gregory is even more traditional and highbrow than James, if that's possible."

"It's not gone down too well with the congregation then?"

"Do you know, I think they've been surprised by how glorious our music now sounds. Gregory can make that old organ of ours sing. The music has become really rather exciting again, and I don't think any of us expected to feel like that. We still have the worship band for the family service at eleven o'clock on Sundays, but the first service at nine-thirty every week is completely traditional, and people are just pouring in. It seems to have hit a vein of need in them – perhaps bringing back memories of being in church as children; maybe simply because of the much-loved phrasing and language of that service, and the familiar hymn words that are just stored there in their hearts and minds, like a spiritual first-aid kit."

"That sounds as if it's working well then."

"But not for the choir, it seems. I mean, most of them aren't a day under retirement age and they've been singing in the choir for as long as anyone can remember. There were only ever about ten of them anyway, and it sometimes felt as if they were just singing for their own enjoyment rather than leading the congregation. I remember when James was installed, he was asked to choose the hymns he wanted, and he made sure they were all really well known, but even then they managed to get the phrasing all wrong so that the words didn't really make sense. A couple of the other vicars who came along for that special occasion were sitting in the choir stalls, and we could all hear them trying to out-sing the choir because they were so terrible."

"Oh dear," said Kath, trying not to laugh.

Ellie started giggling too. "Honestly, Kath, it went from bad to worse. Whenever I was queueing for Communion in the aisle between the choir stalls, all I could ever hear were two voices from a couple of choir members in the back, and neither of them managed to hit any of the right notes."

"And then along came Gregory."

"Along came Gregory," echoed Ellie. "He swept in like a new broom, and insisted that every one of them should audition for a place in the choir – and he ended up inviting only three of them to stay, because the others just couldn't sing."

"Ah, not the most tactful approach."

"You can say that again. The three he chose were so incensed about the others being excluded that they all hung up their robes too, so we were left with no choir at all. But Gregory probably planned that all along, because the following week there was a notice in the local paper describing the content and quality of the choral music he wanted the newly formed St Mark's choir to sing – and applications came flooding in, from music students, trained singers and several members of other established choirs in the area. The end result is that the St Mark's Choral Choir, as it's now called, is more than twenty strong. They have even numbers of female and male members, which is amazing because we've only ever had a couple of male voices in the choir before now. And they're good, really good – which is vindication for James and Gregory, very pleasant for the congregation, but the start of mutiny among all the old choir members."

"Oh dear, what a mess."

"Well, it's a mess that might be coming your way. Pauline Owen – you remember her, the one with the strongest voice that always stands out from the rest because she's usually singing half a tone above everyone else?"

"Oh yes, I know exactly who you mean."

"Well, apparently Pauline went to see Gregory to ask him to explain precisely what was wrong with the choir members he'd sacked, after they'd been perfectly well received for many years at the church. He just told her they had to go because they can't sing."

"He didn't sugar coat the pill then."

"Far from it. She stomped off, called an emergency meeting, and the upshot is that they've decided to form an alternative choir of their own."

"Wow! Good for them. How do they plan to do that?"

"They're coming to see you to ask if they can rehearse at Hope Hall. You may have to choose your time for their rehearsals quite carefully. They've chosen a name that I have no doubt they'll live up to: the Can't Sing Singers!"

Carol glanced at the kitchen clock as she tried to persuade a wriggling Little Joe to put his arms through the sleeves of his winter jacket. Half past eight, bang on time. She hated being late, because she knew how difficult it was for Jen to open up the hall and prepare everything needed for that day at playgroup when she was on her own.

A chilly winter wind took her breath away as she opened the front door and headed towards her car with Little Joe happily singing in her arms. Two minutes' wrestling to get the reluctant toddler into his car seat and she was behind the wheel at last, turning the key in the ignition.

Nothing. Not a peep.

She tried the key again, but the old car didn't even give a groan or a creak. There was just nothing.

With a squeal of frustration, she thumped the palms of her hands against the steering wheel. Little Joe immediately burst into tears of alarm, and she could happily have joined him. Instead, fumbling in her bag for her phone, she rang Phil's number. Perhaps he hadn't reached work yet. Maybe she could just catch him before he got too busy. Her heart was sinking as the phone rang half a dozen times, but then, just as she thought she was going to be leaving yet another message on his voicemail, he picked up the call.

"Babe, I can't talk now."

"Wait, Phil! My car won't start – again."

"Babe, I'm sorry, but I can't do anything about it. I'm at work. You know I can't do anything when I'm at work."

"And I need to get to work. Phil, this car is a wreck, and I'm driving our son around in it."

"I'll speak to you tonight, okay? We'll talk then—"

"Phil, I'm stuck in the car on our front drive. How am I going to get to playgroup?"

"The bus?"

"That could take me an hour, once I've got to the stop, then waited for the next bus to come along. They only run every thirty minutes."

"Good luck then, babe. Ring me at lunchtime, if you like, and let me know how you get on."

The line went dead.

Seething with anger, Carol forced herself to take several deep breaths. What should she do? What *could* she do but ring Jen straight away?

"Hi, Carol! You okay?" Jen's familiar voice brought a warm wave of relief to Carol's frazzled nerves.

"The car won't start."

"Oh, Carol, please don't say that—"

"I've spoken to Phil, but he can't do anything because he's already at work."

"Your Phil wouldn't do anything anyway. He's so irresponsible about that old wreck he sends you out in."

"He says I'll have to catch the bus."

Jen sighed heavily, obviously irritated by this news. "What time do you reckon you'll get in?"

"I'll just nip back indoors to get Little Joe's pushchair, then I'll walk down to the bus stop. The next bus goes at five past nine, so I should be with you by about twenty-five past."

There was silence at the other end of the phone as Jen considered her options.

"I'll ring Marie. Perhaps she can come in a bit earlier to help me out. This can't keep happening, though, Carol. I have to rely on you because you're the second most senior member of staff, and I love you dearly, but if you can't guarantee you're going to be here on time…"

Carol didn't want to hear the rest of that sentence. "I'm on my way, Jen. Bye."

The bus was late. It was gone half past nine by the time a red-faced Carol rushed into the old school hall. Quickly organizing Little Joe, she waved across at Jen as she hurried off to make the morning snacks. Jen gave a small smile back, then returned her attention to the little girl beside her.

In that moment, Carol knew that however strong their friendship was, she was on thin ice as far as her job was concerned, unless she could improve her travel arrangements. As she chopped and buttered, she wondered whether she should simply abandon the car and take the bus every morning, but the length of the journey and the unreliability of the bus service, not to mention the expense of the tickets, made that an option she'd prefer not to have to take. Could she cycle? Perhaps put a seat on the back of her old bike for Little Joe? She thought about the rush-hour traffic with all those impatient drivers determined to cross roundabouts and traffic lights without much care for anyone else, and knew that cycling would terrify her. No, there was nothing for it. She *had* to get a new car. She'd talk to Phil that night. She'd sit him down and tell him in no uncertain terms that she would have to give up her job, and they'd lose all her income, unless he organized for her to have a car that actually worked.

The sharp knife in her hand flashed as she chopped the carrots and cucumber sticks as if she hated them.

They'd had their meal and Little Joe was safely tucked up in bed that night before Carol brought them both a cup of tea and joined Phil on the settee. In retrospect, it was probably a mistake to tackle him on the subject of the car just as *A Question of Sport* was about to start, because his eyes barely left the screen as she said her piece about the difficulty of getting to work that morning, the embarrassment of being late, and the fear she felt about the security of her job if she couldn't guarantee getting to the playgroup on time.

"I know, love," said Phil. "But we can't afford anything different at the moment."

"But you're doing okay at work, aren't you? Have you had this month's bonus yet? You thought you'd done quite well, didn't you?"

"Oh, I didn't get as much as I'd hoped. Sometimes they don't pay a bonus at all these days. Perhaps I'll get a bit more next month."

"I hope so. I mean, we shouldn't be this broke, should we? Not when you've got such a good job and I'm working too?"

He shrugged, his eyes still on the screen. "Everything's so expensive these days."

"But we've got our savings account. How much is in there now?"

"I'm not sure. I haven't looked for a while. Not a lot though. A few hundred at best. Don't forget we had to pay for the new central heating boiler."

"A few hundred? Could we spare that for a car?"

"That would leave us with nothing at all to fall back on, Carol. We can't live like that. I won't let us. We need to keep some in reserve."

"Look, Phil, I'm not asking for anything posh. Just a car that works – please!"

"Frankie Dettori!" Phil yelled at the television, seconds before the presenter Sue Barker confirmed that Frankie Dettori was indeed the answer to the last question she'd asked the *Question of Sport* teams.

"Phil, listen to me. Did you speak to Rob?"

"He called this afternoon, but I was on the road with a client in the car. I couldn't ring back."

"Speak to him now."

"It's too late."

"He won't mind."

"I'll give him a ring tomorrow."

"Do you promise?"

"I'll try. Depends how things go at work."

Furious with frustration, she reached for her tea and stood up. "I'm going to bed."

He looked surprised. "It's only half past eight."

"Well, there's not much company for me down here. Goodnight."

Carol stomped off upstairs. Deciding that a long hot soak in the bath might go some way to calming the anger that bubbled within her, Carol turned on the taps, added some of her Christmas bath oil and lit a couple of scented candles on the shelf in front of the bathroom mirror. Heading back to the bedroom as the bath filled, she tore her clothes off, still incensed by Phil's lack of reaction, or even interest, in discussing her need for a different car. What they needed was money – and Phil had always been the one to keep an eye on their purse strings. He'd been a bit vague about exactly how much was left in their savings account. Perhaps there was more than he thought. Now where did he keep the building society folder? It would be in the banking file, of course: the large box he kept tucked under the dressing table with all their statements and account details in it. Pulling it out, she quickly flicked through the paperwork, cheque-book stubs and bank correspondence, but was slightly surprised to find the building society statement folder wasn't in there. Where on earth would it be? She searched through another couple of folders they kept in the box, then pulled out all the drawers in his bedside unit to see if it was there. Nothing.

Now committed to her search, she went to turn off the bath

taps before directing her attention to the wardrobe. She opened the door on his side and looked across the shelves, the shoe racks and the rail packed with clothes neatly hung on hangers. In a moment of hopeful inspiration, she reached out to grab the jacket of the suit he'd worn to work that day. She patted at the fabric to see if he'd left anything in the pockets, but then, as she pulled the jacket forward to search properly, she caught sight of something stuffed down behind his suits where it would never normally be seen. She stretched out to pull whatever it was into the light. And there it was: the folder he "hadn't looked at for a while", in which all the building society statements and paying-in slips were neatly kept in date order. With fumbling fingers, she turned to the last payment slip.

The payment had been for £492, and it was dated two days ago. Shocked, Carol traced back earlier movements on the account. He was right about the cost of the central heating boiler a few weeks before. That was £672 – a large bill, as he had said. What he hadn't said, though, was that he had been paying significant amounts, probably all those work bonuses he said weren't as much as he'd hoped, into that account for more than a year: £472 the month before, £539 before that, over £700 on one occasion. Her eyes widened with disbelief as she read the final total: £5,365.47. They had more than £5,000 in that account, and he was lying about it. Why?

Still gripping the receipts, she sat down heavily on the bed. She knew why that money was there. She knew what he was saving for. He'd told her often enough how it was his passion to get that old bike of his repaired and restored to its former glory. His eyes lit up as he talked about how he'd like to enter it into one of the big vintage bike rallies so that everyone could see what a wonderful piece of engineering it really was. This money was for his old banger. *Her* old banger was never going to get a look in.

Her fingers stiff with fury, she stuffed all the papers back into the folder. She knew she should challenge him with it. She knew she should demand an explanation. But she was so angry, she feared the words would come out wrong. No, she thought, slipping the folder into its hiding place behind his suits in the wardrobe. She would bide her time. She had to plan this carefully and get it right.

Chapter 4

G ary wasn't quite certain where to go as he ushered the twins through the main entrance of Hope Hall at five o'clock that Tuesday evening. That is, until they stepped into the foyer and heard excited squeals coming from beyond the glass door partition. Any nerves Toby and Max had felt on the way to their first Beavers' meeting were soon forgotten as they tugged their dad towards the fun.

What they saw when they got inside could have been described as bedlam, until a closer look clearly showed it wasn't. Boys between the ages of six and eight years old, all wearing bright turquoise sweatshirts, were deeply engrossed in a complicated team game of tag played under the watchful eye of what seemed to be about half a dozen leaders. One of them, a thirty-something man dressed in a smart Scout uniform, walked across to welcome the newcomers.

Looking down at the boys, he smiled. "Hi, I'm Andy – and I can see you're the twins we're expecting, but which one of you is Toby and which one is Max?"

After introductions all round, Andy sent the boys off with another Scout, who was probably in his late teens, before turning to Gary.

"Let's see how they get on this evening as a trial, and whether they think Beavers is for them. Then, if you'd like to sign them up as members, I can give you the forms to take home so that you can bring back everything they need when they come next week."

"What about the uniforms? Do they need those next week too?"

"You can buy the sweatshirts here. We've always got a supply. Again, leave that until next time, just to be certain they really want to join."

Gary laughed. "Not much doubt about that. Look at them! Toby can often be quite shy, but from the way he's running around and shrieking his head off, I think he's definitely planning to stay."

"Right, well, feel free to stay yourself and watch what goes on. There's a coffee machine in the foyer, if you fancy that – parents sometimes stay out there, or sit in a corner of the hall, whatever works best for you."

"I'll stay here for a while and then perhaps get a coffee later. Thanks, Andy."

Watching from the sidelines, it didn't take long for Gary to recognize that joining Beavers was going to be a perfect outlet for his lively twin sons. Several of the boys in their class at school had already joined, because their sixth birthdays were a little earlier than Max and Toby's. The moment the twins' birthday was behind them, they nagged incessantly to be able to go along too. Karen never got back from work until after seven, which didn't matter because, as a freelance graphic designer, he worked at home with the aim of fitting his working hours around the boys' timetable. After Karen set off for work before seven each morning, Gary would get the boys ready to leave for school at half past eight, and then would be standing at the school gate at half past three to bring them home again. Their arrangement wouldn't suit every family, but they made it work for them. When the boys came along almost immediately after they'd first considered having children, they had been faced with a dilemma. Karen was the main breadwinner. Her knowledge and experience at the sharp end of the IT industry was specialist and sought after. Her salary was three times as much as Gary could ever earn from his design work, but they were a couple, partners in all family decisions. So when Karen said that she'd like to take up the opportunity of going back to work a year after the twins were born, Gary immediately stepped into the role of house parent.

Privately Gary had worried that he would feel under-valued, alienated from using his undoubted artistic skills, cut off from adult company during the working day, but in the end, none of that mattered when he thought about the needs of his sons. From the moment he first set eyes on the boys, he'd adored them. They lit up his life and made sense of everything. He didn't mind getting up in the night. He'd tackle dirty nappies and piles of washing in his own haphazard way. He even managed to cobble together some sort of evening meal to share with Karen when she eventually arrived home, drained and exhausted. During weekdays, they barely saw each other in daylight, and often got through several days without her having the energy or opportunity for anything more than the most basic of conversations. At the weekends, once the boys had been organized with cereal and their favourite television programme downstairs, Gary and Karen were sometimes lucky enough to grab an early morning cuddle, when they'd kiss and talk, and decide that life wouldn't always be like this. They loved each other. They were a team. Their family life might seem odd to others, but they felt it was worth the sacrifice in order to be able to provide everything they wanted for their family.

After watching the Beavers for a while, Gary quietly slipped out of the double doors into the foyer, thinking that a cup of coffee sounded like an excellent idea. On one side, there were three parents, obviously good friends, chatting over coffee cups as they sat around a table, while another couple of fathers were standing in the far corner having an animated conversation about some sport or other. Feeling a bit of an intruder, Gary went over to the coffee machine, which was much more sophisticated than he had imagined. There were two racks of buttons offering variations on the coffee theme – more than Gary thought could ever be needed. What he wanted was a simple coffee with a dash of milk. Among all the buttons, there didn't seem to be one that offered just that.

"If you want a white coffee, you have to push the button for a black Americano," said a voice at his shoulder. "Then you can add as many little pots of milk as you like. They're on the top of the machine in that basket."

Gary turned to see a woman in jeans and a huge winter jumper, with her long fair hair scraped back into a low ponytail.

"These gadgets fox me," he admitted with a wry grin. "All I want is a straightforward cup of coffee."

"Me too. It's taken me ages to work out how to do that. It always seems to want to add sugar, even though I haven't asked for it."

"Oh, I don't want sugar either. Do I have to do anything to stop it?"

The woman stepped forward to check that he was pressing the right buttons, then they waited together until they were both able to walk across to a table with the coffee they'd each chosen.

"Claire," she said, holding out her hand. "Mother of Josh, who's just mad about Beavers."

"Gary, father of twin boys, Toby and Max. This is their first night."

"They'll love it."

"I can see they already do. How long has Josh been coming?"

"About a year now. He was a bit of a late starter really, but he loved it straight away. He's always heartbroken whenever the meetings stop over the holidays, even this last one when there was all the fun of Christmas going on."

"I never got involved with anything like this when I was a kid. What do they do? Is it mostly just playing games?"

"Oh, it's definitely fun, but they do all sorts of things – lots of arty stuff, painting and building structures. Then they sing songs, listen to stories, have parties, go on outings. And what I really like is that they learn about helping others, not just near home but across the world too. In fact, they've got us all saving printer cartridges, stamps and tin cans at the moment, because they can be recycled to raise money for projects they're supporting."

"It used to be Bob-a-Job week, didn't it, years ago?" mused Gary.

"That's how they did their fund-raising. I don't suppose knocking on doors would be considered safe these days."

"What was a 'bob'? An old shilling, wasn't it? I wonder what that would be worth now?"

He laughed. "More like a pound, I should think. How about you? Were you ever a Brownie?"

"Was I a Brownie!" she exclaimed. "Not just a Brownie, but a Sixer! And I had an armful of badges to prove it."

Gary grinned. "So, not just a Brownie, but a *boss* Brownie?"

She straightened up with pride. "A boss maybe, but never bossy. That would have been against the Brownie Promise:

I promise that I will do my best:
To be true to myself and develop my beliefs,
To serve the Queen and my community,
To help other people
And keep the Brownie Guide Law."

"I can't believe you still remember it after all this time. And what was the Brownie Guide Law?"

"'A Brownie Guide thinks of others before herself and does a good turn every day!'" remembered Claire, a note of triumph in her voice.

Gary nodded approval. "That's character-building stuff all right!"

Claire giggled at the thought. "I don't know what went wrong then. What happened to all those good Brownie intentions?"

"Life, work, marriage, kids..."

They looked at each other then, both surprised by the way in which the tone of their conversation had subtly changed.

"Anyway," said Gary, "what time do they finish? They won't be long, will they?"

"Any time now," she replied, getting up from her chair. "I usually wait for Josh over by the door."

Gary didn't follow immediately, but took his time to finish his coffee just before the doors burst open to allow a noisy gaggle of Beavers to stream out. Getting Toby and Max into their jackets was quite a challenge, as the pair of them were too excited to concentrate on anything except telling their dad every detail of how wonderful it had been.

Once they were finally ready, Gary glanced across the room to say goodbye to Claire, just as she looked over at him with the same idea.

"See you next week," she called.

"Definitely – and thanks again for your help in taming the coffee machine."

And with a wave, they gathered their respective offspring and headed towards the car park.

There had never been large numbers of participants in the Knit and Natter Club, but the organizer, Elaine Clarke, really didn't mind. She would have been quite happy if only one other person turned up to share her passion, providing they had a real love for needlework of any kind. Betty and Doris always imagined that, in her younger days, Elaine must have been a hippie, because of her long hair – once auburn, now a dusty shade of strawberry blonde – along with her flowing embroidered tops, and her skirts decorated with Inca patterns.

"She told me once that she studied textiles," said Betty, as she and Doris got out their handiwork that afternoon, "but I don't think she ever worked for anyone but herself. I don't suppose that weaving loom of hers is quite what you find in textile factories these days."

"Oh, I hope she doesn't just go on about weaving rugs and wall hangings again this week. I keep telling her my eyes really aren't good enough for all that tapestry work she likes so much," complained Doris. "I enjoy knitting. I can do that with my eyes closed, So let's hope she just leaves me to get on with this matinee jacket for baby Charlie. I've only got one more sleeve to do. How are you getting on?"

Betty held up the brightly coloured square that she was crocheting. "This is my fourth square this week. I've made so many now that I don't think there can be any babies left in Africa without a blanket to warm them up on cold nights."

The two women worked in silence for a while, not looking at their flying fingers but scanning the group around them in an apparently casual way.

Suddenly, Betty's elbow nudged Doris, and their heads drew together so that they could speak without being heard.

"That Joan doesn't look well, does she?"

"Quite a high colour, don't you think? What can have caused that, I wonder?"

"She swore to me that she'd stopped drinking gin. She promised," hissed Betty.

"I know," agreed Doris. "And with all those medicines she has to take… Well, she's a fool to herself."

"Did we ought to have a word, do you think? Ida said we should."

"Well, Ida would. Ida feels she has the right to an opinion on everybody and everything."

"The trouble with Ida is that she can be so domineering."

"Oh yes, she's always thought she's a cut above the rest of us."

"I'm surprised she's not here today. She doesn't usually miss the chance of a good gossip, a cuppa and one of Maggie's cakes."

"I think she's still taking umbrage because we all said we'd go to the armchair exercise and sing-along dance class tomorrow afternoon."

"Well, if she doesn't want to go," sniffed Betty, "that's fine by me, but I do resent her laying down the law to the rest of us."

"She's so insensitive… and, dare I say, even quite spiteful at times? I hate people who gossip. I really can't stand it."

Just at that moment, Kath came in from her office through the side door of the hall, with Maggie at her side. They stopped for a while just inside the door, taking in the scene in front of them.

"Do you know," hissed Maggie, "those Knit and Natter ladies haven't got a good word to say about each other."

Kath smiled in agreement. "And Elaine doesn't seem to notice at all. I sometimes think she lives on a different planet to the rest of us."

"Cloud cuckoo land, do you mean?" chuckled Maggie. "You know, that sounds like a rather nice place to be."

They glanced back then towards the stage end of the hall, where another group of mostly elderly people, the Down Memory Lane club members, were huddled in twos and threes, poring over pictures of the town in years gone by, with the help of Jean, the dementia care therapist who ran the club.

"Does anyone remember this big shop with double windows that used to be just opposite the town clock in the High Street?" Jean asked, holding up a photograph so that everyone could see.

"Liquorice sticks." Bill Cartwright's rheumy eyes were gazing into the distance as he spoke.

"What – those long black liquorice sticks, do you mean?"

Bill turned to stare at Jean, his expression blank.

Jean tried again. "Or do you remember the liquorice wheels that used to have a bobbly pink sweet in the middle of them?"

"I liked those," injected Ruby, a frail, wispy-haired lady who was sitting in a wheelchair. "And spaceships. And cherry lips. They used to stick to my teeth."

Suddenly she threw her head back with peals of laughter, her parted lips revealing the smooth edges of bright red gums. "They'd be all right now. I've got no teeth left for them to stick to."

"Liquorice sticks," repeated Bill. "Like wood."

"Oh, I remember those!" joined in Celia, clapping her hands with excitement. "Liquorice roots! They tasted awful. My nan said I should suck the flavour out of them because it would keep me regular."

"Did it?" asked Bill.

Celia's face clouded over with concentration. "I don't know."

"Cod liver oil kept you regular," added Bill. "It made me sick though."

Jean leaned down to pull a photograph out of her folder. "And here's a picture of Mr Brown who owned that shop. Do any of you remember this gentleman?"

Celia reached over to take the photo, laying it on the table between her and Bill so that they could look at it together.

"He had a shop," she said at last.

"What sort of shop? Do you remember?"

"Liquorice sticks," said Bill.

"I think you're right, Bill. He probably did sell those medicinal liquorice roots, and lots of other pills and potions. Can you remember what kind of shop Mr Brown owned?"

Bill's face was expressionless again.

The small lady in the wheelchair was bobbing up and down with excitement. "Iron tonic. My mum had lots of bottles of that. She'd send me down to Mr Brown to buy them, and if I had a ha'penny left over, she let me buy some spaceships next door."

"So what kind of shop was this, Ruby?"

The palm of Celia's hand thumped down on the table. "The chemist! It was the chemist shop!"

"Well done, Celia. Well done, all of you. Now, can you remember what other things Mr Brown might have sold in his chemist shop?"

"Ribbons," said Ruby, her eyes narrowing as she tried to recall. "Combs. Moth balls."

"Liquorice sticks," said Bill.

Smiling encouragement, Jean dug into her folder again to draw out another photo, as Maggie and Kath disappeared through the foyer doors.

"By the way, Maggie, I've been meaning to ask you. I've had a request to hold a wedding reception here on the last Saturday in February. Quite short notice, but I get the impression the wedding is a hurried affair."

"I wonder why?" smiled Maggie.

"Well, actually, not the usual reason. Apparently, the groom is in the Army and is just about to be sent on a six-month tour of duty in Afghanistan. The couple have been engaged for quite a while, but hadn't been able to afford the wedding their family wanted for them. But now he's been called up they've decided to just bite the bullet and try to organize everything as cheaply and quickly as possible."

"A registry office job then?"

"Well, no, they're getting married across the road in St Mark's, because the whole family have been going there since the bride and groom met at Sunday school when they were six years old."

"Oh, how lovely!"

"I know. The members of the congregation have clubbed together to make the ceremony really special for them. They've sorted bell-ringers, flowers, and even the choir are rehearsing a new anthem to sing for them."

"And the reception will be here?"

"Yes, but they've come up with the idea of making it a 'bring and share' reception. Everyone in the church is invited along to join with their family and friends – all they have to do is bring something for the buffet table."

"What a great idea! Do they need my help?"

"Definitely. They've asked if they can come and talk to you sometime this week, just to sort out crockery, cutlery and glasses, table decorations, seating – you know, all the usual. If I text over her number, would you mind giving her a ring?"

"Of course not. If there's a large number coming, we might need to work out whether we can trust them enough to ask if we can borrow extra crockery and glasses from the Women's Institute cupboard."

Kath whistled softly. "Oh, that's a serious consideration."

"I'll meet the family to talk over what sort of numbers they have in mind for the reception. If they need more chairs and equipment than we have ourselves, then I'll ring the WI chairwoman and see if she'll allow theirs to be rented out just for the day."

Kath shrugged her shoulders. "Rather you than me. That Barbara Longstone is formidable."

"Wish me luck then!" quipped Maggie as she disappeared back into her kitchen.

It was just turning five when Maggie and her team finally finished clearing up the kitchen after the tea they always provided at the end of the afternoon for the members of both the Knit and Natter and the Down Memory Lane clubs. Many of them had transport home organized by Good Neighbours, and it was always a slow process to get everyone heading off in the right direction with the right driver.

Ray would be along later that evening, probably around seven, to make sure the PA system and bar were set up in preparation for the line dancers, who would arrive in force around half past seven – but for the time being, knowing the hall was empty, Maggie pulled the front double doors shut behind her, and turned the large key in the lock.

"Hello, Maggie."

He stepped out of the shadows to block her way as she walked through the small enclosed garden towards the pavement.

"Dave! What are you doing here?"

"I've been hoping to talk to you for a while now, and not managed it. I thought this would be a good place to find you."

"And you thought you could talk to me here without Steph insisting on being around to keep an eye on you."

"I saw her. Did she tell you?"

"Of course she did. She was furious. She tried to tell me a bit about what was said, but I really don't want to know. I can't cope with it – not yet, perhaps not ever. Please just go away now. Don't do this to me."

"I can't, Maggie. I want to know how you are. I care about you."

Maggie's laugh was hollow. "Huh! You care about me while you're living with another woman? Don't be ridiculous, Dave."

"Of course I care. We've known each other most of our lives. We had our Silver Wedding Anniversary—"

"Oh, you remember? I'm surprised."

"I care – and I'm sorry. I am really sorry I've hurt you. I didn't mean for all this to happen."

Maggie stared at him, this man she knew so well – at least, she *thought* she had. Her shoulders slumped and she leaned back against the door of the hall.

"What do you want, Dave?"

"Well, I just want to sort things out, get everything on a more reasonable footing."

Maggie pulled her collar up against the cold January wind. "Reasonable? What's reason got to do with this?"

"I can't turn the clock back, Mags. It's happened. I've put a bomb under our family, and I know it, but we need to sort out where we go from here."

"Do we?" Maggie's tone was sarcastic.

He hesitated for a moment, uncertain how to continue.

"We've got to sort out the divorce."

She felt the world spin around her, her fingers fumbling to grab the firmness of the hall's brick wall to stop her knees from buckling beneath her.

"I'm not the sort of person who gets divorced, Dave. You know me – I'm the loyal, loving type."

"Yes, you are – and I'm sorry it's come to this, Mags, but I need a divorce."

"Why? What's the hurry?"

Dave looked at her for several seconds before answering. "Mandy's pregnant."

Her head swam, her knees buckled, and from somewhere near she could hear a low wail, as if an animal was in pain. At the end of a long tunnel, she heard him calling her name, felt his hands on her arms as her mind tried to make sense of what she'd just heard. His face was directly in front of hers, this face that was as familiar as her own, saying words that ripped her heart into tiny, wretched pieces. Suddenly she was filled with superhuman strength as she pulled back both her arms before pushing out with every muscle in her body. He fell backwards, narrowly avoiding being speared on the low, spiky, metal fence as he tumbled.

She didn't look at him. She never wanted to look at him again. She staggered out onto the pavement and ran, ran, ran as far away from him as she possibly could.

Della never gave a performance without being certain her make-up was perfect. Today, her eyelashes were black and glossy, if a little unnaturally thick and long. The Christian Dior foundation, bought from duty free on her last cruise, gave her skin a flawless finish on which the curves and dips in her cheeks were accentuated with pale highlights here and dark peach-coloured contouring there. Her lips were a rich shade of coral, shaped by a carefully drawn line from a dusky brown lip liner. She'd skilfully scooped up her long dark chestnut hair into a glorious crown on top of her head, carefully pinned into position so that the blonde highlights shone through the darker strands and fell down in tendrils around her face. She'd chosen her clothes carefully: soft grey tracksuit bottoms teamed with a beautifully cut sweatshirt on which the designer labels were clearly displayed. The look was casual. The effect was elegant. She was ready for her public.

She knew all eyes were on her as she walked into the hall and up the steps to the stage for her first day of lessons. She was aware that the administrator, Kath, looked up from the conversation she was having with one of the drivers who'd brought elderly pupils along for the start of armchair exercise. She heard the buzz of chatter halt as she made her entrance. She caught sight of her pianist, Ronnie Andrews, giving her a wink as she took her place centre stage in front of the class. Good old Ronnie. He'd been the pianist at her mother's dancing school from the time she'd first started lessons there at the age of three. Ronnie was old now, probably more than fifty, but he was a professional. When he was younger, he'd worked for a while as the musical director of summer end-of-pier shows and pantomimes. He understood the business. He understood that the show must go on – and this was *her* show.

She took in the scene in front of her. Chairs had been spaced out in rows across the hall, stretching back until seating was in place for twenty pupils. Some of the chairs in the back two rows were already filled, while other potential participants sat or stood along the sides of the hall waiting for instruction.

Lights, camera, action! Della's face lit up with an electric smile as she beamed at them.

"Hello, everyone! Welcome! Are you all ready for some fun today?"

An embarrassed wave of laughter and chatter rippled through the room.

"Now, don't be shy! We will have a great time together, but most of all we will be gently stretching our bodies and getting fit."

Expressions around the hall changed from laughter to trepidation.

"Take a seat, all of you! You'll see best if you sit at the front, and I promise I don't bite."

After a moment's hesitation, it was Betty who moved first,

closely followed by Flora and Doris as they chose their seats in the second row from the front. Others followed, some quite sprightly as they walked, some plainly struggling with stiffness in their hips, knees and various other joints.

"Okay!" chirped Della, as she launched into a stylish pirouette that took her into exactly the right position in front of her own chair. The class members gasped with admiration. Della let out a tinkle of delighted laughter.

"We'll have all of you doing that before the term's out. So, let's sit down, feet facing front, straight and parallel, with your heels just an inch away from the legs of your chair. Backbones straight, shoulders down, chins up, bottoms pushed right back into your seat. Now, just follow me. Ronnie – music, Maestro, please!"

The half-hour that followed went in a whirl of bends, twists, stretches, legs lifts, standing up, sitting down – and a long, slow "R-e-l-a-x" at the end of each set of exercises. Around the hall, Della could see deep concentration from some, desperate effort from others, occasional shocked disbelief at what they were being asked to do – and lots of giggling when things either went entertainingly wrong or simply weren't achievable at all – yet! A couple at the back got up and walked out, but the rest stayed. The more they tried, the more they realized they could manage. The music was jaunty, the exercises were varied and constantly changing, and overall, as Della had promised, it *was* very good fun.

At the end of that class, on a high from all they'd achieved, most people were happy when their chairs were moved to the side of the hall so that Dance Sing-along "for the old but bold" could begin. Ronnie struck up a medley of songs they all knew – swing numbers made famous by Frank Sinatra or Nat King Cole, with more modern favourites from Buddy Holly and The Beatles thrown in. And there were well-known Glenn Miller Band numbers they could la-la along to as they swayed and turned, sometimes on their own, but mostly holding hands with a partner – bosom to bosom, as no gentlemen had come along to the class at all. They waltzed, they marched, they did the conga, they bopped, boogied and bounced along to cha-cha-chas and rumbas. Nothing was too taxing. Nothing too fast or complicated. It was a half-hour of nostalgia that brought back memories of the dances they'd been to long ago and the music they loved. All that was missing was a glittery ball shining down from the middle of the hall.

They finished up linking arms and kicking legs in a long chorus line as they bellowed out the words of "New York, New York" at the tops of their voices – and Della knew she had a hit on her hands.

"Ida would have loved that," enthused Betty, still getting her breath back.

Doris chuckled. "Do you mean Ida was actually *wrong* about something?"

"Let's call in on her on the way home. Where's Flora? Has she already gone?"

"No, look! She's over there talking to the pianist."

"Why? Does she know him?"

"I'm not sure," replied Doris, her eyes squinting in the hope of getting a clearer view of the pianist's face. "I certainly don't. Anyway, she'll catch up. I need the loo. Coming?"

The tap class that followed went just as well. Nineteen girls and one boy, ranging in age from five to their early teens, turned up. They were greeted by Della, who had transformed into a completely different look. She'd peeled off her tracksuit bottoms to reveal long, shapely legs clad in bright blue tights and sparkling silver tap shoes. She'd changed her top too, into a new one that, on the front, had a sequinned silhouette of a loose-limbed dancer with his trilby hat tipped at a stylish angle, and his feet obviously flying beneath him.

Some of the class had their own tap shoes, others appeared to be wearing heeled school shoes, while a few had come just in trainers. And if some of the older dancers had been to tap classes before, they'd never come across anything quite like this. Della not only drew out rhythms from their feet, but from their voices and their hands too, as fingers clicked, mouths whistled, heels stamped and toes shuffle-ball-changed through a series of deceptively simple steps that had all the style of Ginger Rogers and Fred Astaire. Well, that's how it felt, even if it wasn't *quite* how it looked.

As the class drew to a close with Ronnie playing the final triumphant notes of "Razzle Dazzle 'Em" from the musical *Chicago*, the dancers joined all those watching around the edges of the hall in a spontaneous round of applause. Della took a deep, theatrical bow, knowing that there would be even more tap students the following week.

Fifteen minutes of changeover time later, Della appeared in yet another guise. The blue tights remained, but the sparkling tap shoes had been swapped for feather-light dance trainers. Gone was the tap-dancer top, and instead she was wearing a loose-fitting grungy top, which hung off one shoulder and seemed to have tears of differing lengths strategically ripped into various corners of it. The look of her pupils had changed dramatically too. It was as if they'd just walked in from hanging out on a street corner in clothes that ranged from torn jeans and well-worn tops to studded trousers and designer-look-alike leather jackets that may well have been bought specially for the occasion.

Ronnie, the pianist, had gone too, his contribution no longer required. Della set up her music system and blasted out hip-hop and dubstep, to which the dancers could pop, lock and break.

Not bothering with any formal welcome, Della grabbed the mic, stood centre stage, and simply called out, "Let's see what you've got!" In every corner of the hall, dancers sprang into action, spinning, flipping and jerking their bodies like zombies and robots.

And this is going to work too, thought Della, as she surveyed the scene. She'd known all along that it would. After all, she was a professional.

The minute she got home, Flora picked up the phone.

"Pauline Owen," answered the formal voice at the other end of the line.

"Pauline!" squeaked Flora, shrill with excitement. "I've found him! I've found the pianist we need. His name is Ronnie Andrews, and he says he'll help us. I've got his number... he'll be just perfect."

"Can you come here right now?" said Pauline, the enthusiasm in her voice matching Flora's own. "I'll ring him straight away, and then get on to the administrator at Hope Hall to make us a booking. Flora, I do believe the Can't Sing Singers are on their way!"

When the front door bell rang, Ray opened up to find Shirley standing on the doorstep, grinning widely.

"Hi, Ray. I brought homemade chicken soup for Sara, along with some of those soft bread rolls that she seems to be able to manage. And there's a beef stew here for you. I made dumplings. I know you like them."

"Shirley, that's really kind, but you don't need to do all this."

"I know. That's what you keep saying. But I also know you'd do the same for me, if our places were reversed. How's Sara? What did the nurse say this morning?"

Ray lowered his voice as he led Shirley through to the kitchen. "She said Sara is fading just a little bit more every day. I can see it. She's so tired, and there's no colour in her face. She knows she's going. We can both tell, although we don't mention it. We never give it a name."

"Of course not – but my nan always used to say that where there's life, there's hope, so it's a mistake to assume the worst just because it looks that way."

"It *is* that way, Shirley," was Ray's gentle reply.

Shirley nodded, then squeezed his arm. "Right, I'll put this stew in the oven to warm up for you, but Sara's soup can be ready in no time. Is she awake?"

"She was a minute ago."

"Good. I'll take these daffodils up to her and say hello. And then I'll run the vacuum over."

"Honestly, Shirley, I can do that."

"Yes, I know, and probably much better than me, but I'm still going to do it anyway, because I know how you'll worry if you don't get chance to do it after all."

Ray knew when he was beaten. His head tilted as he looked back at her. "You're a good girl, Shirley Wells – a new friend, but a really wonderful one. Thank you."

"You're not so bad yourself. Now, where's that teapot?"

The storm that had raged all night, with its high winds whistling around the houses and fat raindrops thumping against roofs and windows, was still stubbornly sitting over the town that morning. Carol held her breath as she put the key in the ignition of the car, letting out a huge sigh of relief as it sparked into life. Thank goodness. She just hoped it would keep going. This wasn't the day to be stranded on the roadside anywhere.

Phil had set off early that morning, on his way to a big conference a couple of hours' drive along the coast in Brighton. He had been quite chatty over breakfast about how much he was looking forward to the whole-day event. There would be quite a few potential clients there and, in his business, networking was everything. The managing director of his own company was going to be with their team too, so this would be a good opportunity for Phil to impress with his own business acumen and sharp new ideas. He yelled goodbye to Carol and Little Joe, humming to himself as he climbed into his car and hit the road.

The first call to his phone came at quarter to ten. There was another at ten o'clock, and two more within the next twenty minutes. They were all from Carol. Phil did glance at his phone and saw she'd called, but he had just met up with the team, and the MD was giving them a pep talk. He'd ring back later, if he had chance.

Then Rob rang – at twelve-twenty-five, and again at five to two. At three-fifteen, Carol rang one last time. Phil didn't manage to answer any of the calls.

It was with a great sense of satisfaction that Phil finally closed the car door and drove away from the conference centre. What a day! He knew he'd made a good impression. The MD had said as much when he shook Phil's hand as they were both leaving. There was the whiff of promotion in the air, a management place left vacant by Matt Benson, who'd recently left to head up a department in a rival company. That job would be just right for Phil. He was the perfect fit, and it looked as if the MD was thinking along those lines too.

The phone rang, and he clicked to take the call from his friend Rob.

"Hi, Rob. Sorry I couldn't ring back earlier. Busy day."

"Yeah, well, I've been busy too. Dreadful business with Carol this morning."

"What business?"

"Don't tell me you haven't spoken to her!"

"No, I've been tied up for hours. What happened?"

"Her car broke down on the dual carriageway at the height of the rush hour. It caused quite an incident. Traffic piled up behind her, and tempers got very frayed until the police arrived. She had Little Joe with her and they were both really upset, so the police looked after them until I could get there to tow the car away."

"Oh, I didn't know. Poor Carol."

"The car's a complete write-off. In fact, the police are thinking of pressing charges because of all the things that were wrong with it."

"Oh!" For the first time, Phil sounded as if he might be genuinely worried.

"I think I managed to stave them off by promising that the next stop for that mess of a vehicle would be the breaker's yard."

"What, you mean it really is a write-off?"

"More than that, the police said it was a death-trap."

Rob could practically hear his friend gulp at this news.

Finally, Phil said, "Well, sorry you got dragged into this – thanks for sorting it all out with the police, mate."

"I think it's Carol who needs the apology."

"Yeah, of course. I'll talk to her tonight. I suppose I'll have to look for another car for her now, which we could definitely do without at the moment."

"No problem. It's all organized. A car came into the garage for part exchange yesterday afternoon. It's absolutely perfect for her. Carol loved it the moment she saw it."

"Oh, right…" Phil's voice was uncertain. "How much is it?"

"Three and a half thousand pounds, but it'll last her for a good few years."

"No chance, mate. We can't stretch to that."

"But you already have. Carol nipped down to the building society straight away and drew the cash out. The car is hers. I expect she'll be wanting to show you all its great features the moment you get home."

There was a stunned silence at the other end of the line.

"Got to go," said Rob. "A customer's just come in." He put down the phone and looked across the garage waiting room towards Carol and Jen, who were sipping glasses of Prosecco on the battered settee, with Little Joe propped up between them munching a chocolate biscuit. Suddenly, the room exploded with noise as the two girls shrieked and hugged each other, and Rob roared with laughter.

"He swallowed the whole story just as we thought he would. I don't know how I managed not to laugh out loud when he sounded so shocked at the price you've just paid for your new car, Carol."

"Well," spluttered Jen, wiping tears of laughter from her eyes. "That rainstorm this morning was so perfectly timed. No wonder he believed every word. You told him enough times that your car kept breaking down, so it was absolutely possible that it might just come to a grinding halt on a rainy day like today, in the middle of the dual carriageway in the rush hour, and cause a massive jam."

"I love the bit you came up with about the police threatening to press charges over the state of the car," squealed Carol, helpless with laughter.

"It was a good job we knew Phil had to be away all day at that conference," grinned Rob. "It was obvious he'd never answer his phone, not to me and not to you, whatever trouble you were in. So he did what we knew he'd do – he ignored my warnings, didn't take our calls – so he can see that we had no choice but to sort things out ourselves. Your old car is at the scrapyard, where it belongs, and you are the proud owner of a beautiful new vehicle."

"And all the while," said Jen, raising her glass, "Carol and I were sitting here snug and warm, nowhere near rain or roundabouts or policemen, drinking coffee and enjoying the thought of Phil getting his comeuppance!"

"What happens when he realizes how we tricked him?" asked Carol, her voice now quieter. "What am I going to say to him?"

"Now let me think," retorted Jen. "Oh, I know! When it comes to taking someone for a ride, anything he can do, *you* can do better!"

"I still can't get over the way he lied to me. I really thought we had no secrets."

Jen leaned across to put an arm around her friend's shoulders. "I know, love. You two have got some talking to do."

"We've all got some talking to do," said Rob firmly. "We four are best friends, and nothing's going to change that. But Phil's been acting out of order, and today we've put that right. We're all going back to your house now to welcome Phil home, show him how delighted you and Little Joe are with the new car – and tell the old skinflint that he's going to have to start saving up again for that wreck of a bike of his!"

Chapter 5

Maggie always looked forward to every other Sunday when Darren and his partner Sonia came over for lunch. It was a routine that had worked very happily for the two years the couple had been together. Maggie had hoped that Darren might have popped the question by now. After all, it would be hard for her good-natured, warm-hearted son to find a girl more suitable, practical, devoted and loyal than Sonia. It seemed, though, that the modern generation had a more relaxed attitude to the way in which a couple's commitment to each other should be expressed. While Maggie was thinking about marriage, Darren and Sonia had casually started living together and found they liked it that way. While she thought weddings, they thought mortgages, and even though the possibility of saving enough for a deposit was a distant dream, the couple were determined to put every possible penny into their house fund rather than rush out to choose wedding rings.

Oh well, thought Maggie, in her usual, practical manner. *I look dreadful in a hat anyway.*

So, when Darren suggested a break to the usual Sunday routine, Maggie wondered what could be important enough to have him making a special effort to see her on a Thursday evening. It was probably nothing, but as she watched her stocky, sandy-haired son walking up the garden path, she realized her heart was thumping.

They hugged. Maggie immediately put the kettle on and cut slices of Darren's favourite chocolate cake to have with their tea. They talked about the weather and the latest episode of *EastEnders*. And then, finally, laying his empty cup down on the coffee table,

Darren cleared his throat before searching in his jacket pocket to draw out a long white envelope. Maggie recognized Dave's handwriting on the front straight away.

"Dad asked me to give you this." His eyes didn't meet hers as he spoke.

Maggie made no move to take the letter. "Why? Why couldn't he just send it in the post – or, even better, come himself – if he has anything to say to me?"

"I don't know, Mum, but he said it was important and you should see it. He thinks you might throw any letter that comes from him in the post straight into the bin, and he wanted to make sure that didn't happen. He said to tell you that you must read it."

Her hand was shaking as she stretched out to take it, her fingers fumbling to open the envelope.

"Here, let me," he offered, taking the envelope back from her and sliding his finger along the top to open it.

"I haven't got my glasses," she mumbled.

"Shall I get them for you?"

"No, I don't think I'd be able to make out the words even then. Would you mind—"

"Reading it for you? I will, if you're sure that's what you want."

"I'm not sure of anything, Darren. Nothing at all."

He sat down on the sofa beside his mum, so that they could both watch as he slowly removed the letter to discover that there were two pages, one on top of the other. The top one had Mandy's address as a heading, and was dated two days earlier. The text had been neatly typed before Dave had added his signature at the bottom.

"Dave can't type," snapped Maggie. "That woman must have typed all this and made him sign it."

Darren reached over to take his mother's hand before he started reading.

Dear Maggie

This letter is to inform you fully of my situation. There are several actions that need to be taken at this time, and I hope you will understand that it's urgent we get matters between us formalized as soon as possible.

I am delighted to say that Mandy is pregnant. It wasn't something we planned, but it has happened and we couldn't be happier. I hope you will find it in your heart to welcome this new baby into our family circle.

Obviously, I now have to make arrangements for my new responsibility. Mandy's house is only rented, and really is too small for the two of us when we have Belle and Marlin to consider too. The new baby deserves a more settled start in life than this. Our family needs a house of our own, and because you have always been a wonderful parent yourself, a homemaker and a very kind person, I am sure you are sensible enough to understand that.

So even though this may be happening faster than you would want, I have been to a solicitor to start divorce proceedings. His letter is enclosed with this one. I'm sure you'll agree that we need to put this behind us without delay, so that we can all get on with our lives.

It will mean that our house must be sold. The mortgage is all paid up, and my solicitor says that I am entitled to the full fifty per cent of its value. I have rung Morgan's estate agents on the High Street, and they will be contacting you this week to arrange a time to measure up and give us a valuation. If you're working and can't be there for their visit or any future viewings, do ring me and I'll come to the house to show people round myself. I'd be very happy to do that if it helps make things more convenient for you.

There are certain pieces of furniture and other items I would like to collect from the house, some of which we really need right away. I want the complete contents of the shed, as that has always been more my area than yours anyway. That includes the lawn mower, the new barbecue, all the ladders and most of the tools, except the older ones. Obviously the kitchen is where you prefer to be, but I do intend to take the electric knife, the microwave, the halogen oven, and the crystal whisky glass set that my Auntie Dot gave us when we married. The decanter should come too, so the set stays together.

We're okay for crockery, as Mandy has more modern taste than you, so please feel free to keep all that. You'll remember that when we decided to buy the big television in the lounge, you said it could be for my birthday, so that TV is mine, along with both games consoles and all the DVDs. I'd like the big coffee table too, and the sofa that turns into a bed settee. I'm taking the new vacuum cleaner, because you've got two at the house and the one here isn't working. We need to talk about your car as well. We got that estate to carry your catering things around, but I really need an estate car now. My car is a bit newer, so you can have mine and I'll keep the estate. I think that's fair. Please let me know when I can come with a van to collect all these items and everything else at the house that is rightfully mine.

In my newfound happiness, I still realize how much this has hurt you, and want you to know that was never our intention. I hope that any upset will soon be over and that we can look forward to being good friends and co-parents to our enlarged family in the future.

Yours sincerely

David Stapleton

Maggie let out a squeal of anger. Mild-mannered, gentle Maggie – the woman who was always in the kitchen, always looking after others, always devoted to her family – thumped her fists into the sofa cushions until the tears came and she collapsed into Darren's arms, sobbing until there was no breath left in her. When she finally slumped back into the seat, Darren disentangled himself and went to fetch her a small glass of sherry from the drinks cabinet.

"I don't want that."

"You always said it was good for shock. You're in shock."

"I can't drink it."

"Oh well," said Darren, downing the dark brown liquid in one gulp. "I'm in shock too. I can't believe Dad would write that."

"He didn't. *She* did. Your dad can't string two words together on paper. I've always written his letters. Now she's his secretary, along with every other role in his life that she's taken from me."

"Are you going to reply?"

"What can I say? There are no polite words to answer that insulting, patronizing, selfish, cruel piece of rubbish!"

"But the estate agent? Can you do anything about that?"

"Your dad can't sell this house. It's our home. It's been our home since we married. It's *your* home. It's mine. I live here. Where else would I go?"

"Mum, I wonder if you need to see a solicitor too? You need to know what your rights are. If you're going to fight this, you must get some professional help."

"How am I going to be able to afford a solicitor's fee? They cost a fortune. I'm struggling to pay the bills every month as it is. I've got nothing to fight this with."

"Sonia and I will find whatever's needed for the bill."

"No," replied Maggie, covering his hand with hers. "No, that's very kind of you, but you need the money for your deposit. It doesn't look as if Dad and I will be able to help you out with that now, as we always planned, so you need to keep every penny you've saved for yourselves."

"We won't let you go through this alone, Mum. We're here for you."

"I know, love. I just need to calm down a bit and think."

"Would you like me to stay here tonight?"

"No. I'll be all right. In fact, I think it would be good to be on my own right now. Perhaps my thoughts will be a bit clearer then."

"Are you sure?"

"Yes, you get on home. Give Sonia my love. Will I see you both on Sunday?"

"We'd love to, if you're up to it. I'll ring you first thing tomorrow morning, Mum – and if you need anything tonight, you just call me. Promise?"

"Promise," she agreed, "but I'll be fine."

With one long, emotion-filled hug, Darren finally closed the front door behind him. As Maggie watched him getting into his car, she knew what she had to do. Picking up the phone, she dialled the number she needed.

"Hello?" said a familiar voice.

"Kath, it's Maggie. I've had a solicitor's letter from Dave. It's absolutely floored me—"

"Put that kettle on. I'm on my way."

It was raining the following afternoon as they walked away from the office of Sewell & Co. Kath had known exactly which solicitor could best help Maggie. Brian Sewell and Kath served on the Good Neighbours executive committee together, and had always got on well. When he agreed to see Maggie immediately, Kath insisted on driving her friend to his office, which was more than ten miles away. Maggie had worried about speaking to someone too local, because she had lived in their town all her life, and knew such a wide circle of people, especially because of her role as Catering Manager at

Hope Hall. She was appalled at the idea of people knowing her business. This whole nightmare was so raw and shocking that she was finding it hard enough to cope with it herself, let alone having to pretend she was all right to people she hardly knew. Though some of them may well be genuine and full of sympathy, others were just as likely to be nothing more than nosey parkers.

Kath steered her across the road to a small teashop, its windows steamed up against the miserable weather. Inside, though, the aroma of coffee, the chintzy tables decorated with small jugs of fresh flowers, the serving area displaying cakes, savouries and sandwiches, and a friendly waitress all welcomed them in like a big warm hug. With her professional eye, Maggie peered at each cake and pastry in turn before she made her final choice of a huge slab of lemon meringue pie with a dollop of clotted cream. Then they made their way to a quiet corner table while they waited for their order to arrive.

"I've always wanted a place like this," sighed Maggie. "To have a little café serving every kind of cake under the sun – that's been my dream since I was at school and first discovered that academic subjects weren't for me. Then I started Home Economics – that's what they used to call cookery classes in those days – and I felt as if I'd come home the moment I walked into that kitchen. I'd found my passion."

The waitress brought across their drinks, a pot of Earl Grey tea for Kath, and a hot chocolate topped with whipped cream, chocolate sprinkles and marshmallows for Maggie.

"You know what they say," she said, as she popped a pink marshmallow into her mouth. "A little of what you fancy..."

"... does you good!" finished Kath. "You deserve something good, dear Maggie, with all the rubbish that's landing on you at the moment. How do you feel after that meeting?"

"Better." Maggie looked thoughtful as she dipped a long-handled spoon into the cream on top of her hot chocolate. "I felt totally out of control last night, as if my world was being torn apart and ransacked, and I couldn't do a thing about it. But I *do* have rights, and at least now Brian can be the one to tell Dave what those rights are. He can't just barge in and cherry-pick all the best items from our house, my *home*, simply because he's decided that's what he wants. I mean, having another baby when he's fifty-two years old!"

Unable to stop herself, Maggie chuckled. "And I wish him luck with that. He was never good with our kids when they were babies. He hated being woken up in the night, and he didn't cope very well with all those years of early mornings when they'd want us to get up at six o'clock just because they were awake. I can't remember him ever changing a nappy, or having any patience when they kicked balls around in the lounge or had a Star Wars fight in the middle of his vegetable patch. He hated it when I insisted we all went out for the day in the car. He was always grumpy, and would go off on his own, usually to a nearby pub, so that he could get a bit of peace and quiet before the drive home.

"My Dave likes routine. He likes dinner on the table at six, his shirts all hung up in the wardrobe with the top button done up and all the coat hangers facing in exactly the same direction, and he gets in a real strop if anyone dares to take the TV remote control without his permission. And there he is, bringing up someone else's children, having his meals cooked by a dolly bird with 'more modern taste' than me. He's even having to take an interest in whether the vacuum cleaner works. I didn't think he knew what a vacuum cleaner was before now! And what's more, that grumpy old man is going to have a new baby on his hands. Really, this couldn't be happening to a nicer fella."

"You *are* going to change those locks on all the doors, though," pressed Kath. "You don't want him turning up with a van when you're not there. He knows what hours you work."

"I'll sort that out straight away when I get back home."

"And how do you feel about the divorce itself? It's a very emotional decision to make."

Maggie nodded. "Yes, it is. I can't believe it's happening. We've always been so strong as a couple, as a family. Never a cross word really, nothing that ever worried us. We've been very happy, completely comfortable together through all these years."

Kath reached out to cover her friend's hand. "You will be happy again. You may not feel it now, but you are such a wonderful person, Mags. Everyone loves you."

"Except my husband." Maggie's eyes suddenly filled with tears, and she fumbled for the tissue she kept up the sleeve of her cardigan, to dab them dry.

"Still," she said at last, with a note of determination in her voice, "I have to be practical. After all, that's what Dave is doing. He's sorting out what he wants for his future. I need to do that too."

There was a lull in their conversation as Maggie stabbed a fork into her lemon meringue pie.

"What do you think will happen?" asked Kath as she picked up the freshly made shortbread she'd chosen. "Do you think Dave will stick at this?"

Maggie considered the question.

"Not a chance! That's my gut feeling, but it's based on the character of the Dave I knew. I'd never have imagined he had it in him to do something as dramatic as this. All this change, the upheaval, the inconvenience – none of that would have appealed to the Dave I've known for years. But just look at what's happened, so perhaps I never really knew him at all. I thought we were settled and contented, but maybe he thought our marriage was just boring. He must have wanted something different, something dramatic and exciting that would give him the life he really wished he'd had. I mean, what's exciting about me? I *am* boring."

"No," said Kath firmly. "No, my dear Maggie, there is nothing even remotely boring about you."

Maggie shrugged, as if she couldn't believe that.

"If he turned up at the door tomorrow saying it was all a horrible mistake, and he's sorry and wants to come back, what would you say?"

"I'd shut the door in his face. I am so angry at the moment. I'd tell him where to shove his apology."

"That's the spirit!"

"But I don't know how I'll feel a couple of months down the line. I'm not the sort of person who enjoys living on her own. My home has always been full of family – but the kids have left, and now Dave's gone too…"

Maggie bristled as a new thought occurred to her. "And where will my home be anyway? The solicitor says I'll have to agree to the house being sold. We moved into that house the year we were married, a lifetime ago. Where will I be this time next year? What have I got to look forward to?"

Once again, as tears began to course their way down her cheeks, Maggie's shoulders slumped and her head dropped in an effort to hide her misery.

A classroom on the ground floor of the old school building was booked, and the piano placed there in good time for the first official gathering of the Can't Sing Singers. Pauline and Flora arrived first, followed minutes later by Peter and Olive Spencer (husband and wife, both in their eighties); Brenda Parker (loud voice but stone deaf – always picked a note, any note, and stuck to it); Mary Brownlow and her sister Elizabeth (spinster sisters, members of the St Mark's Church choir since attending Sunday school there fifty years earlier); Sophia Mansell (in her late forties, a contralto who says she was professionally trained when she was a young woman); and Bruce Edison, who used to sing in a rock band. One unexpected latecomer was Keith Turner, a young man with a lovely tenor voice to whom Gregory, the new music maestro at the church, had graciously awarded a place in the prestigious St Mark's Choral Choir. Keith loved a bit of scandal almost as much as he loved singing, so he couldn't resist taking a peep at the breakaway group.

"The St Mark's rehearsals are all so *serious* now," he moaned. "He makes us do scales and vocal exercises before we start – all that na-na-na-na-na and me-me-me-me-me! And we have to read music, which you know has never been my forte. *This* choir sounds like *much* more fun. What are we going to sing?"

"A good question," said the tall figure who walked into the room at just that moment. They looked up from their gossipy huddle to see a man in his late fifties, with thinning hair and very blue eyes that had a definite twinkle in them. Pauline was the first to recover.

"Ronnie! Thank you so much for coming. Shall I do the introductions?"

"I tell you what," said Ronnie, pulling out the piano stool and opening the lid. "Why don't I just play a song or two, and you can all join in whenever you find one you like. If you don't know the words, don't worry. I probably don't either. Remember I'm not expecting much. You've already made it abundantly clear you can't sing!"

They gathered rather shyly round the piano, with Keith, Bruce and Sophia pushing their way to the front, while the others formed an odd-shaped crescent behind them, with sisters Mary and Elizabeth hiding at the back. Peter and Olive didn't move from their seats at the side of the room. Perhaps they thought this was a performance they'd just come along to watch, rather than a rehearsal in which they were expected to take part. It wasn't long, though, before they were joining in with the rest, even though they never left their seats. The music was so infectious. They sang everything from "My Old Man Said Follow the Van" to the "Hallelujah Chorus". They sang "We All Live in a Yellow Submarine" and "All People that on Earth Do Dwell". They sang "Three Blind Mice" in a round, and "Amazing Grace" with an attempt at a line or two of harmony.

That was the point at which Ronnie finally stopped playing. They all held their breath as they looked for his reaction. Were they too terrible for a professional like him to consider? Was it possible that anyone able to play as wonderfully as Ronnie could ever really want to take on a mismatched, out-of-tune, over-enthusiastic but thoroughly endearing bunch like them?

His broad smile came like a ray of bright sunshine. "Brilliant! I haven't been so entertained by singing in years. You are *so* terrible that you're glorious. Can't Sing Singers, you've just got yourselves a musical director."

The following week as pensioners began arriving for the Grown-ups' Lunch, Ida clucked with disapproval as she squeezed past Percy Wilson on her way to join Betty, Doris and Flora at the next table.

"Just look," grinned Percy, nudging Connie to look in the right direction. "There they are – the Merry Widows. Mind you, you can't be merry and look down your nose at the same time, can you? Perhaps that's why they always seem so miserable."

Two old friends, John and Harold, reached them at that moment, and asked if the remaining seats on the table for four had been taken.

"No, lads. Come and join us!" guffawed Percy, his arms thrown wide in welcome. "John, I've not seen you for months. How've you been?"

"I lost Marion. Did you know?"

"I did hear," replied Percy, his voice softening. "She'd been ill for a while, hadn't she?"

"Two years since the diagnosis. She put up a good fight, my girl."

"Well, I'm sorry to hear that. Your Marion was a good 'un. Made the best fruit cake I've ever tasted."

John smiled in agreement.

100

"And Robert, are you still playing bowls?"

"The odd game of carpet bowls once in a while. The outdoor club got too competitive for me – all that spiteful business with people trying to distract players as they bowled, getting in their eyeline at the crucial moment. I only ever went along for the tea at half-time and the company."

"We three go back a long way, Connie. Robert and I played in the church football team, and John, you joined our youth club, didn't you?"

"We all lived quite close to each other, you see," John explained to Connie. "We never had television or any of those computer games the kids have today. We just hung around together."

"Mostly up to no good," chortled Robert. "We stood on street corners hoping our dads wouldn't catch us sharing a fag."

"Well, your dad was always a bit of a hoot," grinned Percy. "All those stories he told about being a painter and decorator, the things he got up to…"

"Oh, he had dozens of tales to tell. He did make us laugh, although I'm not sure Mum always approved."

Percy's eyes sparkled as he thought back. "Do you remember that one he told us about when he was painting Mr and Mrs Smith's outdoor lavatory at number 17?"

"Oh yes," roared Robert. "How could any of us forget that?"

"What happened?" asked Connie.

"Well," said Robert, "Dad was known in the area as a good handyman, able to do a reliable job on anything needed in a house. Mr and Mrs Smith booked him to paint their outside toilet in green and white paint. Dad had done all the gloss paintwork and thought he'd take a break outside, but when he went to clean his brushes, he realized that he'd left his usual paintbrush cleaning rag behind, so he nipped into the lav, pulled off some sheets of toilet paper to wipe the brushes, threw the lot down the pan and shut the lid. He was just outside putting his other stuff away when Mr Smith came hurrying out of the house. He rushed into the smallest room and slammed the door behind him. Apparently, he wasn't allowed to smoke indoors, so he liked to sit on the lav and smoke for a while after lunch.

"Just then, Mrs Smith called Dad into the kitchen for a cup of tea, and suddenly there was a howl of pain, and Mr Smith came flying out of the lavatory with his trousers round his ankles! He'd sat down as usual, and because he was engrossed in his newspaper, he did what he always did, and lit his cigarette with the box of matches he kept on the windowsill. Then he threw the match down the lav between his legs. The toilet paper all soaked in my dad's gloss paint ignited – so, with flames licking at his underpinnings, Mr Smith upped and ran for his life!"

The table erupted with laughter, until eventually Connie made herself heard enough to ask, "Did your dad get paid?"

Robert immediately stopped laughing as he considered the question. "Do you know, I can't tell you the answer to that – but that story is absolutely priceless."

Toby and Max leapt out of the car and belted at full speed towards the main door of Hope Hall in their enthusiasm to get to their second Beaver meeting. Catching up, Gary helped them wiggle out of their jackets and change their shoes before going through to the hall. A small group of parents were in the foyer, some chatting together as if they knew each other quite well, others leaving as soon as their sons were settled. A coffee, thought Gary. Perhaps he'd master the intricacies of the machine a little better this time.

And he did. With triumph he withdrew a cup of hot coffee that smelt okay, even if the colour was a rather odd shade of mucky grey.

"Well done!" said a voice behind him. "You've cracked it."

Gary turned to see Claire's friendly smile as she reached out to take a cup for herself.

"Your boys were keen to come back then?"

"Honestly, they've been counting the days," grinned Gary.

"Josh is just the same, especially now he's earned himself a couple of badges. It's all I can do to get him to take that sweatshirt off. I think he'd sleep in it if I let him."

"Do they have to sew the badges on themselves, or is that the challenge they set the parents?"

"No good with a needle and thread then?"

"Hopefully I can pass the buck on that one. Karen used to like sewing, although she doesn't have much time for anything like that now."

Claire's expression was questioning as she turned back from pushing buttons to get the coffee she wanted.

"Karen works really long hours. She's in IT, and has to go into London every day."

"Oh, that must be exhausting for her, especially in the rush hour. What time does she leave in the morning?"

"She's always on the quarter past seven train, and gets back in the evening around quarter past seven too. At least she manages to see the boys before bedtime, but only just. It's very hard for her."

Claire watched the coffee steaming into the cup for several moments before she answered.

"How are the boys about their mum having to work such long hours?"

"Ah, you know kids, how resilient they are. They can't remember anything different, so they're used to it really."

"And what does that mean for you?" she asked as Gary led the way over to a table where they both sat down.

"It means that I'm a house husband – well, sort of, because I *am* able to work at home, so it's not as hard as it sounds."

"What do you do?"

"Graphic design. Catalogues, advertising material, magazines – anything that comes my way."

"Freelance then?"

"I am now, but I worked in a big design company for about six years before the boys came along, and when I left, quite a few of my clients followed me. That's meant that I haven't had to struggle too much to keep the money coming in."

"Do you miss working in a team with other designers around you? Does that matter in your line of work?"

Gary stirred his coffee as he thought about the answer.

"I suppose I do in some ways. It's good to spark off other people, share ideas and concepts. But I don't miss all the internal politics of working in a large company. Every single meeting we ever had there seemed to start with a discussion about who was eligible to use the company car park spaces."

She laughed. "It's just like that at the school where I work. There are only four parking places on the school premises, because all the other ground is needed as a playground for the children. The spaces go to the headmaster, the deputy head and then two different heads of department on a rota basis."

"How many departments are there?"

"It's a big secondary school. There must be about ten departments in all."

"So the rota is hotly disputed then?"

She chuckled. "You can say that again. The daggers are out, I can tell you."

"Not slicing tyres, I hope!"

"I wouldn't have put that past a couple of them."

"Do you ever get a space?"

"A lowly assistant in the art department? Not likely! No, I got a bike instead."

Gary laughed. "Keeps you out of trouble and in shape too."

"Difficult to balance my art folder, though."

"What kind of things do you do?"

"Well, the kids range from eleven to eighteen, although the

older ones are doing A-levels so I don't have much to do with them. It's mostly for the younger classes – and I do all sorts of work really. I prepare for lessons, of course, following whatever the teacher has planned for them, then clear up afterwards, and make sure all the artwork is kept safely so that the students can add to it again the following week if they need to. And I mount exhibitions of the pupils' best work. I also catalogue and submit the pieces they're putting in as part of their external exams."

"Are you an artist yourself?"

"Perhaps in another life I might have been, but art wasn't really offered as a viable option for girls at my own school. My parents were both professional people who thought the only way forward was academic study, and I suppose I did well enough at all those basic subjects. I was able to do art as part of the general curriculum as I moved up the school, but when it came to exams, my parents made it clear that art was a frivolous subject that would never fit into the career progression they had in mind for me."

"That's awful."

"I didn't realize it at the time, because I just did what I was told. I got four A-levels in Maths, English, Biology and Latin, and before I knew it I was enrolled at university to study medicine."

"Wow, so you trained to be a doctor?"

"For four years, yes, I did. And then, just to prove my complete understanding and grip on all the intricate workings of the human body, I got pregnant with Josh."

"Aah. How did your parents react to that news?"

"Badly. They stopped talking to me for ages."

"And the father?"

"Nigel and I got married."

"Was he studying to be a doctor too?"

"No, he's a chemist. He works in the research labs of one of the big pharmaceutical companies. He loves it. That kind of work is right up his street."

"But your studies had to stop, I suppose, with Josh to look after?"

"Yes, and honestly I didn't mind. By that time I'd realized that medicine was more the choice of my parents than something that really interested me. And I loved Nigel, even though marriage had never been part of our plan until then. It just seemed the right thing to do when we knew Josh was on the way. And becoming a mother made me complete. That's the only way I can describe the feeling that overwhelmed me the moment I first held Josh in my arms – and I've never stopped feeling that way."

"And the art assistant job? How did that happen?"

"Well, with a little boy to entertain, I found myself really enjoying doing artwork with him – drawing, painting, making and building things. I'd have been a great presenter on *Blue Peter*, making something out of nothing – all those creations from washing-up bottles and papier mâché! And then, when Josh started at playgroup, I went along too as a helper, and found that I had endless ideas for things the children could try and enjoy. It was the woman who ran that playgroup who pointed me in the direction of a course at the local college here which would give me a qualification to become a teaching assistant. I thought I might end up working with infant or junior school children, but the only job that came up at the time when I started looking was for the senior school, and I have to say I love it."

"And your parents – did they ever come round?"

"Very reluctantly. It took a couple of years, though. They didn't come to our wedding, and they didn't see Josh until he was six months old. Mum and I managed an occasional telephone call, but we both knew Dad would be furious if she blatantly disobeyed him to see me. It was Dad who was laying down the law about cutting ties with me because I was such a disappointment to the family. Thank goodness my brother was able to do his duty and become a lawyer!"

"So were you eventually able to meet up with your mum?"

"Yes. I was longing to see her, and she couldn't wait to meet Josh. We both just burst into tears. We sat in my car with Josh in the back, and sobbed our hearts out. The problem then was how to bring Dad round."

"But you did it?"

"In the end, it was Josh who did it. I didn't want to go to the house – too many bad memories of huge arguments there – so I suggested that we meet at the park, where there was a playground for little children that Josh always loved. Mum was able to persuade Dad to come and join us, although I could tell Dad was really unhappy about the whole idea. He hardly spoke to me, just let Mum do the talking, but he was watching Josh all the time. Then, when Josh took a tumble, he leapt up and went over to help, and Josh just accepted him being there as if he'd known him all his life. Dad was charmed, and his fascination with Josh has never stopped since."

"And you? Did he soften towards you too?"

"A bit, but for him the main issue was Nigel. Dad blamed him for taking up my time at uni when I should have been studying. He was totally dismissive of our marriage. He thought that I'd married beneath myself and was destined for a life of ruin and domestic drudgery. Dad refused to meet him from the very start, and became more and more entrenched in his views as time went on."

"Which I'm sure went down like a bomb with Nigel."

"He was furious. He *is* furious. He's a brilliant, well-respected research scientist, and he's achieved all that in spite of coming from a family where no one had ever wanted to go to university before. And his family are wonderful – a big, warm-hearted gaggle of relatives that accepted me just as I am from the moment I first met them."

"And how did things with your parents work out?"

"Well, for some time I took Josh round to see them quite

regularly. Dad adores Josh, but it created problems when he kept buying him expensive toys, mostly way beyond his age group. Naturally enough, Nigel really resented him doing that. He got more and more angry whenever Josh came back with an expensive bike, or a tablet or his own mobile phone so that Grandad could ring him directly without having to come through us."

Gary grunted disapproval. "That is not fair. I don't blame your husband at all for being furious about that. You two are Josh's parents. Those special gifts need to come from you, when you know Josh is ready for them, and when you are able to monitor their use as you see fit."

"Definitely. Nigel and I are in complete agreement about that. But Dad always seemed to find a way to give those things to Josh before I even knew they were coming. He just came out with them, and once Josh had seen them, it was impossible for me to take them away again. I asked him so many times not to do it any more, and eventually Nigel sent him a very firm letter telling him that future gifts could only be given when we had prior knowledge and had agreed that the gifts were appropriate."

"How did your dad take that?"

"When Josh and I were at my parents' house a few days later, Dad was out in the garden with him. It seems that he gave Josh a pep talk about what a wonderful and talented boy he was. Then he said that Nigel and I, his mum and dad, simply didn't realize that he was so clever, and we were jealous that we couldn't afford all the special presents that Grandad wanted to give him. Then he asked a four-year-old boy if he wanted to carry on getting presents from Grandad, or whether he wanted to do what his mum and dad suggested and have none."

Gary sighed with disbelief.

"Well, you can imagine Nigel's reaction when he heard about that! He got in the car and drove straight round to my parents' home to meet them for the very first time. I had to stay with Josh, of course, so my heart was in my mouth as I thought about my husband and my father meeting at last. It all went so badly. Nigel was standing on the doorstep shouting at Dad, and my father was superior and insulting, which to Nigel was unforgivable. My mum was tearful and trying to come between them. It was all a complete disaster. In the end, Dad slammed the door shut and Nigel drove home. He stood in the living room, his face purple with anger, and told me that if my parents ever tried to have anything to do with his family again, he would leave me and take Josh with him."

A long breath whistled through Gary's lips as he pulled back from an instinctive desire to put his arm around Claire's shoulders as she sat beside him, distraught and near to tears.

"And now?" he asked at last.

"Now, I speak to Mum on the phone quite often, but I have to make sure Nigel doesn't know, and she only ever rings when she's certain Dad isn't listening. Josh asks about his grandad all the time. He doesn't understand why he can't see him, and he gets really upset because of what my dad told him – that his mum and dad don't realize how special he is, and it is only because we are unreasonable and jealous that he isn't allowed to spend time with his grandad and have lovely presents from him."

"That must make it very difficult for you and Nigel."

"It's driving a huge wedge between us really. He's probably guessed that I still keep in touch with Mum, but he never asks. In our house, my family are a taboo subject, including my brother Dan, who has children of his own now, Josh's cousins. Nigel has never met them either because of Dad's attitude towards him from the start. But Dan's my brother. I love him and have always kept in touch with him, in spite of Nigel's attitude to my family. Apart from anything else, I want Josh to know his cousins as they're growing up. Nigel will have nothing to do with any of them, though, and the atmosphere when he suspects we might have seen them is icy for days."

"That's tough."

"Nigel can't understand why I feel the need to bother with my family at all when his own are so straightforward and welcoming. He thinks they already provide all the love and company that Josh and I should ever want or need."

"But for you that's not enough."

"I try to understand his point of view. I try not to feel resentful. Sometimes I can't work out if I'm more disappointed in my father as a parent or in Nigel as a husband. Surely he can see how unhappy this has been making not just me, but Josh too?"

"But your father was way out of line."

"Absolutely. This is all his fault – and I don't want you to think that I don't love Nigel, because I do. It's just that there's this gaping void inside me that should be filled by the unconditional love and support surely any of us should expect from our own parents. My mum and dad always wanted to control me, to live out their own aspirations through me, and in the end I couldn't bear that burden. I disappointed them, but they have disappointed me too. It's all become a dull ache of frustration and despair that I constantly feel. It colours everything."

Without thinking, Gary reached out to take Claire's hand. She didn't pull away. Perhaps she was so deeply engrossed in her own thoughts that she didn't even notice.

A loud cheer from the Beavers in the hall suddenly broke the atmosphere. Their hands were instantly withdrawn, and Claire quickly rubbed her fingers across her cheeks to wipe away the tears that shone there. A man came across from the other side of the foyer to make himself a coffee, calling out to ask the parents he'd just been talking to whether any of them wanted him to bring them back a drink. Gary and Claire sat quietly together, not able to speak, but both feeling there was so much they wanted to say.

Sometime later, the glass doors opened and the boys came pouring out.

"Dad, we've got to buy our sweatshirts!" yelled Max, beckoning furiously at his father. "Bear's got some ready for us. Can you bring the money?"

Gary shot a wry smile at Claire. "Duty calls."

She nodded. "It never stops."

"You okay?"

"Oh, I'm fine."

"See you next week?"

"Definitely."

He pushed back his chair and picked up the boys' jackets. "Bye then."

"Bye, Gary."

Seeing the deep wells of sadness in her eyes as she looked at him, his heart contracted with compassion. "Bye, Claire. Take care of yourself."

"You too."

And they both walked over to join their boys.

Chapter 6

Kath's home phone was ringing as she put her key in the door. Hurrying to catch the call, she fumbled with her latchkey and bag, throwing both onto the carved box in the hallway as she reached for the phone.

"Oh, Kath, I was just about to leave a message!"

"Denise, how lovely to hear from you! I've been meaning to ring you."

"Yeah, yeah," retorted her old friend Denise with affectionate humour in her voice. "I know you're a country bumpkin now and have probably got lots of jam to make and harvest festivals to organize."

Kath laughed, kicking her shoes off and taking the phone with her through to the living room, where she slumped down to stretch herself out along the length of the sofa.

"And, of course, you'll be fighting off all those gentlemen farmers!"

"I don't know any farmers—"

"And you don't know any gentlemen either. Country life sounds better and better."

"Believe me, Denise, that couldn't be further from the truth."

"But you're happy, aren't you?" asked Denise, her tone more serious now. "This move from London has worked out as you hoped it would?"

"Well, I could have done without having to nurse Mum for all that time. It's horrible to see someone you love suffer."

"I'm sorry. I didn't mean to sound trite."

"Of course you did, my lovely friend, and I wouldn't want you any other way. How are things with you? Are you running that hospital yet?"

"Have I taken over the job you were in line for, do you mean?"

"Oh, that seems like a lifetime ago," replied Kath. "I'm not sure I could manage anything as complicated as that these days."

"Well, your job now does sound very different from what you did here."

"And I welcome that. It's a lovely place, Hope Hall. It's got a good heart."

"Can a building have a heart?"

"I have a feeling this one has. I often imagine it as an old-fashioned Victorian grandmother gathering waifs and strays into the folds of her skirt, where they're safe and warm."

"That's very poetic – and doesn't sound like you at all. You're definitely overdue a bit of R&R in the city. And that's why I'm ringing. You *are* coming to the reunion on Friday, aren't you? I don't think you actually replied."

Kath hesitated. "Well, I'm not quite sure. There is an event on at the hall that night. I might need to be there."

"You need to be *here*, my darling Kath! You need to get yourself on a train and meet up with the gang. We miss you loads. Jan and Paul are going. Wendy's coming down from York, and apparently the physio lot are all planning to come too."

"Oh, it would be lovely to see everyone again." Kath realized in that moment that she really meant it.

"Don's coming, and Carrie – and Jack…"

Jack. Just the sound of his name felt like an electric shock after all this time. Jack. The love of her life. The one who'd never asked her. The one she left behind.

"Kath, are you still there?"

"What's Jack doing now?" Her question was as casual as she could make it.

"He's Consultant Paediatric Surgeon in Southampton."

"That's great," smiled Kath. "He deserves it. He was always destined to go far."

"He sent an email yesterday saying he was going to try to come and was asking who was likely to be there. I gave him the list, and included you on it."

"So he then wrote back saying he'd got a prior engagement, did he?"

"Quite the opposite. He said he wouldn't miss it for the world."

"Oh," was all Kath could think of to say.

"And because you're too polite to ask, Jack is still single."

"Married to his work, I expect."

"Or," retorted Denise, "he's never been able to combine the woman he loves with the right timing in both their lives. It sounds as if he's a lot more settled now."

"You are an incurable matchmaker, dear Denise, but it won't work in this case. Jack and I are a thing of the past, and that suits me fine. But yes, I will come. I'll book the train ticket tonight and see you there. Gosh, it's the day after tomorrow, isn't it?"

"Yes, so you only have one day to sort out a drop-dead gorgeous outfit that lets Jack know once and for all that you *are* absolutely fine without him!"

Clucking with amused indignation, Kath said goodbye and then stared ahead thoughtfully for quite a while before she laid the phone down on the coffee table beside her.

So, what *was* she going to wear? Would there be time tomorrow for her to nip out and wander around the department store to see if she could find something elegantly casual for the occasion? A little outfit with a bit of colour and style that someone who was a country bumpkin would *never* wear... And maybe Mark could fit her in for a last-minute colour and trim tomorrow afternoon? Picking up the phone again, she rang the hairdresser's number and left an urgent message asking him to ring her as soon he could the following morning.

***

Maggie checked the diary to see if she'd remembered everything. The next out-of-the-ordinary big event was just over two weeks away now. She was looking forward to the wedding of Esther and David, the young couple who had grown up together as part of the congregation at St Mark's Church just across the road. It was there they would be getting married on the last Saturday afternoon of February, followed by the reception their friends and family were organizing for them at Hope Hall. The "bring and share" meal that was being planned for them was a wonderful idea, in theory. But it was down to Maggie, as Catering Manager at Hope Hall, to ensure that they didn't end up with too many people and not enough for them to eat and drink. Under the original plan, no one had thought to ask those invited whether or not they were actually coming and, if so, exactly what they intended to bring. It would be all too easy to end up with multiple bowls of salad and no main dishes. Or every variety of crisp and not enough proper desserts. Or dozens of cans of beer and no soft drinks or anything suitable with which to toast the bride and groom.

So when the couple and their parents had come along for the initial planning meeting some weeks earlier, Maggie worked with them to set up a link where guests could confirm their attendance and give a precise indication of what they were planning to bring. Because an open invitation had been given to everyone at the church, as well as a wide circle of family and friends, numbers had been largely guesswork. It soon became clear that so many people were likely to come that Maggie would have to approach the formidable Barbara Longstone, Chairwoman of the local Women's Institute, who had a walk-in locked cupboard at Hope Hall in which the WI kept their supplies of tables and chairs, along with a whole range of crockery, cutlery and serving dishes. From past experience, Maggie didn't relish the idea of going into battle with

Mrs Longstone, who was known to push for a hard bargain when it came to fees for the WI equipment. Wonderfully, those worries were all swept away by the bride's mother when she explained that *dear* Barbara was not only one of her oldest friends, but she was making the wedding cake too!

There had been a terrifying moment the previous day when an ear-splitting scream rang out around the building, closely followed by a bellowing cry of "What's the matter?" which unmistakably came from their cleaner, Shirley. Rushing out of the kitchen, Maggie saw that the person screaming was the bride-to-be's sister, Rachel, who was standing outside the WI cupboard, feather duster in hand, her face the colour of chalk.

"Spider!" she managed to say, her voice a high-pitched squeal. "It's enormous. Must have escaped from a zoo or something. Shut that door – and call the fire brigade!"

"Oh, for heaven's sake!" snapped Shirley. "Give me that!"

Snatching the feather duster out of the girl's shaking hand, Shirley marched into the cupboard with all the confidence of a Ghostbuster and re-emerged triumphantly a couple of minutes later with a clear pudding bowl turned upside down on a flat white plate. Inside the bowl squatted a bemused and totally still spider, with its legs folded up neatly beneath its round, black body.

Flattened against the wall and still trembling with panic, Rachel finally peeped at the vile offender. "Is it dead?"

"Nope," replied Shirley, not breaking her stride as she marched towards the back door. "It's just terrified. And before you ask, I'm sure there are plenty more of this spider's family living in that cupboard. So unless you're going to stop being a complete wimp, could you clear away from the door and leave it to us to get out whatever's needed?"

Kath didn't catch the nine-fifty train from Waterloo that night after the reunion. The train she caught didn't leave until nearly midnight. But then she didn't have to travel across London on her own, because Jack was with her.

His was the first face she saw as she walked into the hospital library. As old friends greeted her, and gathered round for hugs and handshakes, she could feel him watching her from across the room. When the next newcomer arrived to be greeted, she walked towards him – and the years fell away.

"You look lovely."

And there it was: the slight Scottish burr as he spoke, the warm tone of his voice, the gaze of his grey eyes that had always reached into the very heart of her.

Afterwards, she could remember little of their conversation. They must have covered the basics of what they'd been doing in the years since they'd last seen each other. She knew that they talked about old friends and new jobs. They'd swapped tales about the areas in which they were now living and working, and the people who had become their colleagues and neighbours. And although she was longing to know who he'd loved since she'd left him, and who was loving him now, she didn't ask, for fear of hearing the answer. Neither did he ask anything personal about the company she was keeping. Perhaps if he had, she could have told him the truth – that there had been no one since him. Then again, maybe she preferred him to think there just might be someone now who adored her enough to want to share her home and her life.

"You know," he said, as the evening drew to an end, "Southampton isn't so far away from your town. You're not all that far from Portsmouth, are you?"

"Uh-huh," she agreed.

"Could we meet up sometime?"

"Well, yes, I suppose so"

"How are you getting back tonight?"

"The train from Waterloo."

"I've driven up. Why don't I drop you off at the station? I could easily pass Waterloo on my way out of London."

"I don't want to put you out."

There was warm affection in his eyes as he simply replied, "It's no trouble."

Several others in the reunion group also had long journeys home, so were starting to say their goodbyes. Kath did the rounds of swapping phone numbers and making promises to meet up again very soon, leaving her farewell to Denise until last.

"He's still into you, isn't he?" Denise whispered in her ear. "It's written all over his face."

"Really?" Kath asked, glad that the evening light was hiding the flush in her cheeks.

"Be careful, dearest Kath. Jack hurt you badly. Take care of that tender heart of yours."

"I'll be fine – but thank you for your care, and thank you for making sure I *did* come tonight."

"Well, ring me first thing in the morning," hissed Denise. "I want to hear every single little detail."

Jack's car was low and sleek. Obviously not a family car, then, she realized with a touch of relief. As he drove, she found herself watching his hands, long-fingered and achingly familiar. Those hands had touched her face, stroked her hair, held her close. Turning away quickly to look at the road instead, she pushed those treacherous thoughts out of her mind.

"Have you got time for a coffee?"

She meant to say no, but instead found herself agreeing when a parking space loomed up just as they passed a small café where couples were still huddled round tables. The night was cold, and Jack put his arm around her as they walked towards the door, finding a table in the back corner.

Their coffee came quickly, and when Jack reached out to take her hand, she didn't pull away.

"I've thought about you often." He spoke so softly that she had to tilt her head closer to his to be sure she heard him clearly.

"Have you?"

"I've thought back over that time with such regret. I was unsure then what I wanted, uncertain where I would be based, nervous of dragging you along with me when you had ambitions of your own."

"You never asked me what I wanted. I might well have gone willingly and been happy to make a life for myself alongside yours."

"You expected a proposal. I knew that."

She shrugged. "Perhaps. I remember feeling that I needed to know what you really felt."

"Whether my intentions were honourable?" he asked with a grin.

"Whether you could see your life with me in it. Or whether you could imagine a life without me and be okay with that."

"And then your mum got sick and you said you were moving away—"

"I wondered if you might try to stop me. You didn't."

"Because the only fair way to stop you would have been to propose – and I was pretty sure that if I asked you, you'd say yes. That's why I couldn't do it. At that time, your feelings were so much more certain than mine. My uncertainty wasn't about you, because I loved you without any doubt at all. It was about my career, and being free to follow that path wherever it took me. I'd worked so hard to get to consultant level…"

She squeezed his hand. "You did work incredibly hard, and time has proved that you made the right decision for your career. It's probably all worked out for the best."

"Do you really believe that?"

Kath looked down at their clasped hands while she worked her way through her muddled thoughts.

"I don't know," she said at last. "I never expected to see you again, and this evening has knocked me for six. But I need to go home, back to normality, back to my job at Hope Hall. That's where I need to digest all this, and try to make some sense of what I'm feeling."

"So, you *are* feeling something?"

"Oh yes, Jack. I am overwhelmed by what I feel. Did we make a mistake then? Are we about to make another mistake now? Or could we be on the point of making the best and most glorious decision of a lifetime?"

He leaned towards her then, brushing her lips with his own.

"Sleep on it then, my darling Kath. And I will wait for as long as it takes to hear from you again."

Esther and David's wedding day was simply wonderful. The day dawned chilly but bright, with cloudless skies that added a sparkle to the sprinkle of spring flowers pushing their way into view in every garden and window box. St Mark's was packed for the occasion, as this young couple and their families had long been popular members of the congregation there. The hymns were a perfect mix of old and new. James's sermon hit just the right note – and so did the newly formed St Mark's Choral Choir. Not only did they sing a heart-stoppingly beautiful rendition of John Rutter's "The Lord Bless You and Keep You", but they sent the newly married couple down the aisle and out into their new life together in magnificent style by singing "Zadok the Priest" with such emotional fervour that the old rafters in the arched ceiling of St Mark's shivered with pleasure.

"They were all right," sniffed Flora as she crossed the road towards Hope Hall, holding on to the arm of Pauline Owen.

"A bit screechy at times, I thought," replied Pauline, "and frankly very ostentatious. 'Zadok the Priest' at a wedding! That's hardly appropriate."

"Didn't the Queen have it at hers?"

"I think you'll find that was her coronation. Not the same thing at all."

"Well, I thought the choir sounded as if they had plums stuffed in their mouths," commented Betty, who was walking alongside them. "All those rolled Rs gave the impression they'd got something stuck in the backs of their throats. And I reckon the bride and groom probably got sprayed with spit every time they over-pronounced all those Ds and Ts at the end of each line they sang."

"Well," chuckled Doris, as the group of ladies walked through the open doors of Hope Hall, "I certainly wouldn't want to be part of that choir now. They're so stuck up and full of their own importance."

"The Can't Sing Singers are much more fun," agreed Flora, hanging her coat up on the same peg as Betty and Doris's. "Why don't you two come along to our next rehearsal and join in? The more the merrier! You too, Ida. You've got a very strong voice. Honestly, Ronnie is a marvel. The hour just flies, we enjoy it so much."

"I might consider joining a choir." Ida picked a tiny white fleck from the arm of her dark lilac suit jacket, which she wore with a perfectly coordinated floral blouse. "However, I really couldn't consider joining a choir with such a frivolous name."

"Even if it's an accurate description of what we are and how we sing?" asked Pauline.

"*Particularly* if that's an accurate description of what you are and how you sing."

And adjusting her neat cream handbag into a comfortable position on her forearm, Ida marched down the hall with stately elegance as she led the way to their table.

For months afterwards, the wedding breakfast served that day was hailed as one of the best Hope Hall had ever seen. The newly-weds, along with their family members on both sides, had a network of friends that spanned a wide variety of nationalities and cultures. So their Caribbean friends arrived with a huge pot of goat curry, along with platters of sizzling chicken and rice; the Spanish group brought several dishes of paella topped with langoustines and calamari, while their Italian neighbours brought mushroom risotto and tagliatelle carbonara. The bride worked for a French bank, and they sent across a big parcel of elegant cake boxes filled with delicious tarte tatin, plus a selection of colourful macaroons for each table.

The English contingent arrived with trays bearing individual portions of poached salmon topped with grapes and watercress, along with several home-cooked hams cut into thick, moist slices. And then there were pavlovas of all shapes and heights, smothered with lashings of cream beneath layers of strawberries, black cherries, tropical fruits and winter berries. They stood alongside traditional favourites like summer pudding, blueberry cheesecake – and lemon meringue pie straight out of Mary Berry's cookbook. There were bowls of salad, pastas and couscous to suit every taste. There were savoury bite-size appetizers and after-dinner mints. The banquet kept coming, and the crowd kept eating until they could eat no more, and felt they'd never be able to move again. Then the Army band organized by the bridegroom got started with a varied programme of musical favourites for all ages. The crowd waltzed and boogied, bopped and smooched their way through a thoroughly enjoyable evening.

"Oh, these shoes are killing me," sighed Mary as she and her husband Trevor, Hope Hall's accountant, slumped down into a couple of empty seats at the table Maggie was clearing.

"Mine too," agreed Maggie, stacking empty plates onto a large tray. "It's been a busy day with so many wedding guests to feed."

"The food's been wonderful," said Trevor, joining the conversation. "I've never tasted goat curry before and only put it on my plate by accident, but I loved it. Mary, you've got to learn how to make that!"

Mary looked hopefully towards Maggie.

"Don't worry," Maggie laughed, "I've got a recipe for it in my book. I'll let you have it. Mind you, you might have to search around a bit for the goat's meat!"

"I hope, Maggie, with all these people here, you haven't been too busy to dance. This band is terrific."

Maggie nodded in agreement. "I may not be dancing, but I've been singing my head off. They're brilliant."

"Have you seen Kath?" asked Trevor. "I thought she said she'd be here."

"I was wondering about her too. She did a lot of organizing for this evening, so I know she was meaning to come."

"Perhaps she's in the middle of that crowd dancing to 'YMCA' then."

Mary giggled. "Not her style at all. I have a feeling the extent of her interest in dancing is watching *Strictly* on TV. But you've got me worried now. Perhaps she's not well?"

"Come to think of it," said Trevor, "when I saw her yesterday morning, she was quite excited because she was going up to London later in the afternoon for a reunion of colleagues at that hospital where she used to work."

"Oh, that's probably it then," agreed Maggie, a note of relief in her voice. "I expect it finished late and she ended up staying the night with an old friend."

"Well, I'm sorry she's missed this," trilled Mary. "It's a wonderful evening. All that gorgeous food, and this wine is simply delightful…"

Just then the band struck up the familiar intro to "Just Want to Dance the Night Away".

"Oh, this is my absolute favourite," yelled Mary, dragging a reluctant Trevor to his feet. "Come on, they're playing our song!"

Stretched out on the settee, Kath watched the shadows of the leaves on her living room wall as they were caught by the eerie light from the street lamps that glowed through her open curtains.

And it was indeed an old friend at the reunion last night who had prevented her from going along, as she knew she should, to the wedding reception at Hope Hall that evening. She never missed appointments. She could always be relied upon to be exactly where she said she'd be, and do precisely what needed to be done. Kath never let anyone down.

But meeting Jack after all this time had changed everything. She thought she'd succeeded in putting him out of her mind. To get him out of her heart, though – that was a different matter. Last night had proved that. What a fool she was for thinking she would ever be immune to his effect on her! And now Jack was back in her life, living less than an hour's drive away, wanting to see her, saying he may have made a mistake and asking if it really was too late to try again.

Was it? After all, what could he see in her now? She was no longer a powerhouse of people management, order and fashion as she'd been at the hospital. Her fiftieth birthday was only a couple of months away. Her waistline was wider, her skin drier and her hair thinner and tinged with silver – and what's more, she knew all of that mattered so much less to her now. She couldn't remember the last time she'd bothered to go to the beauty salon for a facial or massage, and her nails hadn't had a pampering manicure for months.

She had mellowed. Now, she rushed less and rested more. She was no longer afraid of her own company, embracing instead the orderly comfort of her beautiful flat. She revelled in the sheer pleasure of being able to spend a whole weekend by herself, choosing what to watch, listen to or read until she fell asleep – without the guilty conscience she'd always had in London, worrying about work that needed to be done or people who urgently needed a phone call.

Was she happy? She considered that thought for a while and decided that perhaps the word she would use to describe herself now was "content". No more ups and downs of emotional turmoil.

No depths of despair or heights of passion. Being content was comfortable and calm, a way of life that brought peace and good health. She liked being content. She'd learned the hard way that although passion thrilled and excited, it also stung and wounded. Living without passion was not so bad.

And now, out of the blue, Jack had stepped back into her life again, upsetting her equilibrium, ripping a hole in the carefully woven fabric of her contentment. So unexpected, so breath-taking, so passionate – and so absolutely terrifying.

There was a glorious irony to be found in the contrasting activities that were on offer at Hope Hall every Tuesday. From eleven in the morning until two in the afternoon, the Grown-ups' Lunch gathered together elderly, infirm, lonely and vulnerable members of the community for a hearty, specially planned lunch prepared by Maggie and her catering team. The meal was served to the diners in the foyer, which was set out as if it were a high-class restaurant. There were starched tablecloths, beautifully folded serviettes, gleaming glasses and sparkling cutlery.

The whole experience was far removed from the lifestyle of many of the members, most of whom lived on their own, often unable to enjoy a freshly cooked hot meal at any other time in the week. Some lived without company at all, often with the most basic level of assistance and a sad sense of being so irrelevant to the world beyond their front door that their welfare didn't matter much to anyone. From the start, Maggie's soft heart had gone out to them and she'd determined that while they were in her care at Hope Hall, they would each be treated as VIP guests.

When it came to the menu, she saw early on that what went down best with the appreciative crowd of Tuesday lunchtime regulars was old-fashioned, traditional favourites like shepherd's pie, roast chicken, meat pasties and tasty casseroles, followed by the sweet treats they remembered from childhood, like lemon sponge, strawberry trifle, treacle tart and rice pudding. No calories were spared, no second helpings denied and no expanding waistlines were ever clucked over – unlike the club that met in the more discreet surroundings of the old school hall from five o'clock later the same afternoon.

Members of the Slimming Club (known affectionately by its members as the Fat Club) either tried to slip in unseen by anyone in the outside world, or marched in with heads held high as a symbol of the triumph of their steely determination over both hunger pangs and sugar deprivation, an achievement that surely deserved nothing less than a cheer from the rooftops.

Most of the would-be slimmers were ladies, though the occasional man did dare to make an appearance. Every session started with a weigh-in. The members queued up to step onto the scales with an air of trepidation. There was no hiding from the indisputable reading on those scales. Everyone could tell from the reaction of Belinda, the leader of the group, whether the read-out showed a loss, which was loudly applauded, or had crept up, which attracted an embarrassing array of concerned and sympathetic expressions from other slimmers who were secretly glad that *they* had hit their weekly target when others had failed miserably.

Sally Meadows and her friend Alison usually went along together to the club wearing the lightest clothes they could find in their wardrobes. They would also make a last-minute stop at the Ladies once inside the building so that the dreaded reading on the scales was as low as they could possibly make it. The timing of the club worked perfectly for them because they both had boys who went along to Beavers, which started in the main hall at five o'clock, the same time as the Slimming Club.

On that Tuesday evening, as the Beavers were gathering in the foyer, Sally was trying to persuade her son Jason to change from his outdoor shoes just as Alison arrived with her son Finn. After several minutes of the boys giggling together and tangling in and out of sweatshirts and shoes, the mums sighed with relief as the boys finally disappeared into the hall.

"See those two over there?" Sally whispered so that only her friend could hear.

Alison followed her gaze towards a man and a woman who were chatting as they waited at the coffee machine for their hot drinks.

"They do look very comfortable together, don't you think?"

"That's Josh's mum, isn't it?" Alison said under her breath. "What's her name? Isn't it Claire? She's nice. I met her at the parents' evening just before Christmas."

"And do you know him?"

Alison peered across at the tall man standing beside Claire. "If he turns this way I might recognize his face, but I don't think I've seen him anywhere other than Beavers. His boy started a couple of weeks ago, didn't he?"

"He's got twins. They're in Jason's class at school. He must work at home, I reckon, because he usually drops them off in the morning and picks them up again in the afternoon."

"Oh!" replied Alison, looking at him with extra interest. "Is he a single dad?"

"Oh no, he has a very nice wife called Karen. I've coloured her hair when she's come into our salon. Works all week in London, so she told me."

"And here he is—"

"Sipping cappuccinos—"

"And cosying up with Claire—"

"Who is happily settled with Josh's dad, I assume?"

"Married, I believe."

Alison continued to stare across the room at the couple who were chatting comfortably together.

"I think those two are worth keeping an eye on. Don't you?" muttered Sally.

"Definitely!" agreed Alison, as they both picked up their bags and walked out of the side door towards the old school hall.

Totally unaware that they had become the objects of such interest and speculation, Gary and Claire took their seats at their usual table.

"I'm glad you're here," she said. "I wanted to apologize for pouring out all our family history last week. You must have thought you were in the company of a mad woman."

"Not at all. You've been through a tough time."

"Yes, but I shouldn't have blabbed about it to someone I hardly know."

"Don't they say it's easier to tell your troubles to a stranger?"

"Ah, but the thing is, I'm going to be seeing you every week when the boys are here at Beavers, so I'm not sure that really means you're a stranger."

Gary grinned. "Just strange then, eh?"

She laughed then, her shoulders visibly relaxing. Gary realized that she had probably been nervously preparing her apology for a while before this evening.

"I've forgotten what we talked about last week already," he assured her. "Terrible memory, you know!"

"Well, I do remember you telling me that you're a graphic artist. That sounds like an interesting career."

"It's funny. I never think about it as a career. Perhaps because nowadays I don't go off to work in the morning and come home at night, the way people with careers usually do."

"Is it hard to work at home? I think I'd find there are so many distractions: jobs that need to be done, shopping to organize, washing to put on, television programmes you can't resist watching, meals to prepare. And the kids come back at half past three, so that's your day gone."

Gary finished his last mouthful of coffee, shaking his head in agreement as he put the mug back on the table. "How right you are. That's quite a problem when I'm working on a big project. I really do like peace and quiet to think things through and plan the artwork I need to prepare for my clients. I can be quite single-minded when I'm busy, which annoys Karen, because she can't understand why I don't get more done if I'm at home most of the day. She says it doesn't take a minute to put on the washing machine or put the plates and cups in the dishwasher, but women are so good at multi-tasking, aren't they?

"It takes me ages to gather up all the right colour clothes, search through the pockets for paper tissues and any sticky sweets that might be lurking there, and then to work out what cycle they should be on in the washing machine. Then the clothes have got to be hung out to dry – and that takes me forever too. Don't ask me why I find it so difficult. Karen always gives me precise instructions about where to put the pegs, which way up shirts should be hung, and how to organize socks so that they end up in the right pairs. But I'm terrified about getting it wrong, mostly because I always do."

"Well, Nigel would be just the same. I don't think he's ever used the washing machine in all the time I've known him. Apparently that's what wives are for."

"And I used to feel exactly the same way. I'd always just thrown my socks inside out and shirts all buttoned up into the washing basket, and sometime later they'd appear back in my wardrobe washed, dried, ironed and folded. It was a wonderful service!"

"Well, I guess that everything is more difficult if you have twin boys. Are their clothes and toys all identical? Do you have to make sure you get the right T-shirt back to the right son?"

He laughed out loud. "You can't imagine the trouble I get into trying to sort out what belongs to Max and what is actually Toby's!"

"Who minds most if you get it wrong – the boys or their mum?"

"Mum probably. I'm still trying to remember which one of the Paw Patrol team each of the boys like best, because they've both got pyjamas with their favourite character. Karen thinks I'm not concentrating enough and I should try harder. But honestly, I just can't remember. End of story. The boys think it's hilarious when I get a ticking off. In fact, I suspect they deliberately change pyjama tops just to get me into trouble."

"It must be hard for Karen too, not being able to spend more time with you all."

"I think it was in the beginning – very hard for her, and incredibly hard for me too. She missed them a lot and I really missed her. I was so nervous about being completely in charge, especially as the boys were only toddlers then. I was worried I'd drown them in the bath, lose them at the shops, or poison them with my cooking."

"But you didn't."

"No, I didn't, and I came to understand that kids are really quite resilient. When they were small, we were both terrified about how tiny and needy they were. Karen found it hard to feed two hungry babies, so we ended up bottle-feeding, which meant we could share the job between us. But Karen just got to grips with everything much more easily and naturally than I did. I was all fingers and thumbs trying to put the nappies on, and when it came to preparing baby food for them as they got on to the weaning stage, I made some terrible mistakes. Not that the boys seemed to notice at all. Bath times were what I dreaded most of all. They only need a couple of inches to drown, don't they – just enough water to cover their mouth and nose? I lived on a knife-edge of fear once Karen went back to work, just hoping both boys would still be there and okay when she got back in the evening."

"But you've obviously got used to it. You're great with the boys now."

He smiled. "Yes, I've finally worked out that in spite of their cack-handed, well-intentioned father, they will probably live to a ripe old age."

"And Karen? You said how much she missed them, but did she

eventually get used to the idea of having to be away from them so much during the week?"

"Yes. She rings up each lunchtime, just to make sure everything's going okay, but her job is so demanding and I know that she has to close her mind off to what's happening at home while she's there."

"And how do you feel about that?"

"I've got used to it, I suppose."

"And the boys?"

His expression became more serious as he thought about the question.

"Mostly, they're absolutely fine. It's normal for her not to be there, and they really don't mind too much, because she is such a wonderful mum when she's back home again. But if they're ever ill or in trouble at school or uncertain about something, or they've fallen over and scraped their knee or elbow, then no one else but Mum will do. My cuddles aren't a patch on hers. It's Mum who always knows the right thing to do and say. They adore her. I sometimes think they just tolerate me because I'm the one who has to make them do their homework and tell them off when they're naughty. I'm the parent who really *can't* cook, who gets their toys and clothes mixed up, who forgets where they have to be and when, and always turns up last at the school gate. Compared to her, I'm a bit hopeless really."

Claire smiled. "I think you're doing pretty well."

He smiled too as he asked, "Fancy another coffee?"

"That would be lovely."

"I'll make them. Same as before?"

"Yes, please. And I've just remembered that I brought along a couple of pieces of lemon drizzle cake that were left over in the staffroom after a retirement gathering today. Would you like some?"

"Lemon drizzle is my all-time favourite! Let's make sure we've eaten every crumb before the boys come out and catch us."

***

"Guess what!" beamed Doris, her knitting needles flying along the last sleeve of the matinee jacket she was making for her baby grandson Charlie, without her even looking down. "Ida is talking about coming along to Armchair Exercises. She says she won't come this week, but perhaps next because she wants to see if anyone is still going by then."

Betty looked up from crocheting yet another square towards blankets for babies in Africa. "Well, that's a surprise. I suppose that means her joints ache as much as all ours do, although I never thought she'd admit it."

"She says that she doesn't trust a teacher as young as Della one single bit, and I suspect her aim is to prove her point by moaning about everything we do."

Betty chuckled. "Then again, she might find it really entertaining. You never know."

"Oh, I think we do."

"Do you reckon she'll stay for the Dance Sing-along too? I love that."

"So do I. Tell you what – if Ida stays and stands at the front, we'll find places at the back. Let's just keep out of her way, and if she ends up moaning so everyone can hear her, we'll pretend we don't know her. Agreed?"

A slow smile spread across Betty's face. "Agreed – with brass knobs on!"

Chapter 7

Maggie glanced up from where she was serving a couple of customers at the Call-in Café just as their accountant Trevor walked in, with his wife Mary following several steps behind him. Uncharacteristically, the usually friendly Trevor marched through the foyer without a word, leaving Mary to sit down alone. She cut quite a forlorn figure, so as soon as Maggie was free, she walked over to pull up a chair beside her.

"You okay? You look like someone who desperately needs a coffee."

When Mary turned her face towards her, Maggie was shocked to see that tears were leaving dark mascara tracks rolling down her cheeks.

"Come around the back," said Maggie kindly. "We'll have our coffee in my office."

Minutes later, Maggie put down two cups on the desk and brought over a chair so that she could sit directly opposite Mary.

"Bad day?"

"You could say that," sniffed Mary.

"Would it help to talk about it?"

"You'd be better off talking to Trevor. He's the one who's being unreasonable."

Maggie reached out to pull the lid off the biscuit tin she'd also brought in with her. "Tell me over a biscuit or two. There's nothing in the world that a chocolate digestive can't sort out."

"Well, it was an ordinary morning really. I always go to the supermarket on a Friday, and that's exactly what happened. I did everything as usual: took the trolley round, filled it up, got to the checkout and paid – nothing out of the ordinary at all. But then, when I got back out to the car park, my car was nowhere to be seen. I walked round for ages, but I couldn't find it anywhere. It had been stolen."

"Oh my dear, what a terrible shock for you!"

"A security man there saw what a state I was in, and he put a call through to the manager, who came out and walked right round the car park with me to take another look. He was so kind. He took me through to his office while he called the police, and a lady arrived with a sweet cup of tea from the café. They couldn't have been nicer."

"What did the police say?"

"They came quite quickly. I just told them what had happened, and they asked me for all the details of the vehicle and about what might have been in it. They said they'd be on the look-out for the thieves right away, because they might still be in the area."

"Of course. These car thieves are so clever. How did the police think they got in?"

"Ah, well, that's when I realized it might just have been my fault. Trevor is always telling me off for leaving my key in the ignition. It's so convenient at home, and because the car is way up the drive I've never thought there was any problem about leaving the door unlocked. I've always been dreadful for losing my keys, and that's why I've found that leaving the key just where I need it in the car is a really sensible solution."

"And you think you might have left your key in the ignition at the supermarket car park?"

Mary's answer was no more than a nod as once again her eyes filled with tears.

"And you knew that would be the first thing Trevor would think."

Beginning to understand, Maggie handed over another tissue so that Mary could blow her nose before she began speaking again.

"I knew exactly what he'd say, so I kept putting off ringing him. I told the manager my husband had probably gone to work and I couldn't disturb him. I really didn't want Trevor giving me a lecture while all the supermarket staff were listening. In the end I said I needed some fresh air and went back out into the car park to call him."

"And you got through to him?"

"Eventually, yes. I couldn't get him at home, and his mobile phone rang for quite a while before he answered. But when he did, I just poured out the whole story – about coming to the supermarket, doing the shopping, and then finding the car had disappeared from the car park."

"And?"

"And – well, at first I thought he'd got cut off, because he didn't answer for ages. Then he said, really coldly, that *he* had driven me down to the supermarket that morning because he needed the car. I remembered then. We'd arranged that he'd come back and pick me up."

In horror, Maggie's hands shot up to cover her mouth.

Mary let out a long, guilty sigh before she continued. "So I just asked him to come back and get me straight away."

"Good. Did he come?"

"He said yes, he'd come – just as soon as he was able to persuade the two big policemen who had just arrested him for driving a stolen vehicle to let him go."

When Betty, Doris and Flora told Ida that numbers were creeping up for the Armchair Exercise class and the Dance Sing-along session that followed it, Ida simply dabbed her nose sniffily with her embroidered hankie and made no comment. She showed such a lack of interest that the ladies didn't think she had any intention of following up on her suggestion that she might come along to see the classes for herself. In fact, they'd completely forgotten about the possibility of Ida coming at all, and had already bagged their seats in the second row when Ida lowered herself onto the chair beside them.

"You came!" gasped Betty.

"I may not stay."

Suddenly, Ronnie struck up a fanfare on the piano encouraging applause from the class as Della, this time wearing a pale pink tracksuit, strode into the centre of the stage to accept their adoration. Her eagle eyes quickly took in how much the class had grown since she'd started it.

"I see we have newcomers in our midst," she purred, locking her gaze for just a second with Ida's stony glare. "So come on, the home team, let's show them what they've been missing!"

Again, she led them through a series of deceptively simple exercises that could be practised on, under, round and by their chairs. Their legs swung, their arms circled, their heels pumped up and down, their shoulders heaved, and their necks rolled first this way and then that. Nothing was too difficult, and the jaunty beat of Ronnie's music certainly helped them all to keep going. Some of the frailer members relaxed and watched at various stages throughout the class, and others were panting heavily by the end of the half-hour. But generally there were broad smiles and a huge sense of achievement all round.

"What did you think?" Betty immediately asked Ida. "Are you aching?"

"Of course not. It was all at a very basic level."

"Yes, but did you enjoy it?" Flora wanted to know.

"I'm going to get a drink and take my place for the next class. Dance Sing-along, did you say?" Ida retorted.

"That's right – and you're going to know all the words," enthused Doris.

"But surely this is meant to be an exercise class. It is always detrimental to each element if you try to combine art forms." And after turning round extremely stiffly, Ida haughtily made her way over to where she'd left her bag.

"She's aching," smiled Doris. "And she's having a good time."

In fact, everyone in the hall enjoyed every minute of the Dance Sing-along. The songs were all familiar, and the tempos changed so that they were waltzing one minute and doing a calypso the next. Somehow, because they were having such fun singing old favourites, they hardly noticed that they were exercising every part of their bodies at the same time. Thirty minutes shot by so fast that a genuine sigh of regret echoed round the hall when the class came to a euphoric end.

"We're going to get a cold drink from the machine. Are you going to join us, Ida?" asked Betty as the four friends gathered up their bags and squeezed their feet back into their outdoor shoes.

If Ida was trying to appear cool, her bright red cheeks and her heavy breathing gave her away. In fact, she was glowing, her eyes sparkling with enjoyment as much as everyone else's.

"You go and get a table," she ordered as she headed to the Ladies. "I'll be with you in just a minute."

By the time the four of them had worked out how to get exactly what they wanted from the drinks machine and collapsed with happy exhaustion around a corner table to down their drinks, fifteen minutes had passed. Then, from inside the hall, they could hear Ronnie strike up the piano again.

"I ought to go," said Ida.

"Me too," said Betty as they gathered up their belongings. However, when Doris wandered over to the door that led through to the hall, rather than making for the outside exit Ida, Betty and Flora followed her. Their heads touching, they all stared through the glass windows to watch the tap class that had just begun.

The age of the pupils ranged from about five years old to some girls who were probably in their early teens. There was deep concentration all round as they tried to follow the lead of Della, who was dressed in smart black trousers and a short black jacket over a crisp white shirt. She was shouting out precise instructions in time with Ronnie's music:

"Heel, heel, toe, toe.
Ball change, ball change, ball change, clap!
Step, shuffle ball change, stamp!
Step, shuffle ball change, clap!"

"I can do that," said Ida. "I learned tap as a child. You never really forget."

"Me too!" exclaimed Doris. "I always loved it."

"It looks hard," said Betty, squinting through the glass to see just what Della's feet were doing as she danced on the stage at the other end of the hall.

"Tuition of tap is wasted on this modern generation," stated Ida. "They could never understand its place in dance history."

"I was in love with Gene Kelly," sighed Flora.

"I always fancied myself as Ginger Rogers," added Betty dreamily. "All those gorgeous dresses she wore—"

"Wasted!" declared Ida. She turned away and marched towards the exit door, with the other ladies scurrying along behind her.

Kath glanced down at her phone. No call from Jack today. Nor yesterday either.

But he *had* rung just a couple of days after their evening together in London, and that reassured her that he was sincere in his delight that they were in contact again. As ever, their conversation during that phone call was relaxed, in the way it usually is between friends who know each other well and are comfortable in each other's company. That said, she found she didn't mind that their conversation was only on the phone. In fact, she was quite relieved, because it took away the giddiness that had swept over her again at the reunion, when she'd looked into those grey eyes of his and noticed how his smile was still delightfully lopsided. It meant that the memory of running her fingers through his strong, wiry hair could be held at bay, and the honey tones of his familiar aftershave were unable to intoxicate her senses. They had talked for more than an hour, and when at last they said goodnight, she had climbed into bed in a warm glow, falling asleep instantly as the image of him invaded her dreams.

After that she longed for him to call, but he didn't ring for several days. That started a pattern of the two of them sharing long, chatty, gently flirty conversations on the phone. Then they would say goodbye and head back into the reality of their own lives, until eventually they spoke again several days later.

Already she could feel herself wanting more. She longed to see him, and yet she was nervous at the thought of him asking her out. Where would they go? How would it be? Could she bear it if he dangled the prospect of them being together again, only to change his mind and break her heart as he had before? Could she bear it if history repeated itself and he never actually got round to asking the question she was longing to hear from him?

She wouldn't ring him. She would not come across as a desperate ex-girlfriend longing to turn back the clock. She would let him see she was independent and established, with a responsible job and a circle of friends who cared for her. Her life was just fine. She didn't need a man to make her complete. It was important that he recognized that.

But did he need *her* to make *his* life complete? With a shiver of doubt, she sensed what the answer might be. Better not to call. Better not to meet up. Better to walk away right now.

Looking down at her mobile for the second time in as many minutes, she willed it to ring.

It didn't.

Probably just as well, she decided. She really didn't mind.

But she checked the screen again before putting her phone into her handbag, which she zipped up with a flourish.

Several streets away, Maggie stared miserably into her cup of Horlicks, her thoughts too tangled to remember to drink it.

Things were happening far too quickly. The solicitor had put a stop to Dave's assumption that he could just turn up at the house and take away whatever he fancied, but there was no way to stop the process of her home being put up for sale. She had stood miserably in the kitchen as the estate agent came round, measuring here, assessing there, opening cupboard doors, counting radiators, peering into the garden shed and taking copious photographs from every possible angle, both inside and out. A copy of the sale details arrived a day later, and she gasped at the value they now put on the house. They had been so excited when they managed to scrape together enough money to put down a deposit to buy the three-bedroomed semi-detached house back in 1995 for what seemed the huge sum of £52,000. Of course, they'd done lots of work on it, modernized the kitchen and bathroom, and added a conservatory at the back, but when the agent announced that they would now be putting the property on the market for £350,000, Maggie's head swam. No wonder Dave wanted to get his hands on fifty per cent of a figure like that!

And today, the first prospective buyers had arrived. She said that she would prefer them simply to take themselves round, and she would answer any questions they had at the end. From her bedroom where she had taken herself off to hide, she could hear some of their conversation through the open door.

"Oh, I don't like that. We could knock that out, couldn't we?"

"What a terrible colour to choose for these walls!"

"If we dug up the front garden, would there be room for both of our cars?"

Didn't they know that Steph had chosen the colour for the walls in her room when she was a teenager, and Maggie had never had the heart to change it? And that Darren had built that shelving unit while he was taking woodwork lessons at school? It may not be the most modern bedroom fitting, but it had always worked well enough for them. And these awful people wanted to dig up the front garden and concrete over her beloved shrubs and the flowerbeds where the spring bulbs were now in their full glory!

Flying down the stairs, she grabbed her car keys and slammed the door behind her as the astonished couple stood assessing the front of the building.

"I've got to go out. Sorry!" she mumbled, as she ran to the car and drove off round the block without a backward glance.

And now here she was, back home and staring at her Horlicks. On the table in front of her was her mobile phone on which she'd listened over and over again to the message from the estate agent telling her that the couple had made an excellent offer on the house. And the great news, he said, was that the potential buyers had already sold their own property, so it would be a cash purchase. No problems, no mortgage companies, no delay! Please could she ring him immediately? Oh, and as he hadn't managed to get through to her as he'd hoped, he would now ring her husband instead.

Maggie carefully laid down the cup on the coffee table in front of her. Then she bowed her head, clasped her arms tightly round her waist, and rocked backwards and forwards in despair.

"Is Maggie here?" asked the young woman who strode into the Call-in Café at half past nine the following Tuesday morning. She was carrying two large trays of eggs, and was followed into the hall by three teenagers from the local school.

Maggie's assistant, the ever-competent Liz, was already well ahead with preparations for the Grown-ups' Lunch Club as the newcomers made their way into the kitchen.

"Hi, Tess. You've brought eggs. Great. I'm making quiche Lorraine for lunch today."

Tess laid the eggs down with care. "The bill for the eggs is here. Mum put the salads and vegetables on the invoice too, so it can all be paid together."

"That's fine. I'll pass that on to Trevor."

"Where's Maggie?"

"She's a bit under the weather at the moment, so she's taking the week off."

Tess nodded without comment. News had soon gone round that a For Sale sign was on show outside Maggie's house, and Dave had often been seen in the town proudly walking around with his new girlfriend and her children as if they were the happiest of families.

"Give her my love."

"Thanks, Tess. I will."

"Right, you know Gemma and Jess, I think," said Tess, slipping from her unofficial role as delivery driver for produce from her parents' farm to her proper job as teacher at the local senior school. "They've done work experience here before and they're both good in the kitchen. You want to work in catering, don't you, Gemma?"

"Yes, Miss."

"Well, this is a great opportunity for you both."

Tess then glanced outside towards the foyer, where the teenage boy who had also arrived with her was casually taking in the scene.

"And that's Kevin. He's mad about cookery. He's going to be the next Jamie Oliver, so he tells me. He's going to change the eating habits of the whole country through the television series he's already planning!"

Liz, a grandmother herself, knew a thing or two about teenagers and smiled understandingly. "A bit of a handful then, is he?"

"Kevin," called Tess through the hatch. "Can you come in here, please?"

When Kevin appeared in the kitchen, Tess did the introductions, which he seemed to ignore as he strolled across to look at the food Liz was already preparing.

"What are you cooking?"

"Lasagne and quiche Lorraine."

"Basil in the lasagne? That's a classic Italian herb, you know."

"I do know," replied Liz, as she handed him a potato-peeler. "And you're on potato-peeling duty. There's a big bag of Desiree over there for the mashed potato. That's a classic British food, you know."

By eleven o'clock, enthusiastic members of the Grown-ups' Lunch Club started to arrive, some delivered by Good Neighbour drivers, others turning up alone or in small groups from their nearby homes.

Percy was always one of the first to arrive, choosing his favourite table nice and early so that no one else could pinch his seat. The other tables were filling up fast before his friends Robert and John took their places, with Connie being brought to the table on the arm of Pat, one of the Good Neighbour volunteers.

"There you are, dear," said Pat. "Let me help you with your coat – and can I get you a cup of tea?"

"Yes, please," said Percy. "Two sugars for me. Robert, you like your tea milky, don't you – and strong with no sugar for you, John?"

Pat looked a bit harassed at being given such a large and unexpected order, but she good-naturedly repeated all the instructions before heading off to the serving hatch.

"And a plate of biscuits, please, love," shouted Percy. "We like the chocolate chip ones best."

"Percy Wilson, you'll spoil your appetite for lunch," smiled Kath, who happened to be passing on her way up to the balcony lounge.

"Nothing ever spoils my appetite for lunch," Percy beamed. "What have we got today?"

"Quiche, I think, with a nice salad."

"Euck, rabbit food! Is that all? Nothing more suitable for a growing chap like me?"

"I saw a beautiful lasagne being prepared in the kitchen. I'll make sure you get a big portion, okay?"

"With chips?"

"I think they're on the menu too."

Percy huffed his approval, leaning forward on his elbows to speak to his three lunch companions.

"I hate salad. Far too healthy – and green. If it's green, you can never be quite sure what you're eating. Do you remember Donald who used to live down Third Avenue when we were lads?"

"Donald Bacon, do you mean? His dad was the undertaker?"

"That's the one. Little Don took over the business and made a fortune. Everyone needs his services sometime, don't they! Anyway, he's over on the new estate now in a posh place with an attic and a summer house – and *two* bathrooms. Whatever does he do with two? His wife left him for that travelling salesman years ago."

"He was always a bit odd, though, if I remember rightly," frowned Robert. "Didn't he used to keep creepy-crawlies in glass tanks – and lizards and big hairy spiders?"

"He showed me his snake once," Connie commented. "He must have thought I'd be impressed because he'd caught it himself. He tried to tell me it was a viper and deadly poisonous, but I knew it wasn't because I used to see those brown ones in the long grass at the back of our house. I was terrified of them, all the same! Any self-respecting young girl would be."

"Well, perhaps that's why Mrs Donald left him for the Tupperware salesman – because apparently up in the attic of that new house of theirs he has dozens of tanks lit up and kept at the right temperature to make sure all his reptiles and spiders are alive and kicking."

"Oh!" grimaced Connie. "I'd have left him too. What does he feed them?"

"Special stuff from the pet shop: crickets, maggots, dead chicks – things like that."

Connie was turning a distinct shade of green. "How revolting! What sort of person would want to do that?"

"Someone very strange," agreed John. "That's not a usual pastime at all."

"Well," said Percy, leaning forward to make sure they were all listening properly, "the police apparently thought the same thing. They raided his house the other day."

"My goodness!" exclaimed Connie. "Is it against the law to keep spiders then, in case they're man-eaters or something?"

"Apparently," confided Percy, warming to his storytelling, "the police had launched an undercover operation to watch Don carefully when they saw from one of those police spy helicopters or drones, or whatever it is they use, that there was a big room in his house which they could see from the sky was unnaturally warm. It glowed bright red on their electronic machinery. So they stormed the place in the dead of night. Loads of coppers with battering rams and armoured suits."

"Why? All for a handful of spiders?"

"Ah, but they didn't know that. They thought Don had a cannabis farm up in his attic, and that he was a dealer of some sort. They were all ready to cart him off to the police station for interrogation."

Robert chuckled at the thought. "Don Bacon, seventy-six years old, five foot tall, thick glasses, with a penchant for burying people and keeping tarantulas and snakes for fun. Hardly your typical drugs baron, is he?"

"So the police discovered. They were expecting to find his attic full of bright green plants all basking in artificial light to bring them on."

"I bet it really spoilt their day to find a load of lizards instead," giggled Connie.

"But," said Percy, his face very serious, "that's why I stay away from salads. I never allow anything green to pass my lips. I like to know what I'm eating!"

"That probably explains your expanding waistline, Percy," laughed John.

"Quite right! I play it safe and eat cakes instead."

At that point, Pat came back to their table balancing a tray carrying their tea orders. After all the right drinks were sitting in front of the right people, Pat laid a colourful flyer down on the table.

"Have you all seen this? They're looking for teams. Why don't you four go together?"

Robert picked up the leaflet and read out loud:

"BEETLES AND PUDS!
Saturday 7th March   Hope Hall 2 – 4 p.m.

Could your team of 4 win the Hope Hall Beetle Drive?
12 games, one overall winner
Could you be King or Queen Beetle?
Followed by Maggie's delicious puddings
Come and join us!

In aid of Good Neighbours"

"That sounds right up my street," said Connie. "What do you think? Shall we form a team of four?"

"Definitely!" they all agreed.

Percy threw back his head in a hearty laugh. "And those Merry Widows won't get a look in!"

Upstairs in the balcony lounge, Kath and Ellie were just finishing their coffees.

"So," said Ellie, "can I bring Gerald, that lovely old chap from church, along to the Grown-ups' Lunch Club next Tuesday? I'll bring him myself, because he's a bit lost since Phyllis went into the care home."

"Is he living on his own now?"

"He has carers coming in morning and evening, but he's really lost without his wife. I don't think he can even boil an egg, and he seems to have no idea about housework of any sort."

"Poor man."

"He's a real sweetie, though, such a lovely Christian. In fact, let me tell you how endearing he is. He's had a car for years, and he's still driving now, although I'm not totally sure he should be on the road. His daughter told me that she was in the car with him the other day when he shot across a roundabout, and bumped into another car. Before she could stop him, he leapt out and ran across to pull open the door of the other car, and promptly told the driver, 'I forgive you!'"

"Oh, I bet that went down well."

"You're absolutely right, because when he came back and got into his own car, he said to his daughter, 'I don't know why, but that driver seemed very angry!'"

"Oh, Gerald sounds delightful."

"Well, his daughter told me her mother didn't always think so. Apparently at one great family gathering, where she'd been working around the clock to produce a banquet of a meal for everybody, they were all sitting at the table about to tuck in when Gerald stood and announced that he wanted to say grace. So everyone bowed their head, and he just looked up to heaven with his hands stretched out, and said, 'Thank you, Lord, for all this wonderful food, which just seems to have come from nowhere..."

Kath roared with laughter. "I bet his wife felt like lobbing a bread roll at him for that."

"She loves him to bits, though. They've always been wonderful together. It's hard to think of them being apart now."

"Couldn't he live with her in the care home?"

"I don't think their children feel that's right for him at the moment. They're worried that if he's cut off from his friends, his church, the community he knows so well, he will go downhill himself. I think they're probably right, for the time being at least."

"Well, we'll look after him here next week. Let's hope he enjoys the lunch enough to want to come again. It's a great way of keeping in touch with other people."

"Talking of keeping in touch," said Ellie, moving closer to Kath so that she wouldn't be overheard, "have you had any more conversations with Jack?"

"He rang on Sunday evening and we chatted for half an hour."

"Lots to talk about then."

"There seems to be, but it's mostly about his work, the operations he's done, the lack of sleep that drives him crazy. He asks about my job here too. And, of course, we talk about friends we both knew up in London."

"But do you talk about anything a bit more intimate? Meeting up, for instance?"

"No. He's not actually suggested that."

"Do you think he's waiting to take his cue from you?"

Kath considered that possibility. "Maybe, but he hardly needs my permission to ask. I can always just say no."

"Perhaps he doesn't want to risk that. Better not to ask than face a rejection."

"That sounds like history repeating itself," sighed Kath. "I couldn't bear to be hurt that way by him again. I've built a new life for myself now. I'm settled and happy here."

"And he's turning your safe, comfortable world upside down..."

Kath smiled. "Yes, he is – and I'm not sure if I'm more terrified that he'll cause havoc by blasting his way back into my life again, or if the worst possibility is that he won't even try."

"You are quite a catch, you know, Kath. Don't underestimate yourself."

"I think we know each other too well for him to think like that, and that's why we're both really nervous. When you're nearing your fifties, as we both are, you're inclined to be rather stuck in your ways. We're not love's young dream any more, which means we're aware of how easy it would be to let our emotions rule our heads."

"Oh," smiled Ellie, "we all need a little romance in our lives. I sincerely hope some comes your way." She started to gather up her bag then and get to her feet. "I have to go. There's a prayer group at our house in five minutes."

"Thanks for popping in."

"Oh, I nearly forgot," added Ellie, turning back towards Kath. "The Can't Sing Singers – how are they getting on? Did it all come to nothing?"

"Far from it. They've got themselves a fantastic pianist as their musical director, and it seems their numbers are swelling as all the others here who can't sing a note hear how much fun they're having and want to join in too."

"Well, I never did! What a surprise," grinned Ellie. "I can't wait to drop that little nugget of information into the conversation at the St Mark's Choral Choir rehearsal this week. Gregory will choke on his high notes."

And with a cheery wave, she disappeared down the stairs to hurry home.

"You lot, pick that up!"

Shirley's voice bellowed right down the length of the hall from the stage to the back of the foyer. Heads shot up in alarm, and the group of teenagers at the far end jumped in fright as they realized that the command was aimed at them. They looked down at the mess they had created around them – abandoned jackets, scarves, make-up bags, sweet papers and drinks bottles – as they prepared themselves to look as cool as possible for Hip-hoppers, Della's street-dancing class. One of the girls instantly bent down to pick up all her own discarded bits and pieces, and quickly stuffed them back into her bag. Some of the others in the group followed her lead, although they were still not sure just where the voice had come from and who was shouting at them. They weren't used to being reprimanded at all. Even at school, these days, the teachers had an obligation to treat them with respect and politeness. If pupils didn't want to do something, there were always ways to wriggle out of it, and the staff really couldn't do much to change that. They couldn't believe they were being told off and shouted at when they weren't even *in* school. Some of the lads looked ready for a fight – if only they knew who they should be fighting.

"I am watching you," warned the disembodied voice. "I'll be down there to give you a clip round the ear if you don't move it."

A physical threat! That wasn't allowed. Nevertheless, one by one the boys, even the toughest of them, shoved their jackets, phones and cans of beer back in their bags, then they stood around in groups, trying to look as if nothing had happened.

"As I was saying before I was so rudely interrupted," continued Shirley, who was tucked away at the side of the stage helping Della change into ripped jeans and a top that looked as if it had been made out of a used fishing net. "You're doing brilliantly, Della. I'm really proud of you."

"Really, Auntie Shirl?" asked Della. "This isn't the sort of dancing I'm used to - you know, the big show spectaculars with gorgeous costumes and money no object – but I think these lessons are working. Did you get a chance to see much of the classes so far today?"

"I wasn't around for Armchair Exercises, because I was cleaning up the kitchen then, but I did see quite a bit of Dance Sing-along, and that looked like fun. I mean, they're a bunch of old crocks really, aren't they? But they were singing their socks off, and most of them were keeping up with the dancing too. You've hit just the right note there."

"Did you manage to see any of the tap class?"

"I had to be in the kitchen then, but I left the hatch open so that I could watch from there. And there's another hatch into the foyer, which I had open as well. I have to tell you, what I saw going on there really cracked me up."

Della, who was staring into a magnified mirror so that she could make good use of her long acrylic nails to tweak and re-arrange each individual eyelash into position, stopped with her hand in mid-air.

"Why?"

"Well, you were teaching more than just the dancers in the tap class. You had some hangers-on too."

"Who?"

"Four of the old ladies from the class before. I think they planned it. They stayed out in the foyer supposedly getting a drink from the machine there, but just before your tap class started, they delved into their shopping bags and all pulled out shoes with stumpy heels, a bit like tap shoes but without the metal plates on the bottom. Then, everything you were doing inside the hall, they were trying outside!"

"How did they get on?"

"They were terrible. They tried so hard to keep up, and they laughed a lot at themselves – except one old dear, who was taking it all very seriously. She was the funniest of the lot."

"Oh, *sweet!*" trilled Della. "I wish I'd seen them."

"I think they'd have run a mile if they thought you could."

"Do you think they'd come in and join the class next week if I asked them?"

"They're not allowed – are they? Isn't it supposed to be a kids' class?"

"Well, maybe I should allow it to be a *big* kids' class too – for those old ladies, at least."

"Perhaps you should take a peep at them first, to see if it's worth your while. Trouble is, if they're only doing their thing out in the foyer, from where you are up on the stage you'll be too far away to see them properly."

"Do you know who they are? Did you recognize them?"

"I'm pretty sure I've seen them at the Grown-ups' Lunch. I'll keep an eye out next week in case I can spot them."

"Tell them I'd like to have a chat with them during the change-over period between their Dance Sing-along class and the tap dancing. And then I'll think about whether to invite them to join in, just at the back, so they don't disturb the rest of the class."

"You'd better go," said Shirley, glancing out across the stage to the hall below. "It looks like you've got a full house. All those kids out there are dressed like they're teenage gang members in downtown New York!"

"Bye, Auntie Shirl. I'll tell Mum I saw you… and that terrifying voice of yours, it seemed to come from the gods when you blasted those kids earlier on. I might need to take advantage of that again if I have any trouble with this lot."

"Just yell for me if you want me to yell at them," grinned Shirley, giving a cheeky wink in her niece's direction.

Over on the other side of town, Gary glanced at the time displayed on the bottom of the television set in the kitchen, and ran his fingers through his hair with frustration. It was just gone seven, when Toby and Max were at their wicked worst. They'd had a long day at school, and by this time they were always overtired and overexcited. At the moment, they were screeching at the tops of their voices up in the bathroom, with the sound of water splashing everywhere.

"Boys!" shouted Gary, rushing up the stairs from where he'd been trying to fix dinner for himself and Karen. She was always starving when she got home, as mostly she didn't even manage to stop for a snack during the day. She often said that the best feeling ever was when she opened the front door as she got back home, and immediately smelt the lovely aroma of something tasty cooking in the oven.

He was running late. He hadn't finished clearing up after the boys' tea two hours earlier. For some reason the washing machine door wouldn't open, and the school jerseys and clean trousers the boys needed for the morning were all stuck in there. The phone hadn't stopped ringing, mostly about the big design project that was demanding all his attention right now. What must the client have thought when their conversation had to compete with the din of children's television and two boys duelling with their Star Wars lightsabres blaring in the background?

When Gary reached the bathroom door, his jaw dropped as he saw the total carnage the boys had made of the room. Dripping bath toys had been thrown out of the bath all over the floor, along with two soaking wet flannels, one of which had plainly hit the big mirror over the sink, leaving a long, soapy stain that was still channelling its way down the wall. The boys' pyjamas, which he'd left clean and dry, hanging over the radiator, had been knocked to the floor, where an open shampoo bottle had been tossed across the room and landed on them.

He just saw red. He heard himself shrieking in anger at them, ordering them to pull the plug and get out of the bath. He wrapped them both roughly in big bath towels, while he went to fetch other pyjamas for them from their room. Once they were dressed, he snapped out curt instructions at them to tidy up the mess, which the boys plainly didn't want to do.

"You will do as you're told!" he shouted angrily. "You made this mess and you will clear it up. I can't trust you for a minute.

But you've got to learn. You two are grounded for the rest of the week."

Bedlam broke out as the two boys wailed with anguish. It was just at that moment Karen appeared at the bathroom door.

Toby was the first to run crying into her arms, hotly followed by Max, as both boys tried to explain how unreasonable and grumpy Dad was, and they wouldn't be grounded, would they?

Karen avoided the question, just as she avoided eye contact with Gary. Without a word, he stomped off to the boys' bedroom to pull the curtains and put on the nightlight, trying not to notice that the boys were no longer wailing and that there were even giggles coming from the bathroom as Karen supervised the bedtime routine of cleaning teeth and brushing hair. Bristling with frustration, Gary marched downstairs to the kitchen and stared at the mountain of washing-up that was piled high in the sink. With a heavy sigh, he had another go at trying to get the washing machine door open as he heard Karen's voice softly reading the boys a story once they'd finally tumbled into bed.

"Have you made a cup of tea?" Karen asked a few minutes later as she walked into the kitchen and surveyed the scene.

"Not yet," snapped Gary, grabbing the kettle and filling it awkwardly because of all the dishes below the tap.

"How's dinner coming along?"

"It's not. I'm a bit behind. Sorry."

"Gary, have you any idea how it feels to come back to chaos like this at the end of a frantic day like the one I've had?"

"Yes. I am very inefficient. I apologize."

"How can it be so difficult just to get a few basic things done when you're here all day?"

"Because I may be here, but I'm *working*. You know – how you *work* all day in that office of yours which is designed to be a working environment. I am trying to deliver that huge Denison contract while I'm based at home, at the same time as I'm trying to be babysitter, washerwoman, caterer, cleaner – and a million other things."

"Oh, for heaven's sake. Women juggle work and run a house and family all the time."

"Unfortunately, you married a man, not a superwoman. Now, if you go and sit down, I will bring your tea and your evening meal just as soon as I can."

Her expression was a mixture of exasperation and exhaustion. "Don't worry." Her voice was unnaturally flat as she spoke. "I'll do this. Why don't you go and clear up the lounge so that we can find somewhere to sit in there later?"

Seething with resentment, Gary didn't go to the lounge, but instead went up to his office, slamming the door behind him. This was the box room, the smallest room in the house, filled with the widest piece of equipment – his drawing board, the major tool of his trade. The space was cramped and inefficient. It was impossible to succeed in a highly competitive marketplace when his premises and equipment looked like this.

He stayed in his room for some time, knowing he was too filled with anger to come out and talk to Karen. Eventually, he heard her call up the stairs that dinner was ready. He went down to find the kitchen was clear, the washing machine door open, the boys' uniforms were hanging neatly on the rack to dry, and his dinner was waiting on the hot plate for him. He put it on a tray and carried it through to the lounge, where Karen was deeply engrossed in a television documentary as she ate. They finished their meal in silence. He cleared away the dishes without a word, then came back in with a dishcloth to wipe the coffee table. She looked exhausted. Well, tough! He was exhausted too.

"Come and sit down," she said suddenly.

"I'm going up now."

"Just for a while, please?"

He sat down on the settee, leaving the middle seat empty between them.

"I'm sorry, Gary. I know it's difficult for you to look after the boys and the house, and get your work done too."

He felt the tension in his stiff shoulders melt away at the kindness in her voice.

"Oh, look, just ignore me," he replied. "The boys really wound me up tonight, and the washing machine locked up, and I forgot to take the meat out of the freezer for our dinner, and the client from Denison's kept ringing me at all the wrong moments…"

"How's it going?"

"Slowly. It's hard to find time to think ideas through and get some original inspiration when my feet feel constantly stuck in a mire of domesticity."

"I can understand that. I'm sorry."

"And I haven't done their packed lunches for the morning yet."

"I'll do them."

"No, I can see you're worn out – and I'm just having a sulk. Everyone's allowed a sulk sometimes, aren't they?"

"Can we sulk together?" she asked.

"I can think of better things we could do together." His smile was slow as he moved along the settee towards her.

"So can I, and if I thought I could stay awake long enough to enjoy it, I'd love to. But—"

"I know," he said, running his fingers down the side of her face. "I do know. I could murder another tea. Could you?"

Five minutes later, when he came back in with the tea, she had slumped to one side on the settee and was sound asleep.

He kissed her forehead gently, then turned the lights down a little as he went back to the kitchen to sort out the boys' lunch boxes for the morning.

Chapter 8

Spring arrived with the month of March. The bitter chill melted away along with the easterly winds, leaving behind blue skies and pale sunshine that touched the trees with blossom and carpeted the ground with nodding daffodils and the promise of brightly coloured tulips. The previous November, a group of volunteer gardeners had spent a day digging and planting up the narrow garden and the window boxes around Hope Hall, and the fruits of their labour were now plain to see in the blaze of golden narcissi peeping their heads through clouds of purple pansies.

I love the spring, thought Kath as she turned her face towards the sun, closing her eyes and inhaling deeply. When she opened them again, she saw that Maggie was just about to join her as they reached the main door of Hope Hall at more or less the same moment. The change in Maggie over the past few weeks was really quite alarming. Her face seemed to be thinner and there were dark smudges under her eyes.

"Got time for a coffee before you start work?" asked Kath.

"Probably not, but let's have one anyway."

Maggie went to organize a couple of things in the kitchen while Kath headed for the coffee machine to collect two cappuccinos, which she carried through to the back office where Maggie was poring over the diary.

"I've been meaning to ask you," said Kath, as she gingerly sipped at her coffee, knowing that the first few mouthfuls were always burning hot. "You know the Beetle and Puds event that's coming up? The various clubs that run activities at the Hall have decided to take the competition really seriously. They're forming teams and discussing strategy as if it's the Eurovision Song Contest. Anyway, I've had several of them nagging that we ought to have a management team too, and I wondered if you might join us?"

"I'll be doing the puddings."

"I realize that, but I've also known you long enough to be certain you'll have them all organized long before they're needed. And Liz is scheduled to be here, so she can run the kitchen. Come on, Mags, it will be a laugh, and you haven't had many of those lately."

Maggie's eyes glistened as she pulled up her office chair.

"Tough at home, is it?" asked Kath gently.

"It doesn't really feel like home any more, with all the packing boxes and charity bags. There's a quarter of a century of much-loved clutter in that house, and although it's not worth a fig to anyone else, it's breaking my heart to throw some of that stuff away. The paintings the kids did at school. Their baby shoes and their old school reports. I've got every birthday card that anyone in the family's ever been sent. On the wardrobe I've got Darren's A-level Technology project, which is a huge helicopter thing that never really flew – and there's the pair of pyjamas that Steph made in her first year of Needlework. And the photo albums – we've got a whole cupboard full of them, and another that's stuffed to the top with rolls of film, negatives and dozens of packs of photo prints. How can I throw them away?"

"Wouldn't Darren and Steph like to keep some of them?"

"They've not said so. They're a social media generation, aren't they? They've got thousands of pictures on their phones, which they can store on their laptops in the blink of an eye. They're not interested in packs of old prints in which most of the pictures are naff. A lot of them are out of focus – one or two might be worth them having a look at and a giggle, but then they would want to chuck them out. Those photos are *my* memories, because the kids don't really remember the occasion or the other people in the picture or the funny things that happened."

"It's good to have those mementoes of happy times. They're memories worth cherishing."

"Except that Dave appears in so many of those pictures. He was never that much of a hands-on dad, but there he is manning the barbecue, raising his beer glass, driving the caravan or putting up the tent when we went camping. And there are photos of birthdays and Christmases and all our anniversaries…"

Kath could think of nothing to say.

"I still can't believe this is happening," Maggie went on. "I made my vows on our wedding day never dreaming for one minute that we wouldn't grow old together. I thought I knew him completely. It was beyond my imagination that there would be a notion in his head that I wouldn't understand and share. Where did all this come from? Did I ever really know him? Was he just playing the part of the family man while he waited for something better to come along?"

"There is nothing better than you, Maggie. Dave's situation may be very different and exciting right now, but you don't honestly think it's going to last?"

"I shouldn't care, should I? He plainly doesn't care about me."

"Have you seen him?"

"We agreed that he could come over on Saturday to clear out the garden shed, the attic and the garage. I made sure I was working, so I didn't have to cross paths with him, and Darren volunteered to be there to keep an eye on things. That was a mistake. Darren knew why I wanted him to be there, but he still let Dave pick out all the best bits to take back with him, and left all the rubbish for me to clear up."

"Oh, Mags—"

"I hope our lawn mower blows dirt all over her, that the barbecue burns her sausages and that our big paddling pool springs a leak all over her best outfit!"

"That's the spirit!"

"The solicitor says we could be in a position to exchange contracts on the house in about six weeks' time, and then I'll have to move out, whether the divorce is finalized or not. I'll lose my home."

"Have you thought about where you'll live then?"

"No."

"You know I have a big spare room and I'd love your company."

"Thanks, Kath, but that wouldn't be fair."

"You'd do the same for me."

"No, I wouldn't," grinned Maggie. "I'd tell you to pull yourself together and go out and choose a brilliant new home that's just perfect – not too small but big enough, cheap to run, close to work, near the shops—"

"A nice little garden?"

"Not likely. I won't possess a lawn mower, barbecue or paddling pool, and I'm blowed if I'm going to buy new ones. Window boxes will do me fine."

Kath laughed. "Determined and formidable. You're just the sort of person we want on our management team for the Beetle Drive!"

Maggie's face dropped. "Oh no, Kath, honestly—"

"Honestly, I won't take no for an answer. Forget about all the other rubbish just for an hour or two. It will be a laugh."

"It will be a battle to the death, or I refuse to get involved."

"A battle of the beetles it will be then. Heaven help the other teams!"

"What's this, Claire?" Nigel was holding up an envelope on the front of which her mother's handwriting was clearly visible.

"It's for Josh."

"You've seen your mum then, have you?"

"You know I see her once in a while. She's my mother. She's Josh's grandmother."

"And *you* know how I feel about your family. I don't want Josh having anything to do with them."

"I understand your reservations about my father. He did behave badly."

"Well, your mother's no better. There's a twenty pound note in here with a card for Josh saying that he should buy the computer download he needs. What computer download, Claire? What don't you understand about me not wanting your parents to buy Josh anything, *anything* at all?"

Claire's heart thumped in her chest as she cursed her mistake in leaving the envelope on the kitchen table when she should have put it away.

"It's a language tuition program in the form of a game that they were talking about at Beavers the other night. You know Josh is going to take his French speaking badge in a few weeks' time, and when we bumped into Mum in the town the other day, he was telling her about it."

"Don't lie, Claire. You didn't bump into your mother. You arranged to meet her."

"Actually, we just met her in Sainsbury's. I had no idea she was there."

"Even if I believed that – which I don't – having met her by accident, you still stayed together long enough for Josh to work out what present he'd like from her, and to make sure he told her all about it. You *know* how I feel about your parents buying their way into his affections, and you still let that happen."

"Actually, I didn't hear their conversation. I was up at the counter buying tea and a drink for Josh."

"You shouldn't have stopped to speak to her at all."

"You don't understand. Josh and I were already in the café. You know how he loves having tea in there. You were working late and I knew we wouldn't be having our meal until later, so I promised Josh that if he was a good boy while I did the shopping, he could choose whatever he wanted for his own tea in the café there."

"So you met your mum, completely by accident, and you ended

up having tea together, completely unplanned – and she gave this money to Josh."

"No, he doesn't know anything about it."

"Which must mean that you've seen her again so that she could give this to you."

"She left that envelope in a plastic bag that she stuck under my windscreen wiper today when my car was outside the school."

"I don't believe you."

Claire turned angrily and stormed over to the kitchen bin. Rummaging through the rubbish, she pulled out a clear plastic bag with a piece of paper still folded inside it.

"I know I shouldn't do this," her mother had written, "but I hope you will accept this money, not from your father but from me, for that computer language game that will help Josh with his French speaking badge. If you'd rather not accept this, I'll understand. I'll be very sad, but I do realize this puts you in a difficult position. How I long for this dreadful feud between Nigel and your father to be over! Lovely to see you yesterday. Take care of yourself, my darling. Mum x"

"So she knew she was putting you in a difficult position, but she did it anyway. She's as bad as your father. They just assume they know better about our son than we do."

"Nigel, Mum's not like that. Josh is their grandson. She loves him. She loves me. She's just trying to help out when she can. Grandparents do that."

"Well, we agreed, you and I, that we don't want your parents' help. You *did* agree, Claire. You know how furious I am about all this, and in view of that I frankly find it unforgivable that you should go against my wishes in this way."

"I haven't done anything yet. I haven't passed the money on to Josh. I haven't really decided what I'll do."

"There's no decision to make. I don't want your parents seeing Josh at all, *ever*. Do I make myself clear?"

Much to her dismay, Claire felt her eyes fill with tears.

"And don't try turning on the tears, because I won't change my mind on this. You've let me down, Claire. I thought you were better than this."

He turned on his heel and started to walk out of the kitchen towards the stairs.

"And I thought you were a better husband, a better father – in fact, a better man. You're hard work, Nigel. I can't *agree* that I should never see my parents, because I'm their daughter and I love them, and that is an unreasonable thing for you to ask of me. What happened was that you laid down the law and snapped your fingers and expected me to obey you. Well, I've got news for you. Among all the promises I made when I married you, I didn't promise to obey, because I don't think that's the way marriage should be."

"Please stop talking, Claire. Don't say another word, because we will both regret it."

"That's the problem, though, isn't it, Nigel? You think you should do the talking and I should just shut up and do what I'm told."

"Works for me," he shouted, stamping up the stairs and slamming the bedroom door behind him.

"We've got lots of entries for the Beetles and Puds afternoon," said Kath, surprised to find that there were fifteen tables already booked when she totted up the list.

"Do you think it's Maggie's puddings that are bringing them in?" smiled Trevor. "It can't just be the idea of the Beetle Drive, can it? I haven't been to one of those for years."

"It was James, the vicar at St Mark's who first mentioned it. Apparently they had quite a few fund-raising Beetle Drives at his old church, and they always went down really well."

"And how about the idea of combining puddings with the event? Where did that come from?"

"Well, Maggie is on the Good Neighbours committee, as I am, and when she suggested she might bake a cake or two if we organized our own fund-raising Beetle Drive, we bit her hand off. It was Maggie herself who said it would be a good twist to have puddings with nice dishes and cutlery, and tea to go with them – and it seems to have hit just the right note, because the tickets are disappearing like hot cakes!"

"Who's signed up for our management team then?"

"You're our captain, of course, and Mary will be your beautiful assistant, with Maggie and me trying our best to keep up. Then there's a team coming from St Mark's, led by James and Ellie. Oh, I see that their new musical director, Gregory Palmer, and his wife Fiona are making up their number, so that will be interesting, because the Can't Sing Singers have formed a team too."

Trevor chuckled. "That should cause a few fireworks. Who else has booked in?"

"There are a couple of teams from the Grown-ups' Lunch Club. There's one team of ladies who've listed Ida as their captain. She's terrifying. Heaven help her team members if the dice don't land as she wants them to! And dear old Percy Wilson is bringing along his gang of four who always sit together. He's a hoot. If anyone's going to cheat, it will be him."

"He sounds like my kind of captain."

"I'll pretend I didn't hear you say that," laughed Kath, as she continued to work her way down the list.

"There's a team from the playgroup, another from the line dancers – and the Money Advice Service counsellors told me they were coming too, but they haven't put their entry in yet. Oh, and Della is bringing her mum and our Shirley."

"Shirley our cleaning lady?"

"Apparently Della's mum Barbara and Shirley are sisters – and Shirley's husband Mick is coming along to make up the four."

"The way things are shaping up, I think this could easily become a very cut-throat affair. I can see at least some of those teams taking it all too seriously…"

"Yes," giggled Kath. "Beetlemania!"

Trevor turned back to the other papers on the desk. "I've been trying to find out a bit more about the Carlisle Charitable Trust that gave us that grant recently. Apparently, Sir Bernard Carlisle grew up in these parts in a very ordinary farming family, but he always had a gift for mechanics and machinery. He ended up creating his own range of farm equipment that revolutionized the way in which planting and harvesting could be achieved more economically and efficiently. Carlisle became the most popular brand of farm equipment throughout the British Isles and is now one of the leading names for farm machinery across the world."

"It's interesting that an international company like that should have a family trust with funds that are given primarily to local projects."

"Old Sir Bernard never forgot his roots. He felt that he owed his education and values to this community, so he left money to ensure that future generations of young people would be encouraged in the same way. And as he got older himself, he expanded the remit of the fund to include all community projects, especially those supporting families and the elderly."

"Are there still Carlisle family members living in this area?"

"Our cheque was signed by Richard Carlisle, who seems to be the managing director of the company now. It might be worth inviting him along to one of our events some time. Perhaps he'd like to see for himself what their money is achieving."

"Do you think they'd like to make up a Beetle and Puds team?"

"I don't know," laughed Trevor. "Perhaps I should ask."

At that point, Kath's mobile rang. Glancing down, her heart skipped a beat as she saw Jack's name displayed.

"Take it," said Trevor, burying his head in the accounts spreadsheet. "I'm fine here."

Kath picked up the phone and walked out of the office before answering the call.

"Hi, Jack. How are you?"

"I've just finished an all-night shift that came up at short notice – and that was after I'd already worked for eight hours yesterday. We got a match for a heart transplant patient who's been with us for a long time. She's only four years old, and we were beginning to think we were going to lose her before a heart came up."

"And did it all go okay?"

She could hear the weariness in his voice as he recalled the previous few hours.

"It wasn't straightforward – a bit touch and go at times, to be honest."

"You sound bushed."

"I am, but you know what it's like. My mind is racing, and I know it's no good trying to sleep just yet."

"A hot bath then? A warm drink?"

"A warm hug from you is what I would really like."

A trickle of excitement coursed down her backbone. "I'd like that too."

"You're working, aren't you?"

She sighed with frustration. "Yes, it's a busy one today. The accountant's in."

"Ah, well, I'll settle for just hearing your voice then."

"Shall I sing you a lullaby?"

"I've heard your singing before. I might pass on that one." He hesitated just a moment before speaking again. "I would like to see you, though, Kath."

"I wasn't sure you wanted to."

"I was nervous, I suppose. I wanted to suggest something, but wasn't quite certain how you'd feel; whether it was the right thing…"

"I know. I understand."

"Would you like us to get together?"

"Yes."

"When?"

"Whenever you're awake and you can."

"How about tomorrow night? It's Saturday. We could meet halfway. Do you know the Brewer's Arms?"

"Of course. That's such a well-known landmark."

"Shall we meet there about half past seven? I'll wait in the bar."

"I'll look forward to it. What are you going to do now?"

"I'm going to stretch out on the sofa and watch yesterday's rugby match that I missed. I already know that my team lost, so that should send me to sleep. How about you?"

"Well, I'm just sorting out the teams for our Beetles and Puds event coming up the weekend after next."

"What? You mean an old-fashioned Beetle Drive? My mum used to take me along to those. They're great fun."

"Well, we may have a space on our management team. Perhaps you'd like to come and make up numbers?"

"Don't be silly. I'm a doctor. I'd get all the body parts in the wrong places."

Sara was going downhill fast. Ray had seen a change in her condition during the last few days that filled him with dread. There were long periods when she was either deeply asleep or not quite awake. He felt he was becoming part of her fretful dreams as reality seemed to escape her grasp.

The Hospice at Home team had become his lifeline. Their visits throughout the day, and the calls he was able to make to them at night whenever he felt out of his depth, were all that kept him going. He wanted to make sure he was doing everything he could to ease her pain and keep her calm and peaceful. He was worried about showing fear in his face as he watched her struggle with weakness and pain. Just a few days before, she had still been able to have short conversations with him, but speaking was difficult now.

Guttural sounds came from her throat, which seemed to be closing up on her. His heart broke. His eyes stung. His body ached. He was losing her. His beloved Sara was slipping away from him.

"I'll sit with her now." Jane, the hospice nurse, touched his arm as he slumped uncomfortably in the armchair beside Sara's bed. "You're exhausted. See if you can get a bit of sleep in the spare room for a while. I promise I'll wake you if there's any change."

"How long?"

"The doctor's coming this morning. He'll tell us more."

"Is she in pain?"

"Probably not. The medication takes care of that."

"Does she even know I'm here?"

"Oh, I think she always knows you're here for her, Ray."

"I don't want to leave her side if she's…"

Jane knelt down so that he could see the kindness and concern in her eyes. "I'm here to look after you as well as Sara. You need some rest. If there's anything at all to tell you, I will come and get you straight away."

"My son's coming down this afternoon."

"Then you'll need a rest before you see him."

"Nothing will happen before he comes?"

"Sleep now, Ray. Come on, let me give you a hand."

I'll never sleep, he thought, as he allowed her to guide him through to the bed in the spare room, where he climbed in and pulled the bedclothes up round his ears. But by the time Jane was pulling the door closed, he was already sliding into exhausted slumber.

All week long, the Call-in Café attracted a steady flow of customers who either enjoyed their drinks and snacks down in the foyer, or took them upstairs. The comfy chairs in the balcony lounge meant that people sometimes worked their way through hours of chat, at least a couple of cakes and several drinks before they left again. Saturday mornings, though, were always the busiest time, when the café was regularly run by the deputy catering manager Liz, whose greying hair and slight build belied her quick mind, boundless energy and ability to cope with at least a dozen things at once. On Saturdays, she organized everything with the help of a couple of part-timers while Maggie had her day off.

Out of the corner of her eye, Liz had been dimly aware of a figure hovering in the background watching the proceedings rather than joining the queue, but she was too busy to take much notice as she got on with making fresh coffee, preparing a variety of sandwiches, making up ploughman's lunches, baked potatoes, quiches and salads, along with a couple of hot dishes. There were the puddings too, of course, for which the café was well known, as well as a delicious array of mouth-watering cakes.

Liz had just turned towards the sink to wash her hands when she heard a voice.

"Hello, Miss."

She turned to see Kevin, the would-be Jamie Oliver who had started doing work experience at the Grown-ups' Lunch Club. He looked different out of school uniform, although fashion plainly wasn't his thing from the look of his battered denim jacket and jeans, and his hair that was spiky not from a razor-sharp cut, but because it simply did stick out in spikes.

"Hello, Kevin. Have you come for lunch?"

"Only if I can help make it," he replied. "I want to work here."

"Kevin, you're still at school. There are rules and procedures in place for work experience."

"I'll work for free. I just want to be here at this café."

Liz wiped her hands, her face curious. "Why?"

"If I told you my favourite television programme is *The Great British Bake Off*, would you understand?"

She smiled then. "You fancy yourself as a baker, do you?"

"I just want to cook. I love cooking anything, from bacon and eggs to all sorts of meals. I like making something out of nothing – you know, just with things from the cupboard, and trying a few different spices to give it a bit of a twist. But it's baking that I really love most – bread, yeast-based buns, sponges, fruit cakes, icing, sugar and chocolate work. I've seen it all on telly and I just can't take my eyes off it. There's no chance of me trying out anything like that at home. My mum thinks worktops and sinks were designed to be somewhere that you pile up all the dirty plates. Cooking doesn't interest her, and there's never any money for extras anyway. So I'd like to come and learn here because of the baking you do. I'll just stand in the corner and watch, if that's all that's allowed, although I'd be happy to help out if you'd let me."

Liz looked at him thoughtfully. "You did a good job spud-bashing the other day."

"Did I?"

"And I saw you taking an interest in everything I was preparing."

"Yeah?"

"I even saw you adding extra basil to the lasagne mix when you thought I wasn't looking."

His face fell. "I'm sorry. I shouldn't have done that without asking."

"No, you shouldn't – but actually I'm glad you did. The sauce tasted much nicer for it."

His face lit up. "Did it, Miss? I love basil in Italian-based sauces. Did you see me put in extra garlic as well?"

"No, because you'd have been out on your ear if I had. A lot of our diners have special dietary requirements. Garlic can cause an unpleasant reaction in some vulnerable people, especially when they're elderly. You should never add anything to someone else's dishes without checking first."

His face turned an interesting shade of puce. "Sorry, Miss."

"How old are you, Kevin?"

"Sixteen, Miss."

"And what are your plans for the future – *before* you take over from Jamie Oliver?"

"Well, I just want to cook."

"So will that mean going to college?"

"My mum's on her own. I'm the eldest of four of us. I want to get working as soon as I can."

"But cooking is a skill you have to be taught. College is usually the first step."

"You have to pay to go there. I want to be paid as soon as I can. Mum will need me to bring money in."

"So you hope to learn the trade—"

"By working in a place like this, or a baker's shop somewhere. And I can watch a lot online too. I know I won't be earning for a while, but this is what I want to do, and I'd like you to teach me."

"Well, Kevin, I'm not the baking expert here, so you need to talk to our catering manager, Maggie, who will be in on Monday. Could you pop in some time to see her?"

"I could come straight after school about four o'clock?"

"Fine. I'll put that in the diary."

"What's the catering manager like, Miss? What do you think she'll say?"

"I think she'll be very interested to hear what I have to say about you."

"You won't tell her about the garlic, Miss, will you?"

Liz struggled not to smile. "Well, that's for you to ponder, isn't it, Kevin?"

Kath changed her mind about what to wear three times before she finally settled on the soft blue jersey. Whenever she wore it, someone seemed to comment that the colour matched her eyes. Perhaps Jack would think so too.

She recognized his car immediately as she turned into the car park. With a quick glance in the mirror to check that she didn't have dark mascara splashes under her eyes or lipstick on her teeth, she climbed out of the car and made her way through the pub to the bar at the back.

And there he was, so dear and familiar – and there went her heart again, thumping in her chest at the sight of him standing up to greet her. She simply walked into his arms, and they stood there for a while, wound around each other, remembering how wonderful those hugs had always felt.

"You're early," she smiled, allowing him to draw her into the seat beside him.

"And you, as always, are bang on time. I've never known you be anything but punctual, my dear Kath."

"Have you been working today?" she asked, noticing the lines of tiredness around his eyes.

"Just for a few hours. We've a few children in intensive care at the moment who've been through very complicated surgery. I like to keep a close eye on them."

"And, as always, you will put in whatever hours are needed to care for them."

He shrugged. "As a doctor, I want to do the best for my patients. As a human being, I also want to do my best for their parents. I've seen such despair and anguish, as well as unbelievable courage, in the mums and dads who spend days, sometimes weeks, in hospital with their sick children. Often that devotion comes at tremendous cost to themselves and to other members of their family. They need all the support we can give them."

Kath smiled as she slipped her hand into his and gave it a squeeze. "You're the right man for that. Being a doctor was never just a job for you; it's a vocation."

He smiled back at her. "And you? How's your job suiting you?"

"I love it. Hope Hall has a wonderfully warm feel to it. Everybody in the town comes through its doors at some time – babies and children, teenagers, OAPs who are full of life and able-bodied, as well as others who are coping with the effects of getting older – loss of memory, hip replacements, health problems. Then there are people from all corners of the community who come in for special reasons – to find help with debt, or alcohol, learning English or losing weight. They come in to sing, dance, play games, drink coffee, eat cakes! Hope Hall welcomes them all."

"And you make it happen?"

"With the help of a great team. I mainly do the admin and paperwork."

"You forget how well I know you. Admin and paperwork will just be the starting point of what you do. Anyway, would you like a drink? And they do lovely meals here. Have you eaten?"

"No. Shall we take a look at the menu?"

An hour and a half later, following a delicious meal, Jack slipped his arm around her shoulders and drew her close. "I've missed this. I didn't realize how much until I saw you at the reunion."

"I thought I was over you."

"And me you." Jack looked down at their clasped hands. "It's not gone away, though, has it? We still get on so well. There's no learning curve between us. We understand each other."

She nodded, feeling so much, wanting to choose her words carefully. "We are in very different circumstances now, though. We live and work in different worlds."

"That might be a good thing," he suggested. "Hospital life up in London was a bit like a pressure cooker – constantly working, studying, so many people around us all the time. It sometimes felt like being under a microscope."

"And was I part of that pressure? Did you think I was expecting too much of you?"

"Kath, we lived in each other's pockets. We were together all the time. You had a right to expect commitment from me, some sort of plan for continuing our life together…"

"But you weren't ready for that."

"No, I wasn't."

She looked up to gaze directly at him. "And I'm not ready now just to pick up where we left off. We're no spring chickens, Jack. For heaven's sake, we're both heading for fifty. We're independent people, probably stuck in our ways, however much we think we can compromise."

He smiled. "That's my Kath. Say it like it is and don't pull your punches. I've always appreciated that about you."

"But when decisions had to be made about Mum, it felt as if my leaving didn't matter to you. You were so cold – you cut me out as if I were a cancer in one of your patients. That hurt…"

He pulled her closer as her voice faltered.

"I can't go through that pain again, Jack. I'd rather turn away from this right now than take that risk."

"And yet there *is* something here still," he said quietly. "Something deep and dear that I don't want to lose again, not without finding out what this could bring us, both now and in the future." He tilted her chin so that their faces were a breath apart. "Let's just take it slowly. No pressure, no promises, no time limit. There's old love here, but where that love takes us is for us to discover – together."

He held out his hand to her then. For several long moments, she didn't move – and then, winding her fingers around his, she leaned forward until their foreheads touched, her reply no more than a whisper.

"Together."

Tess rang Maggie back on Monday morning, as soon as she had a break between lessons. The two women were old friends – well, to be precise, the oldest friendship was between Maggie and Tess's mum and dad. They had all been at school together, and remained friends as the couple married and worked endless hours on the family farm that they eventually inherited. Maggie had been at Tess's christening, and had watched her grow into a fine young woman who always loved the countryside, but decided as a teenager that she didn't want a lifetime of working on the farm. Her parents seemed slightly bemused when Tess went off to get a degree in Social Sciences followed by her teaching qualifications. After her marriage to a quantity surveyor, who was offered a post in her home area, the couple were delighted when they were able to buy a cottage that Tess had always loved not far from the family farm. Now with young children of their own, she often brought in the vegetables, salads, fruit and eggs that Maggie had ordered from her parents.

"Sorry I missed your call, Maggie. You need to know about Kevin Marley?"

"Yes, he's coming in to see me after school today. He wants to learn to cook here. Says he's really keen on baking."

"Yes, he is. He's an odd sort of lad because he doesn't really socialize with any particular group at school. It's not that he's unpopular. He just walks his own path. I think he has a lot of responsibility at home. There's no dad, and his mum has got a bit of a mouth on her."

"Liz said he was rather cocky last week when you brought him along for work experience, but then he took a real interest in the cooking. He even added a couple of extra ingredients into the pot, and actually they were good ones – but we won't tell him that. He needs to learn discipline in the kitchen, more than anything else."

"Well, I think this might be the chance he needs. He's got to learn to walk before he can run, but I know you and Liz will keep him in check."

"He's not going to rob the cash box and knock over little old ladies then?"

"Actually, he often speaks of his gran. She sounds quite formidable, but he adores her. No, I think he's fine with older people. This could be the making of him."

"Right, I'll see how he gets on with work experience during the lunch on Tuesday, and if that still seems okay, I'll invite him along when we need an extra pair of hands."

"Thanks, Mags." Tess hesitated for a moment. "I spotted Dave in town the other day. It was all I could do not to give him a piece of my mind."

"He probably wouldn't be interested. He's in l-o-v-e – so he keeps telling everyone."

"Well, he was in l-o-v-e with you for how many years?"

"We met when I was sixteen, married when we were both twenty-two. We had our silver wedding anniversary less than six months ago. And you're right. We were in love. We never talked about it, because we never needed to. We just loved each other, end of story."

"You're going through the worst patch now, but it will get better. You'll come through this, and you *will* be happy again."

"Maybe. Thanks, Tess. I'll see you tomorrow then. Will there be three students again, including Kevin?"

"That's right. Bye."

Kevin couldn't keep the smile off his face as he put on his overalls to join the team in the kitchen the following morning to prepare the Grown-ups' Lunch. Once their guests started to arrive, it was all hands to the pump to get each course ready and served.

Among the first guests to arrive was a rather gangly smiling gentleman wearing a beige blazer, cream slacks and leather moccasins. His white shirt was open at the neck, and on his head he wore a straw hat at a delightfully saucy angle.

"Great Scott of the Antarctic!" he announced, taking off his hat in salute to all the people he saw gathered in the foyer. "It's a party. How charming."

"Come on, Gerald," said Ellie as she took his arm to guide him over towards where Kath was waiting to greet them. "There's someone I'd like you to meet."

"Gerald, welcome to Hope Hall," smiled Kath. "Have you been here before?"

Gerald looked about him with an expression that conveyed both delight and confusion. "I don't know. I might have. Phyllis would know. I'll ask Phyllis."

"Phyllis isn't here today, Gerald," Ellie gently explained. "Do you remember that she's not at all well now, so she's getting a bit of rest over at Forest View Nursing Home? We went there this morning. You took her some daffodils. She was very pleased. Do you remember?"

His eyes clouded over for a moment before he smiled broadly. "No, I don't. I might later. Is that tea I see? Am I allowed a cup?"

"You certainly are. Let me take you over to your table. You know Judith and George Merrill from the church, don't you? They've kept a seat for you, and here's your cup of tea now."

Once Gerald was settled, Ellie made her way across to where Kath was chatting to another group sitting at a nearby table. Kath looked up with a smile, but noticed immediately that Ellie's expression was unusually sombre.

"Can I have a quiet word with you, Kath? Something happened this morning that James thought you should know about."

Immediately, Kath led the way out of the hall and back towards her office.

The clock ticked round towards two o'clock. The plates were cleared away, teas, coffees and after-dinner mints were on the tables, and washing-up was in full swing. That was the job Shirley always liked to supervise, and Maggie smiled to herself as she heard the cleaning lady's shrill voice shouting out commands to a flustered Kevin, who was obviously trying his very best.

The door to the kitchen opened, and Kath walked in, her expression sad.

"Maggie, Liz, Shirley, can you come here a moment, please?"

Wondering what awful mistake they must have made, the three women gathered round her.

"I just wanted to let you know that Sara passed away this morning."

"Oh, no!" Shirley's eyes immediately filled with tears, and she pulled a hankie out of her sleeve to stem the flow. "She's been so brave," she managed to say. "So has Ray."

"Apparently Ray has their son and his wife there, and I know they'll be taking care of him and all the arrangements too. I've got a card here that I thought each of us could sign straight away, just to let him know we're thinking of him."

"I can drop it in on my way home," said Maggie.

"Thanks, Mags. Sorry to be the bearer of bad news, but I know all of you were very fond of Sara. And we all love Ray, of course."

The group nodded in agreement as they gathered to sign the card. It felt as if a light had gone out around them.

"Hello," smiled Claire. "I was just wondering whether to make a coffee for you too."

Gary's face lit up when he saw her. "We're running late tonight. Toby and Max got incredibly excited at the idea of coming to Beavers, and when they're excited, it's impossible to communicate with them. Is it just me? Am I a terrible parent?"

"Oh," sighed Claire, "I seem to be surrounded by people who can't communicate properly at the moment."

Gary eyed her with curiosity as he held his coffee cup under the steaming spout of the machine. "Tough week?"

"You could say that."

"You go and grab our table and I'll bring these over."

Once he'd sat down and taken a gulp of his coffee, Gary watched Claire as she circled the spoon absent-mindedly in her cup.

"You're going to wear out the bottom of that cup."

She noticed then, and smiled a little.

"Do you want to talk about it?" he asked.

"I don't know. I probably shouldn't."

Gary said nothing as he picked up his coffee.

"We had a row. Nigel was furious because my mum left a card under my windscreen wiper with twenty pounds in it for that computer game a lot of the boys here have got. You know – the one that helps them prepare for their French speaking badge?"

"I don't think that's been mentioned to my two yet."

"Well, it's just a silly little computer game really, but it's a good way for kids of this age to learn a bit of colloquial French. Josh tried it at his friend's house the other evening and loved it."

"And your mother knew that?"

"Yes, Josh ended up telling her about it. I didn't think she'd remember really, but I should have known better."

"Are you still seeing her then?"

"Not as much as before, but I missed our time together, and I am so angry with Nigel for thinking he has the right to come between us like that. I feel awkward about going to the house, because he's strictly forbidden that, but Mum and I sometimes meet up at the supermarket, so we can have a cuppa and a snack after we've each done our shopping."

"And Nigel doesn't know about that?"

"Well, he didn't – but then I stupidly left Mum's envelope with the money in it for Josh's computer game on the kitchen table. I can't believe I did that."

"And Nigel found it?"

"He went ballistic. He was furious about the money; furious that my mum was impertinent enough to disobey his orders not to buy gifts for Josh without his permission; furious that I'd accepted it; furious that I'd met my mum at all. I told him Josh and I had just bumped into Mum by accident—"

"Which wasn't true."

"No, and I hate telling lies, but he was so angry I didn't dare tell him the truth. He's suspected for a while that I do still see Mum, and that sometimes Josh comes as well, but this is the first time he's had real proof. He knew I was lying, of course, because I'm terrible at it. That only made the whole thing worse."

"So how are things now?"

"The atmosphere is unbearable. Even Josh has noticed, and I can see it's upsetting him. Nigel only speaks to me when he can't avoid it. If I walk into a room, he walks out. He's been working extra hours, which he never normally does. Then he comes home late, saying he's already eaten and not touching the dinner I've prepared. It's just awful."

"Will this blow over, do you think?"

"You know, I'm really not sure. It's certainly not getting any better so far. Nigel is completely adamant that his attitude to my parents is right. I know Dad behaved badly, but my mum just loves us all. It breaks my heart that my family are blocked out like this."

He realized that she was crying, trying not to let him or anyone else see. Under the table, he stretched out to put a comforting hand on her arm. She didn't move it away. She didn't seem to notice it was there.

"And the thing is, he's not the only one who's angry. I'm angry too – and more than that, I'm disappointed. I thought better of him. The man I married was kinder than that, and I thought he understood the importance of family – not just his, but mine too."

"Claire, I'm so sorry."

As if suddenly aware that she might be making a spectacle of herself in front of others in the room, and perhaps even him, she made an effort to pull herself together.

"Don't be," she replied. "We all have our ups and downs. Marriage is like that, isn't it?"

"Oh, yes."

She looked across at him. "Yours too?"

"Karen and I had words this week as well."

"Anything to worry about?"

"Well, to be fair, I think it's more my fault than hers. I know I'm being unreasonable, but I just can't help it. I'm working on a really big contract at the moment for a company that could give me a lot of business in the future. They went out on a limb to choose a sole trader like me, and they're really putting the pressure on."

"And how's it going?"

"I can do the work easily – and it's what I love to do. I know I'm good at it. But getting it done is quite another thing altogether. The box room I work in barely has space for my drawing board, and everything is so cramped. I need a table top to keep all my drawings in constant view, but if I leave anything on the dining room table, not only is it all the way downstairs, but the twins will have scribbled over it in indelible pen before I know it."

"So how do you manage?"

"Well, that's the trouble. I don't feel I am managing very well right now. I'm not good at doing two things at once. The fact is I'm a house husband now. I'm not complaining about that, because that is what Karen and I agreed, for the simple reason that she earns so much more than me. But I'm just not capable of running the house, organizing everything the twins need, and keeping my job going all at the same time. I end up doing nothing very well."

"And are your work clients picking up on that?"

"They seem to choose to ring me when it's bedlam at my end, with the kids running riot. That can hardly give them confidence, can it, when half the time I can't even hear what they're saying because there's so much din in the background?"

"Surely Karen understands that?"

"Yes, she does, but there's not a lot she can do about it. She works such long days. She's always worn out when she gets home. I can't blame her for just wanting to spend a bit of time with the boys, have a meal ready for her, and collapse in a heap."

"In an ideal world, yes, but kids have a habit of getting in the way of that."

"The boys constantly play up for me, but when Mum comes home, they're little angels."

Claire smiled. "I don't think that means you're doing something wrong. It's just that they miss her, and want nothing more than her company when she's back with them again."

"Well, I feel a bit like that about her too. I miss her. I'd like to have some quality time with her, like we used to – but she's always too busy, too late, too harassed, too exhausted…"

"And can the two of you talk about it?"

"Yes, we have talked – and yes, she gets the point, but that's just the way our life is."

"I suppose so."

"I think that what I really miss is going to work, sharing ideas with colleagues, and feeling that what I do is respected and valued."

"Is she interested in your work?"

"She used to be. Not much time for that now."

"And are you interested in what she does at work?"

"I don't really understand it. She's an IT genius; that's all I know. She's really clever. Perhaps that's the problem. I'm not as clever as she is. She's a talented, sought after, inspirational and admired superwoman, who is a super*mum* too. I'm just an ordinary fella who sometimes feels very inadequate and in her shadow."

"Have you told her that's how you feel?"

"In a roundabout way. She says I'm imagining things."

"Could she be right?"

"Perhaps," he sighed.

They barely noticed the two women who were making their way over to the coffee machine at that moment.

"Hello!" said one of them in Gary's direction. "I know you from school, don't I? Aren't you the twins' dad?"

Gary smiled. "That's right. I'm Gary."

"Nice to meet you," replied the woman, beaming with friendliness. "And is this your wife? I don't think we've met."

"Oh no," spluttered Claire. "I'm Josh's mum. We've just met here because our boys are all Beavers."

"Ours too," commented the woman. "Well, we must go. We're off to the Fat Club."

Gary looked surprised.

"The Slimming Club, to give it its official title! It's on at the same time as Beavers, but over in the school hall. See you both later then. Bye!"

Alison and Sally waited until they'd walked out of sight before they turned to each other and giggled.

"Well, we can all see what's going on there."

"Did he have his hand on her knee?"

"I'm not sure, but they were certainly very close."

"Perhaps they're old friends?"

"Perhaps they're more than friends…"

And with a peel of laughter, they hurried towards the school hall.

Chapter 9

They arrived early. Long before the Beetles and Puds event was due to start at two, the competitors came pouring through the door. The ladies formed chatty queues as they disappeared off to "powder their noses" while the gentlemen had been given orders to bag the best tables and organize drinks and snacks from the bar.

"Coo-ee! We're over here." Shirley's voice jangled every window in Hope Hall as she called across to her sister, who was just walking in. Barbara Lucas was an elegant woman, well known for her many years of running a dance school in the town. Alongside her was Della, the next generation of teachers in this dance-devoted family, who acknowledged the greetings of many of her pupils as she glided gracefully into her place beside her Uncle Mick.

"Do you think that's Shirley's husband?" hissed Betty, narrowing her eyes to get a better look at the stocky, muscular man sitting next to the popular cleaning lady. "Past his best now, I suppose, but he must have been quite a hunk. He's a dead ringer for Rock Hudson."

"He wouldn't have done you much good then," retorted Ida haughtily. "Didn't he bat for the other side?"

"I saw every one of his films. I thought he was dreamy," sighed Doris. "Oh look, here's Flora. Our winning team is complete."

"There they are," snorted Percy from a couple of tables away. "The Merry Widows! I knew they wouldn't miss an occasion like this."

"Oh yes, I see them," smiled Connie, waving to get their attention. "Shall we go across and say hello?"

Percy gave her a withering look. "And give away our tactics? Sit down, woman! Robert and John are just coming in now. We have a victory to plan."

On the other side of the hall was the table booked by the playgroup. It had been generally agreed by both the staff and the parents whose children attended regularly that their team would be best represented by the playgroup leader and her deputy – and their husbands, of course, to give the team a good balance. Jen and Carol were staring in the direction of the bar, where their husbands were waiting to buy drinks. This was the first time Rob and Phil had actually seen each other since the day of the "car incident". In fact, the two men, old friends who usually spoke once a week, had not rung each other at all in the weeks since it happened.

"I think Phil's embarrassed," said Carol, anxiously peering across towards her husband.

"Well, nothing will be said unless Phil brings it up," replied Jen. "Rob's pretty disgusted with him, though – hiding all that money away without telling you, and then pleading poverty even though you desperately needed a reliable car."

"Phil just loves his old bikes. He says that the one he's working on is such a classic that it will be worth a fortune when he's done it up."

Jen turned to her sharply. "And you fell for that, did you? He won't ever sell it. You know he won't."

Carol sighed. "Well, I guess he *will* find it difficult to part with."

"Honestly, Carol, if he were my husband, I'd find it difficult *not* to part with *him*. He only ever thinks of himself, but he's got a fantastic wife and a gorgeous little boy. It's about time that man grew up and got his priorities right."

"Don't say anything, Jen, please! Let's just have a nice time together so we can get our friendship back to normal."

"Your Phil thinks it's all forgiven and forgotten," huffed Jen. "You shouldn't let him get away with it, Carol. You're too soft on him."

"Please, Jen, don't!"

Thumping back into her seat with frustration, Jen was beginning to wish she hadn't come.

At that moment, the St Mark's Church team entered the hall, greeting many friends and parishioners on the way. Ellie stopped several times to chat with and sometimes hug people she knew, as the group headed for their table. Her husband James cut a more formal figure, a priest who never forgot the grace and decorum of his calling. Eventually they sat down along with their other two team members, Gregory Palmer and his wife Fiona.

The new musical director of St Mark's was now familiar to most people in the church community. His remarkable transformation of the choir from a gaggle of well-intentioned amateurs to a choral group of high musical acumen was still causing ripples in local church circles. Some were admiring and proud of his success as the reputation of the St Mark's Choral Choir spread. Others dismissed him as high-handed, uncaring and even – dare it be said? – unchristian! But Gregory had no time for gossip and ill-informed opinion. He was simply employed to create a highly competent choir who could sing their praise to God with the skill and commitment that the almighty Father deserved. He was on a mission – and it obviously had God's blessing because the results had proved beyond doubt that the end justified the means. He had pruned out the dead wood, and now St Mark's had a glorious choir in which to take huge pride. Yes, he *was* proud of his achievement. There simply was no one else who could have knocked the music of St Mark's into shape, from the frankly laughable to the obviously superb.

"James, do you see Pauline Owen over there?" said Ellie, acknowledging Pauline's wave. "Gregory, you probably know the group on that table. They all used to be in our choir."

Gregory didn't move a muscle except for his eyes, which darted across to focus sharply on the group in question. Yes, he recognized

Pauline Owen, the choir member he sacked because she only ever sang a semi-tone above everyone else. And Sophia, the dreadful woman with a plummy operatic voice who, if she ever had training, must have gone to someone who taught football, or cooking for beginners, rather than anything to do with music and vocal techniques. And there was Keith Turner, the traitor! He had been granted a place in the newly formed choir, and had come along to most of the rehearsals, but his presence on that table meant that, in spite of the beautiful tone of his tenor voice, he was of no further interest to Gregory. Keith was undisciplined. He talked too much and listened too little. He also kept the worst kind of company.

"That's the Can't Sing Singers' table," explained Ellie, determined to ensure that Gregory understood clearly what heartbreak and uproar he had caused when he unceremoniously turfed out long-serving members of the church choir. "They are doing wonderfully well, so I hear. That's their new musical director on the table with them – Ronnie Andrews. Do you know him? He's worked professionally on all sorts of productions and musical shows for many years. He's very accomplished."

Gregory did not reply. He'd never heard of the man. He was of no consequence whatsoever.

Through the hatch where drinks and snacks were being sold, Maggie glanced up from the kitchen area where she and Liz were putting the finishing touches to the puddings and cakes. Long-necked glasses of lemon syllabub, chocolate mousse and elderflower jelly stood tall next to plates of pavlova meringues topped with bright red berries. Cheesecakes and flans were adorned with an array of exotic fruits. Darkly sumptuous toffee and chocolate sauces had been piped through sundaes piled high with toasted nuts and freshly baked finger-sized stem ginger biscuits. Hot desserts were ready to go into the oven at just the right moment: cinnamon-flavoured bread and butter pudding, melting chocolate fondants and hot lemon sponges that could be served with warm egg custard, home-made vanilla or chocolate ice cream, or crème patisserie. There were biscuits and cakes of all kinds: flapjacks, brownies, rocky road bars and crispy cornflake chocolate cakes. All made with love, no calories spared and every single one destined to disappear before the event was over.

Kevin was at the freezer, pulling a tray of frozen sweets out to defrost, when he spotted a familiar figure taking her place at a table quite close to the hatch.

"There's my mum!" he exclaimed. "She's brought my nan. I'm not sure what you'll make of her. And that's Tracey, our next-door neighbour, and Sonia her daughter. Sonia's got a car, so she brought them all here today. Nan says she can't walk far, but she's pretty good on her legs when it suits her."

"How old is your nan?" asked Maggie, leaving the desserts and moving across to the hatch so that she could see through to the table where Kevin's family were sitting.

"Nan has told us for the last four years that she's sixty-one and deserves lots of special presents. Even Mum isn't sure exactly how old she is, because she's lied about her age all her life."

"Doesn't anyone have a birth certificate for her?"

Kevin shrugged. "Don't think so. She comes up with different dates every time she's asked about when she was born. On her pension book, it says she's seventy-three now – but honestly, I'm not sure. She's looked just the same for years."

"I'd like to meet them all," decided Maggie. "Can I do that, before things get too busy here?"

It wasn't clear from his expression whether Kevin was pleased or appalled at Maggie's suggestion, but he laid down the tray and followed her out of the kitchen into the foyer and through to his family's table in the hall.

"Well, Kevin, don't you look posh in your chef's overalls!" cried his mother, getting to her feet as her son and Maggie reached them.

"I'm Deirdre. Everyone calls me Dee – and if that son of mine gives you too much lip at any time, you have my full permission to sort him out."

"There's no need for that," smiled Maggie. "Kevin has a natural flair for cooking, although I guess you know that."

Dee shrugged. "Oh, he's always whingeing on about wanting to cook this and that. I don't take much notice really. This is my neighbour Tracey and her daughter Sonia. We only asked Sonia because we needed her car. She's not looking forward to this – are you, Son? She's a bit serious – always got her nose in some book or other. This kind of thing is not really her cup of tea."

Sonia smiled up at Maggie shyly, her cheeks pink with embarrassment. "I am glad to be here," she mumbled. "I like the fact that the afternoon is raising funds for Good Neighbours, because they help out with Lily a lot." She gestured towards Kevin's grandmother, who was concentrating on working her way through a packet of chocolate biscuits.

"When are they serving the puds?" Lily asked, staring at Maggie. "I'm starving. Are they ever going to feed us?"

"Well, we've got lots of lovely cakes and puddings lined up, Lily. They're not quite ready yet because we're serving them during the break in the middle of the Beetle tournament."

"What have you got?"

Maggie rattled off the selection of puddings, putting the ones she thought Lily was most likely to enjoy right at the top of the list.

"How much are they?" Lily demanded to know.

"Your ticket allows you to have a pudding of your choice, and then they're a pound each after that."

Lily's eyes filled with tears. "But I'm so hungry. I'll need at least three, and I'll never be able to afford them on my pension…"

Maggie looked down at the elderly lady with sympathy before leaning over to whisper in her ear, "Well, I'm taking part in one of the teams here too, but when it's break time, you and I can go up together and I'm sure I'll be able to treat you to an extra cake or two."

189

Dee clapped her hands triumphantly. "Great, the whole crowd of us will bring Nan up when you go – and then we can tell you what *we'd* like best too."

Knowing she had been completely outmanœuvred, Maggie said her goodbyes and started walking back towards the foyer with Kevin at her heels.

The moment they reached the comparative quiet of the kitchen, Kevin grabbed her arm to hold her back. "I'm sorry. My family are a nightmare. And don't believe a word my nan says. She always gets what she wants, and she doesn't care how."

"Yes, I think I'm beginning to realize that."

"The other day the police knocked on the door to talk about what happened when she went over to that supermarket on the other side of town a couple of weeks ago. Apparently, she'd caught sight of a bloke walking in on his own, and targeted him before he'd had time to start his shopping. Then she just stood there staring at him with her eyes all watery, blowing her nose on a soggy tissue. The man got worried and walked over to ask her what was wrong, and she came up with some story about him looking just like her dead son who'd lost his life while he was serving with the Army."

"Oh, I'm sorry to hear that," said Maggie kindly.

"It was a load of rubbish. But once she'd turned on the tears, the poor man was desperate to do something to comfort her, so she said that it would make her feel better if he would give her a big hug, just like her boy used to."

"And did he?"

"Of course. He was practically in tears himself."

Maggie frowned, wondering where this was going.

"Anyway, Nan seemed much calmer after the hug and as she walked off with her shopping trolley towards the check-out, she called out across the shop floor, 'Goodbye, son!'"

"Oh, how touching."

"It was – until the man finished his shopping and was told at the check-out that his bill was £87. He'd only bought a couple of pints of milk, a loaf of bread and a frozen dinner, and when he told the cashier that, she said that his mother had said her son would be paying for her shopping too."

At two o'clock sharp, Derek Simmons, well known in the town as master of ceremonies, compère and comedian for just about every significant local occasion, got to his feet.

Taking his place in front of the microphone, he welcomed everyone to this special event aimed at raising money for Good Neighbours, and hoped that they would all be good neighbours themselves this afternoon, even though competition would undoubtedly be fierce between the twenty-two teams that had crowded into the hall. He then made sure that everyone was clear on the rules.

"Each of the numbers on the dice represents a part of the beetle's body. You need a 6 for the body, 5 for the head, 4 for the wings (you need two of those), 3 for the legs (six for each beetle), 2 for the antennae (they have two), and a number 1 for each of their two eyes. I will count down to the start of each game, and then all teams begin playing at the same time. Every player has a sheet in front of them with twelve boxes in which to draw their beetles, one for each of the games we have in the tournament this afternoon. All you have to do is throw the dice, and draw in the corresponding body part. The dice is passed round the table with each player throwing as quickly as possible. The minute any player in the hall gets all the body parts they need, they shout out 'Beetle!' and the game stops immediately. That person is the overall winner, but each team member also has to count up the total of all the body parts they've managed to collect. That gives us a figure for each player, as well as for each team. Is everybody clear? Let's start then! Ready, steady, go!"

A frenzied panic erupted as dice were shaken, orders shouted and body parts scribbled onto the pages around the room.

"Beetle!"

The voice was so quiet and ladylike that the MC wondered if he'd heard it right, but he obviously had when a huge sigh of disappointment echoed through the crowd as they strained to see who had called out. Shyly, Connie stood up from her seat next to Percy, who was grinning as if he himself had won. The master of ceremonies walked across to check the win and, on every table, totals were totted up and pencils resharpened for further battle.

The next game was won in record time by the Can't Sing Singers, who immediately got to their feet to bellow out a tuneless version of "Congratulations". At the sound of their singing, a cheer of delight echoed around the hall, while on the St Mark's table, Gregory shuddered with distaste.

Time seemed to race by and before they knew it, the six games were concluded and tea was announced. Maggie had already left her seat on the management table, and was at the serving hatch with Liz and Kevin as the crowd stampeded towards the cakes.

Within minutes, Maggie saw Kevin's family making a beeline for the front of the queue, with Dee parting the crowds in front of her as she called out loudly, "Excuse me, please! A very elderly lady coming through. Give her a bit of space, thank you!" But when they reached the front of the queue, in spite of shouting loudly, Dee found it impossible to catch the eye of either Maggie or Kevin, who seemed to be totally preoccupied with the customers they were already serving. In the end, the only one who responded to them was Liz, who said she had no idea about them having extra cakes, and could they please just make their selection and allow others behind them to be served too?

Kevin could feel the furious eyes of his mother on him as he worked. He'd be in for it when he got home, but it was such a glorious moment that he didn't mind at all.

At the end of the tournament, a thrilled but red-faced Connie was declared Queen of the Beetles, and the line dancing group were acknowledged as the most successful team.

"And, ladies and gentlemen, taking into account the raffle as well as the tickets, plus the money you donated for all those extra cakes you worked your way through this afternoon, I am pleased to tell you that you have helped us raise £383 for the Good Neighbours scheme. That will mean so much to this wonderful cause. Thank you, everyone. Safe journey home."

Sara's funeral was a family affair, with the addition of a few close friends and neighbours. As she was lowered into the family plot in the churchyard at St Mark's, where Ray's parents and grandparents had already lain for many years, he wondered if there would be room to squeeze him in too when the time came.

The following morning, as Kath was just about to start the usual weekly management meeting with Maggie and Trevor, Ray walked in. He'd lost weight, most noticeable in the gaunt hollows of his face, but his expression was determined and businesslike. Before they could register their surprise, he pulled out a chair and looked across the desk at them.

"It's been awful, but that time is now over. I'm ready to get cracking again. What's coming up next and what do I need to organize?"

A couple of hours later when Shirley was cleaning the glass windows in the foyer doors, Maggie walked past her on the way to the kitchen.

"Did you see Ray? He's back and raring to go. Isn't that great news?"

Shirley smiled and nodded before turning back to buff up a stretch of the glass that she knew she'd already polished.

That's me gone, she thought gloomily. They only took me on temporarily while Ray needed time at home with Sara. Now he's back, I'll be getting my cards any minute. And with a small sigh, she moved across to the other door, where she sprayed and polished so hard, there was a real danger the etched pattern might disappear forever.

Claire looked down at the new number she'd listed in her mobile phone as "Beavers". It wasn't the number of Bear or any of the other scouting team who ran Josh's Beaver class. It belonged to Gary. He had insisted she take it just in case she needed someone to talk to if things got difficult at home. He'd taken her number too. It was a simple, friendly gesture, nothing more. So why did she feel so guilty as she found herself staring at it for the second time that morning? And why did she sense just the smallest disappointment that he hadn't felt the need to ring her – to check something about Beavers perhaps? To ask her a quick question about activity badges or uniforms? Or simply to hear her voice, just as she found herself longing to hear his.

This was ridiculous! She snapped the phone shut and shoved it into the deepest pocket of her handbag. She was behaving like a silly schoolgirl instead of a grown woman, wife and mother who'd had the occasional pleasant conversation with a fellow parent.

But she couldn't recall ever being able to talk so comfortably to anyone before Gary. He listened. He asked the right questions. He suggested practical answers. He was kind and sympathetic. He understood. He was the complete opposite of Nigel.

At the thought of her husband, she was aware of the now familiar mix of anger, frustration and despair that coursed through her. They were barely speaking. She suspected that even if she could persuade him to sit down and talk things through in a rational way, there was nothing she could say that would make a difference. The situation was black and white to him. He found her resistance disloyal, and disloyalty was something he could not abide.

She knew he was talking to his family about her. She had always enjoyed the warmth of their welcome and support, and had got used to catching up with his mum or sister every few days. Neither had rung for more than a week now, and her messages to them had remained unanswered.

Her world was falling apart. The solid loving relationship she had taken for granted from the moment she first met Nigel now felt uncertain and vulnerable. It was hard to believe, but undeniably true, that the two of them were taking separate paths rather than walking together. His life revolved around work, hers around Josh. He thought his family was enough for both of them. She knew that the past few months of turning her back on her own parents had crushed her. She was at breaking point. So was their marriage. At least, she thought bitterly, she cared about what was happening to them. Nigel was making it clear that he couldn't care less.

On the other side of town, Gary glanced at the clock with exasperation. Half past twelve already! He'd taken the boys to school and then rushed round the supermarket picking up essentials. When he got home he'd sorted out a load of dark clothes, which he stuffed into the washing machine, cleared up the breakfast things, run the vacuum over the floors, hung out the washing and made the beds. And during that time, he'd taken three complicated calls from his big client, promising to get back to them with answers before the end of the day. No chance! He'd been nowhere near his drawing board all morning.

Almost without thinking, he pulled his phone out of his pocket and stared again at Claire's number. It would be good to ring her. He'd tell her about his disastrous day, and they'd laugh together. She'd wonder what he was working on, and ask questions that showed genuine interest. They'd swap silly stories about what their boys had got up to that morning, and they'd say goodbye knowing that they'd be meeting up as usual by the coffee machine. It was nothing. But it *was* something. There was something in her conversation, her teasing, her understanding of what frustrated him, that made him long to push the button on his phone that could connect them. She'd probably be busy. Maybe Nigel would be with her. And in any case, what would he say? There really wasn't anything they should be talking about – and yet he knew that the two of them could chat for hours and never run out of conversation.

Two years earlier, with the prospect of the one hundredth anniversary of Hope Hall looming, Kath had brought together a few key individuals to form a Centenary Committee. The members had come from both within and beyond Hope Hall, and each of them represented a local organization or was in a position of influence within the community. They turned out to be a very capable and enthusiastic team, coming up with all sorts of imaginative projects that were going on throughout the year in schools, the library, the town square and at Hope Hall itself.

The first big event in the Centenary calendar was the Easter Fayre, a traditional event held annually on Easter Monday at Hope Hall. This year there were plans to turn the clock back to capture the spirit of the town a century before. Roger Beck, the chairman of the town's Rotary Club, was in charge of this event and was channelling in contributions and practical help from every quarter. The schools were planning displays, with the children all dressed in costumes from a century before. There was to be country dancing, a maypole, and children's games with hoops and skipping ropes. The Women's Institute members, under the direction of the formidable Barbara Longstone, were in charge of the many stalls which, weather permitting, would form a ring around the old school playground that stood immediately to the left of the main hall itself. The enthusiastic music teacher at the senior school was gathering together anyone in the town capable of making a sound on a brass instrument, and the race was on to form the motley crew into a new town brass band. It was hoped that the band would be able to take their place along with other performances being planned by groups old and young throughout the town as part of a grand concert. This would be the highlight of the events at Hope Hall on Easter Monday afternoon.

As Shirley was helping her elderly neighbour Blanche take off her coat before settling down at a table of old friends at the Grown-ups' Lunch, she found herself listening in on a conversation taking place nearby at the side of the foyer. A group of lunch club members were chatting with some of the Good Neighbour volunteers as they all looked at the new poster that had just gone up on the board about plans for the Easter Monday Centenary Fayre.

"Are they going to make it look like a hundred years ago then?" asked one man, who'd been hard of hearing for years. "I think I might remember that long ago myself. How old am I?"

The volunteer next to him laughed at the thought. "Not that old, Fred."

"We're not far off, though, are we?" countered Eric, who was sitting at a nearby table. "I'm ninety-three. If they're looking for local history, I'm it."

"I've got all my mum's bits and pieces up in the attic," said another lady. "They must date back years before 1920. She was born in 1883."

"And I've got a chest full of old clothes my grandma used to wear," commented another. "My ma could never bear to throw them away, and they've been wrapped up with mothballs ever since."

Shirley couldn't help herself. There was a gem of an idea here, and she was the girl to get things going. She marched across towards them, her voice so full of purpose and volume that even Fred could hear clearly.

"You're right, you know. You *are* the genuine history here. So why don't we celebrate that? We could all think about what we've got at home – clothes, bits and pieces from life with our families, photos, papers, even stories we can remember – and come up with something really special for the Easter Fayre. I don't mind pulling it all together and organizing any costumes we need. I just know there'll be lots of willing helping hands, especially from all you Good Neighbours volunteers. We could ask Ronnie, the pianist from the dancing classes, to help us out with some music. You lot should be the stars of the show."

"Costumes?" asked Elsie, her dentures moving at a slightly different pace to the words she was actually saying. "I'm not taking my clothes off."

"No, Elsie," said Shirley firmly. "You'll all be putting clothes on. You'll be putting on the style – and looking great."

A buzz of excitement went around the foyer as others gathered round or simply listened in from wherever they were seated.

"Did you say we could tell stories?" asked Percy. "I know lots of good stories."

"Absolutely, Percy! What do you think then? Will the performance by the Grown-ups' Lunch Club steal the show?"

A cheer went up as sticks banged and hands clapped.

Right, thought Shirley. Looks like I'm going to be busy!

Maggie's daughter turned up at Hope Hall just as her mum was putting away the last piece of crockery following the Grown-ups' Lunch.

"Come on, Mum! We're supposed to be there in ten minutes. We can walk. It's only just round the corner."

"I'm really not sure about this," Maggie said, as she grabbed her coat to follow Steph out of the door.

"Mum, your house sale is going through without a hitch and you haven't even looked at anywhere else yet. You have to move everything out in just a few weeks' time. What are you going to do when the time comes and you've still got no idea where your next home will be?"

"I just can't face looking, love. I've had a really busy day and my head is thumping—"

"You're making excuses, and I don't blame you. This place might not be right, but you know I've already gone round taking a look at quite a few, just in case I managed to find something I felt you ought to see. This one feels a bit special, Mum. Just wait until you see it. If it's not for you, then we'll just go home for a cuppa and pack up a few more boxes."

Maggie walked beside her daughter in silence. She was bone weary, not from work in the Hope Hall kitchen, but from the whole nightmare of having to dismantle her beloved home. Steph had been a wonderful help, but she'd also been part of the problem. She was very tough on Maggie about not taking too much with her. What she didn't understand was the deep sentimental value of every stick of furniture, every piece of paper, every item in the kitchen, every ornament and forgotten trinket in every corner of every shelf and cupboard. This was Maggie's life, and it was being ripped away from her. She felt as if she were losing limbs from her body. Maggie was now beyond tears. They were too superficial for the depth of pain she was feeling. Looking down, she deliberately put one foot in front of the other, resenting every step she was taking. She couldn't bear the thought of creating another home – not when she wasn't at all ready to leave the one she loved.

Steph led the way round a corner into a leafy road that Maggie used to walk down years ago on her way to school. In spite of her reservations, she found herself wondering exactly where they were going. Her mind flew back to how these houses used to look as she and her brother walked past each morning. If they timed it right, the milkman would be making his deliveries and would sometimes give them a wrapped butterscotch sweet from a paper bag he kept in his cab. She smiled as she recalled how the fierce brown dog at number 10 would always bark loudly, sending them scuttling off as fast as they could run. Sometimes, when she'd looked across at the big bay window upstairs in number 13, Mrs Hadley had waved as she held baby Frank in her arms. And a huge ginger cat had always seemed to be sitting on the gate post by number 16.

"Here we are!" announced Steph, stopping outside number 17.

As Maggie looked up at the solid detached house ahead of them, with its sandy-coloured walls half hidden by clematis and wisteria just coming into bud, and the front garden colourful and fragrant with blossom, the years fell away. She knew this house. Her best friend Susan had lived here with her two younger brothers. The boys were both such a pain, but she and Susan had always known exactly how to handle them. Susan's father ran the haberdasher's shop in town, and her mother's kitchen always smelt of baking. This family made her feel as if she was family too. She *loved* this house.

Steph's voice broke into her thoughts. "The house has been divided into two apartments, and it's the top one that's up for sale now."

"I know this place."

Steph smiled, taking Maggie's hand. "I had a feeling you did. Shall we go in?"

They walked in through the original front door, which was at the side of the house, but the hallway Maggie remembered well from her childhood visits had since been split into two by a new wall, so that the staircase now led up to another hard oak door. The young lady estate agent had seen them arriving and immediately invited them in to take a look around. She showed them into one room after another, giving a non-stop commentary on all the features, benefits, energy and efficiency ratings, the council tax bracket, sockets, local shops, schools and churches, commenting on the view from each window, the attic trap door above and the beautiful garden below.

But Maggie barely heard a word. She remembered every nook and cranny of these rooms, still recognizable even now after years of other owners and constant renovation. What had previously been Susan's parents' bedroom stretching across the width of the front of the house had become an elegant sitting room, still with its original tiled fireplace, but it felt warmer now with its new golden window drapes and soft yellow walls that matched the evening sun. The bedroom that Susan's brothers had shared was now decorated in complementary shades of taupe, darker for the carpet and a soft browny-grey for the walls. Floral curtains picked out the same grey, along with a variety of pinks that added colour and texture.

As soon as she walked into the back bedroom, she instantly pictured the bunk-bed she had so often shared on sleepovers, always in the bottom bunk because Susan pulled rank to claim the top one. This room was now a mix of different green shades that shouldn't really have gone together, but they did – just as all the different greens in the garden beyond worked together in perfect harmony. Oh, that garden! There had been an old metal swing right in the middle of it in those days. Now the garden was beautifully kept with gloriously planned areas of bedding that were already displaying a riot of spring colour.

"Mr and Mrs Ronson who live down below are very keen gardeners. You'll see that there is a privet hedge running across the bottom of the garden, but actually there is also a small area of grass beyond that which comes with this flat. So all the garden on this side of the hedge is owned by the couple below, but beyond the privet there is enough room for you to have a rotary washing line, perhaps some play equipment if you have children visiting – and there's a small locked shed there too. So you are in the lovely position here of having a beautiful garden to look at and enjoy, but just a small area of grass to look after yourself."

Maggie took so long gazing down at the garden that Steph had to call her to see the other rooms. She gasped in wonder as she saw how the old family bathroom had been turned into a smart new tiled area, with a roll-top bath standing on four carved legs at one end, and an ultra-modern shower unit at the other.

"I've never seen a bathroom as posh as this," she whispered to Steph. "This looks like something out of a magazine. I'd be terrified of making a mess in here."

"You'd absolutely love making a mess in here, believe me," grinned Steph.

"And this is the kitchen," announced the estate agent with pride, as she turned into what Maggie remembered as the fourth bedroom.

"When the house was split into two separate flats," continued the agent, "the owners at that time decided to extend the kitchen below and match its size with a similar extension on the top floor, creating what I think can only be described as a first-class kitchen area. Do you have any interest in cooking?"

"Just a bit," mumbled Maggie as she took in the state-of-the-art range cooker, complete with its own hot plate, deep fat fryer and barbecue grill. A large microwave oven was built into wooden units that were carved and decorated to look as if they belonged in a country kitchen. There was a wide work surface stretching down each side of the room, and a pair of sinks, complete with a waste disposal unit and draining area, sat just below an enormous window that looked out over the garden and across the parkland beyond.

"I'll leave you to look round at your leisure then. I'll be downstairs if you need me."

"Can I afford this?" Maggie hissed urgently at Steph.

"Yes, you can. I've done the sums, and if we plan things really carefully, yes, you can."

"Are you sure?"

"Are you?"

"I've never felt more sure about anything! I belong here. This is my place."

And giving her mum a quick hug, Steph led the way as the two women went downstairs to speak to the agent.

Chapter 10

When the doorbell rang, a sudden panic gripped Kath. What would Jack think of the apartment she'd come to love? Would he find it too quiet, too suburban, too boring for someone who was used to big city life? She pushed the button to speak to him as he stood downstairs at the outside door.

"Come on up! Number 6 on the second floor."

She knew he never took a lift if he could avoid it, and could hear his footsteps approaching as he made his way up the stairs. And suddenly he was there, smiling at her welcome, drawing her into his arms, then pulling back to look into her eyes before he kissed her.

When they finally drew apart, she stood back to invite him into the flat.

I'm talking too much, she thought, as she rattled off reasons why she'd put a certain piece of furniture in one particular corner, chosen those curtains for this room, and decided to have the television in just that position. The tour of the apartment didn't take long and she watched his expression closely to see what he thought.

"It's lovely, Kath. It's stylish and practical – so typically you."

"Well, what do you fancy doing now? I wondered if we might pop over to the Call-in Café at Hope Hall for lunch. They do a good selection, and it would give me chance to show you round my new workplace."

"That sounds good," he nodded, his gaze teasing and affectionate as he looked down at her. "Although I'd be quite happy if we both just made ourselves at home here."

She caught on immediately, but hesitated before answering.

"Too much too soon?" he whispered in her ear.

She stepped back a pace. "We're taking it slowly, aren't we, at your suggestion? Anyway, I've already booked us in for lunch—"

"And you'd like me to see the place."

She smiled, slipping her hand into his. "I really would."

"Come on then, let's go!"

Their arrival at Hope Hall caused a bit of a stir. Through the foyer hatch, Liz saw them walking through the main door.

"Hey, Mags, Kath's here with Jack – and he looks nice."

"Like a very successful doctor," added Maggie as she looked over Liz's shoulder.

"Indeed," Liz agreed, smiling as they all took in his handsome face, stylish hair with a touch of silver fox at the front, the excellent cut of his brown jacket and cream chinos.

"He reminds me of George Clooney," whispered Maggie.

"You should get out more," giggled Liz. "You've been watching too many American emergency room dramas!"

Kath and Jack made their way over to the foyer hatch.

"Maggie, Liz! I'd like to introduce you to Dr Jack Sawyer. We worked together in London."

"Dr Sawyer, welcome to Hope Hall!" smiled Maggie, wiping her hands on a teacloth. "Let me come out and say hello properly."

"I'm just Jack," he smiled, holding out his hand to greet both Maggie and Liz.

"Busy in the café this morning?" asked Kath.

"We were run off our feet earlier on," answered Maggie. "A group of about ten ladies all came in together. I think they'd been working out at the gym, and after that nothing but a whole selection of sticky buns would do."

"We've got quite a few booked in for lunch as well," added Liz, "including you two, if that's still your plan."

"Definitely!" said Kath. "I wondered if you'd like a tour of the building first, Jack – or are you desperate for a coffee before you go anywhere?"

"A coffee would be welcome, but I'd like to take a look round first."

She started by taking him up to the balcony lounge area, where groups of people were chatting, drinking and eating as they looked out from the large semi-circular windows across the town, or else over the balcony towards the main hall below.

"They're setting up down there at the moment for the Knit and Natter group, which is held at this end of the hall in about an hour – and then, at the same time down at the stage end, we have the Down Memory Lane Club. Jean who runs that group is a memory therapist who's been trained by the Alzheimer's Association. They had something like this at our hospital in London – I don't know if you ever came across it? Anyway, Jean organizes lots of art and music therapy, and brings in memory-joggers like photos and newspaper cuttings with her each week. Often the members come along with their family or their carers, who find the techniques really helpful when they're at home too."

Jack said little as Kath took him back downstairs and through the side door that led to the old school building. She showed him her office, which had been created from what was previously the headteacher's room, laughingly telling him that she felt it still had the feel and smell of its former life. She led him into the hall, where the playgroup was in full swing, and then upstairs, where there was a Money Advice Service interview going on in one room and an English for Foreign Students class in the other.

She showed him the plans for the Centenary celebrations and the Easter Fayre, and she watched closely for his reaction. This was all very different from the high-powered, life-and-death work he was involved in every day. What would he make of it?

After a while, they went back to the café, where they both chose shepherd's pie after Kath told him that Maggie's was the best she'd ever tasted. They found a table up in the balcony, where they chatted a little about her work and then much more about his – the challenging operations he'd done that week and the quiet conversation he'd had a few days before with the chief executive of the hospital, who let him know that he was being considered as a future member of the Board of Directors.

She noticed, as they chatted, that he had subtly glanced at his watch on several occasions.

"Do you need to leave?"

"I ought to really. I said I'd call into the hospital on my way back tonight."

She nodded with understanding, and led the way down to the foyer.

"Goodbye, Jack!" called out Maggie from the kitchen. "Come and see us again soon."

But I don't think he will, thought Kath, as she watched him drive away with a cheery wave. He'd been preoccupied and perhaps even a bit bored today. Hope Hall and all that happened here really didn't interest him much. She knew him well enough to recognize the signs. And that simple, heartbreaking fact knocked her sideways.

"Hello." He spoke quietly, standing close enough to whisper in her ear.

"Hello, Gary." Claire turned to look at him, her mood instantly lifted by the warmth of his smile.

"I hoped you were about to arrive. I've got our coffees."

She followed him over to their table, noticing that her chair was a little nearer to his than usual. *Good*, she thought, leaving it exactly where it was as she sat down.

"How was your week?" he asked, gazing intently into her eyes.

"Lousy. Yours?"

"Frustrating. I'm still finding it hard to get any proper work done at home. I nearly rang you…"

Her head shot up. "I almost called you too – several times."

"I thought I shouldn't, in case you were with Nigel. Hopefully things are settling down between the two of you now?"

"No, they're not. They're worse, if anything. We're hardly speaking at all."

"Oh, Claire, how difficult for you. Is there anything you can do to ease the situation?"

"Give in. Say he's right. Promise not to see my parents ever again. Apart from all that, no!"

Beneath the table, he clasped her hand. She didn't move away.

"And how are you and Karen getting on?"

"I've barely seen her awake. She's been at a conference in Birmingham for the last three days."

"So you're Mum *and* Dad this week?"

"I am. What I definitely am not is a graphic designer with a huge project that I am going to be able to deliver successfully on time."

"Is there any point in talking to your client, to explain your challenges at the moment?"

"I can imagine how well that would go down."

"What a pair we are!" she sighed.

His gaze was intense, his face so near. "I wish we *were* a pair..."

"Right at this moment, Gary, so do I – but we hardly know each other. We've just met at a time when we're both unhappy and vulnerable."

He nodded, squeezing her hand even tighter. "I know that's true, but I just can't stop thinking about you."

He felt her fingers tighten around his.

Suddenly, the foyer doors burst open and several of the Beavers came pouring out, followed by Bear and another member of the scouting team.

"The boys are coming to give you mums and dads an invitation to the Centenary Fayre on Easter Monday here at Hope Hall," announced Bear. "The Beavers have been working very hard for several weeks to prepare a special performance for the occasion that will also feature boys and girls from all the scouting groups in the area. It would mean a great deal to them if their family and friends could be there to cheer them on. You'll find all the details about where and when in this letter. Do come and talk to me if you have any questions."

Josh ran up to push a letter into Claire's hand just as Max and Toby came rushing across to Gary with a letter each.

"You'll come, won't you, Dad?" urged Max.

"And we've brought two letters," added Toby. "This one's for Mum. She's not been here to see us in our uniforms yet."

Josh had climbed up onto Claire's lap and was watching her expression carefully as she read the invitation.

"Daddy has to come too," he said firmly. "Daddy's *got* to come. You have to come together!"

Above the children's heads, Claire and Gary's eyes locked for just a moment before Toby grabbed Gary's hand, pulling him to his feet.

"Come on, Dad. We need to go. I'm starving!"

Among the flurry of coats and shoes, and squealing, giggling boys, there was no chance to say anything more than a hurried goodbye – but Claire knew that what she'd glimpsed in Gary's eyes mirrored what she was feeling herself.

"Bye then!" she called out to him, as they walked out of the door and turned in opposite directions.

From the moment of madness when Shirley and the members of the Grown-ups' Lunch Club had first looked at that Easter Fayre poster and triumphantly decided to get involved, a ripple of enthusiasm had spread through practically every group and gathering at Hope Hall. Lines became blurred between one club and another as it was recognized that the talents and abilities of one group were very useful to another. In particular, the needlework skills of the Knit and Natter Club were in great demand as costumes were planned and outfits altered.

"Baby Charlie will just have to wait for his matinee jacket now," trilled Doris, as she stuffed her knitting creation away with just the sewing up to be done. "I hope he doesn't grow too fast, or this jacket will have to go to my great-niece instead. She's expecting her first in May and she already knows it's a boy. Takes all the fun out of it, don't you think, if you know what you're having before it arrives?"

She glanced across to where Elaine, the Knit and Natter organizer, was in deep conversation with dance teacher Della and her mum Barbara, along with the cleaning lady Shirley, who seemed to be pivotal in pulling the whole thing into shape. They had pushed four oblong tables together to create a work area that was already stacked high with costumes and outfits at various stages of completion. On one table there was a huge pile of floaty pale blue material, alongside some paper patterns that presumably were the templates for whatever the pretty material would become. On another, there were bright red taffeta jackets with strips of silver sequins set alongside them, ready to make the braiding that needed to be sewn onto collars and cuffs. Lined up on a nearby table was a row of about twenty trilby hats, black with a silky red ribbon around the rim, in a range of sizes from those that might fit a small child right up to more generous sizes for larger adults. At the other end of the hall, Jean, the dementia care therapist, had brought in big cardboard boxes full of old family photos, pictures of the town in years gone by, household items from early twentieth-century homes, sheets of old music and children's toys and books with covers that were familiar from childhood. Several of the club members gathered around an ancient gramophone that needed to be wound up to play the jumble of old 78 rpm records piled next to it in their distinctive brown paper sleeves. There was great delight whenever the speed wound down so that the voice on the disc sounded like a growling bear until the handle was turned again.

Della had doubled up on her dance classes, fitting in extra rehearsals on several afternoons and evenings, some of which she took herself, while others were led by her mother, who slipped back into the teaching role as if she'd never left it.

Even the children at the playgroup were keen to join in with the fun, as enthusiastic mums came up with ideas for activities and costumes, and Jen and Carol taught the youngsters old songs with simple movements knowing that, from the moment these charming three- and four-year-olds stepped onto the stage, every heart in the audience would melt just at the sight of them.

Overseeing it all was Kath, working closely with the Rotary Club members, who called in a lot of favours around the town to get staging, a powerful PA system and a few other special items that were requested for the performance. It was decided that this Grand Finale of the Easter Monday Centenary Fayre should take place outside, weather permitting, so that Hope Hall itself would provide a glorious backdrop. However, because a wide-ranging display of 1920s memorabilia was also being staged inside the main hall, it was generally agreed that if, on the day, it was either too cold or too wet to stay in the playground, then the performances could definitely take place on the stage inside the hall with no problems at all.

The Beavers were very excited about the part they would be playing during the Easter Monday Fayre too. The plan was that all the boys' uniformed organizations, including the Cubs and Scouts, would be teaming up with the girls' equivalent groups, the Rainbows, Brownies and Guides, for a special joint presentation of their own.

Their performance was the topic of excited chatter from Toby and Max all the way back from their last Beavers' meeting as Gary walked them home. He was hardly listening. His mind was full of his conversation with Claire, and the daunting prospect that both their partners, Nigel and Karen, would most likely be at that Easter Fayre event, when all the parents were encouraged to come along and see what the Beavers had been practising.

The minute Karen walked through the door that night, the twins threw themselves at her, begging her to be there the following week to watch them. She said she'd definitely see what she could do, although Gary could tell from the glance she shot in his direction that, having just arrived home, her mind was too full of work problems to be able to commit to anything that far in advance.

Over at Claire's house, Josh was just as excited as he showed the invitation to his dad.

"You will come, Daddy, won't you?" Josh begged. "Bear said all you mums and dads *must* come."

"Of course I will," said Nigel as Josh's arms shot around his neck in a big hug. "If it's okay with Mummy, we'll all go together."

Claire looked up to see that Nigel was looking straight at her. There was wariness in his expression, but a flicker of warmth and kindness too, which came as a surprise after the stony silence of the previous few days, when he could hardly stand to be in the same room as her.

"Is it all right with you, Mummy?" Josh demanded to know.

Claire smiled across at her son. "Of course. I'm looking forward to it."

"It's time for bed," said Nigel, ruffling Josh's hair. "Why don't I come and run your bath, and then we can read a bit more of *Horrid Henry* once you're all tucked up?"

"Cool!" grinned Josh, slipping off Nigel's lap and rushing upstairs. "I'll race you."

"Have you got something planned for dinner?" Nigel asked Claire before he left the room.

"I wasn't sure if you'd want anything. You haven't eaten any of the dinners I've cooked this week."

"I know, and that was stupid and cruel – and all it achieved was that I ended up hungry," he said wryly. "I'm sorry, Claire. Look, how about you just order our usual take-away while I sort out Josh, then perhaps you and I can spend a bit of time together this evening?"

Claire nodded dumbly, both pleased and apprehensive about what this sudden change in Nigel's temperament might mean.

"I'll ring that through now," she said, picking up her phone to find the number for the local Chinese take-away.

Before long, she heard Josh's screeches of delight as his father pulled him out of the bathtub, tickling the wriggling boy as he wrapped him in a big, fluffy towel to get dry. She went out into the kitchen to switch the oven on low to warm the plates. Her mind was racing. What did Nigel want to talk about? Was it possible for the two of them to have a civil conversation after all the hurtful accusations that had been hurled? The gulf between them seemed too deep. Could they ever step back from it?

Well, if it was Nigel's intention to try, then she would gladly meet him halfway. She had always thought of him as her best friend, but this whole business concerning her parents had made her question whether she could ever feel that way about him again. Pulling a bottle of chilled white wine from the fridge, she reached out for two glasses and started to load up a tray to take into the lounge. Whenever they had meals with Josh, they would sit at the dining table, but if they had chance to eat alone, then they often preferred to have a more relaxed meal at the coffee table, from the comfort of the settee. Perhaps the familiar intimacy of that would help their conversation this evening.

In fact, their conversation was fairly stilted at first, soon lapsing into discussion of safe subjects: people they'd seen, news they'd heard, the weather, the television, the garden. And finally, when neither of them could think of another banal thing to say, they both knew they had to tackle the elephant in the room: the deep and wounding division between them.

"Claire, I'm so sorry. I've hated the way we've been with each other over this. I hear myself saying things I know are unfair and unkind, but I just can't seem to stop them coming out. I don't want to carry on like this. I miss you. I've missed *this!*"

Claire reached out immediately to touch his hand, huge relief in her voice as she spoke. "Oh, so have I! It's just awful—"

"And I can see it's been affecting Josh too."

"It has. He's not daft."

"Yes, he's obviously got a fairly clear idea about what's been causing the arguments between us."

"The trouble is," said Claire, "the two of us are seeing things so differently, and the differences are fundamental. As long as that's the case, I can't see how we can come back from this."

He put his arm round her shoulders and drew her to him. "I've felt hurt and excluded by everything that's happened, as if suddenly I was on the outside of our family unit, looking in. Your parents have always made it clear that they don't think I'm good enough for you, so when they started throwing all this money in our direction, it seemed like an accusation directed at me, that I'm not providing well enough for you and Josh."

Claire stared at him, moving even closer. "Well, whatever misguided impression my parents might have, we both know you're a wonderful dad – Josh and I have all we need. But what we need most of all is you, just you."

"I've been terrified of what you must think of me. I heard the things I was saying, and how spiteful I sounded. I'm not a spiteful person, Claire – you know I'm not."

"Of course not!"

"But I overreacted. I backed myself into a corner and didn't know how to dig my way out."

Claire's arms were around him, her voice muffled as she spoke. "Well, you've done that now. We're together. We're *always* together. Nothing can ever change that."

He kissed her then, overwhelmed with relief and the deep sense of belonging that had always been at the heart of their love for each other.

"So," he said, when at last he pulled away, "I've been thinking. This event on Easter Monday that Josh keeps going on about – do you think your parents might like to come along and watch it with us?"

She gulped with shock at his words. "Are you sure?"

"There'll be lots of people there. It'll be noisy and there will be plenty to look at, so the pressure will be off, because we won't be able to talk about anything difficult. We'll just all be there for Josh."

"He'll love that. So will Mum and Dad. Believe me, they have been devastated by what's happened, and their role in causing this situation."

"No more expensive presents for Josh, though, unless we all talk about it first. Will they agree to that, do you think, providing they know there will be no issue if they want to talk to us about something in particular that feels right, like that language computer game for Josh? That was a really good idea, but I should have known about it myself. I didn't, because I haven't paid enough attention to things like that. I just leave everything to you, and that's not fair. I want to be more involved in Josh's life – in *our* life together."

Pulling him closer, Claire was too choked to speak.

"And the fact is," Nigel continued, "your parents and I don't know each other at all – we've only met once, even though you and I have been together all these years. It's ridiculous that such a lot of distrust and dislike has grown up because of our ignorance of each other. Every journey starts with a first step, and I feel it's up to me to take that step. I don't know how it will work out, whether we could ever get to a point of actually liking each other, but I want to try. In the end, what we already share is our love for you. I'd like to think we can build on that."

"I do love you," she said softly.

He kissed her then, once, twice, a third time, before they drew apart and he spoke again.

"Would you like to ring them now? The invitation might come better from you – unless you think I should speak to them too?"

Claire nodded, her eyes filling with tears. "Oh yes, please. Yes *please!*"

Later, Maggie was able to pinpoint the exact the moment she finally fell out of love with Dave. She had soldiered on for all those weeks and months after he left her, feeling shell-shocked and abandoned by what had happened.

The fact that he had left her for a younger woman was humiliating, but totally understandable to her whenever she faced the mirror and took a critical look at the way she'd let herself go over the years. The thought of him making love to anyone else at all, after the lifetime they'd spent together, made her feel physically sick. The knowledge that a new partner was now expecting his child, a baby who would be a brother or sister to their own grown-up children, Darren and Steph, was just an unbelievable nightmare. The reality of him leaving the family he shared with her to play happy families with another woman and different children was like a knife in her heart.

But then came the day when she found this answerphone message waiting on her mobile:

"Hi, Mags. Dave here. I hoped to speak to you, but you're not there. How are you doing, anyway? We're all doing fine. Mandy is halfway through her pregnancy now, so I'm having to make sure she gets lots of rest. She took herself along to the doctor's for a check-up the other day. She told me the doctor is worried about her and says she should really get a lot of bed rest and keep her feet up most of the time. She stays upstairs whenever I'm home, because she feels most comfy up there watching telly – which I do understand, if that's what the doctor says she must do.

"Hey, do you remember how you had a longing for cream cheese when you were expecting Darren – or was it Steph? Well, Mandy is mad for those huge milk chocolate bars, battered sausage and chips and strawberry milkshake – would you believe! I can't tell you how many times she's sent me out late at night to find extra supplies when she gets her pangs.

"It's quite difficult for me working all day and then looking after Belle and Marlin when I get home. I suppose it's because it's such a long time since our children were small. I've forgotten a lot. I was thinking the other day about how, when you were expecting, you always went into nesting mode. You just kept cleaning and cooking all the time. All those lovely dinners and puddings. I wish I'd noticed a bit more about how you made all those nice dinners now I'm the one in charge of cooking.

"Anyway, I'm really ringing to arrange a time when I can pick up your estate car. You remember I told you before that it would be better if you had mine because it's a year newer than yours. Then I can have the estate, which will be so much easier with the kids and the new baby. Can I come round and pick it up this week? And if you're around, it would be nice to have a chat over a cup of tea and a slice of your chocolate cake. How about Thursday? I might have to bring the kids with me if Mandy isn't up to looking after them. That will be all right, won't it?

"So, can you give me a ring to let me know? This is Dave."

Maggie didn't hesitate for one second before typing out her reply in a text:

NO to you having my car.

NO to you bringing that woman's children into my home.

NO, you don't get one jot of sympathy from me for the difficulties of your new life.

You jumped into that bed. Enjoy it!

If any of this is unclear, please contact my solicitor.

And with one simple press of the Send button, Maggie felt a huge load lift off her shoulders. She was going to be fine without Dave. She was going to be absolutely fine.

Once the schools had broken up, rehearsals for the Easter Fayre stepped up a pace. When accountant Trevor arrived one morning to talk over the finances with Kath, his wife Mary was drawn to the sound of loud music coming from the main hall. Peering through the etched windows, she drew in a sharp breath as she watched Della putting a group of teenagers through their paces.

"They look as if they're dislocating their hips and shoulders when they dance like that!"

Shirley came up to join her and they both stared at the body positions and jerky movements that the Hip-hoppers, the street dancing team, were deeply engrossed in learning during their extra rehearsal that morning.

Shirley chuckled. "When I was their age, a bit of disco dancing round our handbags was all we girls ever wanted."

Suddenly, the two women gasped in horror as one of the boys unceremoniously picked up a girl, turned her upside down and flipped her over his shoulder.

"Haven't they ever heard of a nice waltz or foxtrot?" sighed Mary. "That's a lot more fun."

"Ah, well, during the Easter Fayre event we're trying to represent all sorts of dancing, music-making and entertainment from the past hundred years. But looking at what young people call dancing nowadays, it makes you wonder what they'll be doing in another hundred years' time."

Mary stared at Shirley. "So for this Centenary Fayre, you're interested in all sorts of entertaining skills from the old days, are you?"

"The more variety the better!"

Mary's face lit up. "Then I've got something to show you. Come into the kitchen."

It was the Thursday before the Easter weekend and, as Kath drove towards Southampton, she hoped that the blue skies were a good omen for the next few days to come. With the Centenary Fayre just around the corner, everyone at Hope Hall was frantically busy, including her. The list of jobs on her desk that she had to finish or organize was dauntingly long, but she nevertheless made the decision to take time off this Thursday afternoon, as she often did in light of the fact that she frequently ended up working over the weekends. Hers had never been a weekday-only job.

This afternoon, she had special plans. When Jack had rung suggesting that she might like to take a look around the city hospital in which he now seemed to be moving so quickly up the ranks, she agreed immediately. She wasn't going because she wanted to know how *she* felt about it. What she longed to find out was what it meant to *him*, how he fitted in, how comfortable he seemed there. In the past, their ideas for their individual futures had been very different.

There was a frenetic air of bustle as she walked in, typical of the entrance foyer of every major hospital she'd ever visited. Patients were in wheelchairs or walking down the corridor on the arm of a friend. Worried visitors huddled round tables in the small café. Staff in various department uniforms were coming and going. They were all there, along with the smell, sound and slight sense of chaos that seemed so familiar from her hospital management days in London.

She took a seat in the waiting area, and sent Jack a text saying she'd arrived. She wondered if she had time to pop into the Ladies to check that she looked okay, but decided against it. Ten minutes later, when she'd still not heard from him, she wished she had gone when she'd had the chance.

After twenty minutes of waiting, just at the point when she was wondering whether to text him again, she saw Jack walking at a leisurely pace towards her. He was deep in conversation with a female colleague, and for a moment she thought perhaps he'd forgotten completely that she was due to visit him today. The two of them stopped quite close to her, their conversation intense and urgent. Kath tried not to stare at how attractive Jack's companion was, and how familiar they seemed to be with each other. Then, as a decision was obviously agreed between them, the woman touched Jack's arm with a smile, and turned away to walk back up the main corridor.

"Kath!" he called, his voice warm with welcome. "I'm so sorry I've kept you waiting. You know how it is! Come upstairs to my office. We can have a coffee there."

If she had hoped for some conversation as they made their way through the maze of corridors, covered walkways and lifts to his office, she was mistaken because, time and again, Jack was greeted or stopped by people they met. He was obviously well known and liked here. In the huge London hospital they'd worked in, it was easy to feel that even life-savers like Jack were largely anonymous and unknown. In this hospital, which served fewer people in a smaller city, he seemed to have become a familiar figure around the place. She watched as he returned greetings here, checked notes there, and chatted with a porter in the lift, as well as sharing a comforting word with the patient who was lying on the trolley the porter was pushing.

Jack ushered her into a small office in which files of papers were stacked around the computer that stood in the centre of the desk. He picked up the phone and asked whoever was at the other end of the line for two coffees. Then he turned to Kath, stepping forward to take her into his arms.

"I'm sorry," he breathed into her ear. "I'd like to say it isn't always like this, but I'd be lying. Were you waiting long?"

"No problem. How long have you been here today?"

His brow furrowed as he tried to remember. "There was an emergency op this morning, so they rang last night to ask me to get in at six. What's the time now?"

"Nearly three. You've done more than a normal day's work already. Can you stop now, for a while at least?"

He reached down to pull open his desk diary. "A meeting at four-thirty and another operation at six."

"You must be worn out."

He shrugged with a grin. "It goes with the territory. You know that."

She nodded, saying nothing as she looked at the deep shadows of exhaustion that lined his face.

"Don't worry about showing me round. I'd rather you just sat for a while. Can I get you anything? Have you eaten today?"

He looked blank. "I think so. It was this morning, wasn't it, that I had those scrambled eggs?"

"Do you feel hungry?"

He rubbed his hand wearily across his cheeks and mouth. "Honestly, no."

"Just sit then. It's really quite warm outside. Do you fancy finding a seat in the garden? Perhaps there you could stay out of sight from all those people who need your attention *now*!"

He smiled. "That sounds lovely, but perhaps we'll just hide up here for a while first. The coffee will come soon."

At that moment there was a knock on the door and a young nurse walked in carrying a couple of plastic cups full of a liquid that looked far too orange to be coffee. It tasted all right, though, Kath realized with surprise.

"Can you check your emails, Dr Sawyer? Dr Gooderston has sent through the details of the operation at six, and there's more in your notes about the other two procedures scheduled for tomorrow morning. Sister Thurman is expecting you to call in to see her two patients this afternoon, if you have time – and don't forget you have that department meeting upstairs at half four. There are a few other messages on your desk pad too. And Dr Freeman popped in. She needs to speak to you urgently."

"I've seen Monica. We met in the corridor."

"Anything you need me to do?"

"No, that's fine, thanks."

After the door shut, there was silence as Jack looked through the messages on his desk pad, his attention completely taken as he drew a line through some and scribbled notes against others.

"Perhaps we won't go and sit in the sun then," said Kath softly. "You're busy, Jack, and I'm in the way."

He looked up sharply. "No, Kath, honestly it's fine. I just need to get on top of a few of these things—"

"Of course you do. And I need to get back to do a million and one jobs in preparation for this weekend."

As she started to get to her feet, he looked alarmed. "Don't go, please. I'm sorry. I didn't mean it to be this way. It was supposed to be my quiet afternoon."

She walked round to stand behind him, and placed her hands on his shoulders, massaging her fingers into the muscles of his neck, which were rock hard with tension.

"Jack, it doesn't matter. I understand. You know I do. In fact, I understand a great deal more now I've seen how busy your time is here."

"We're understaffed. It will get better."

"Perhaps. I hope so, for the sake of your health and sanity."

His head lowered and relaxed as her fingers continued to work on his aching muscles.

"I was so looking forward to you coming. I really wanted to show you round. You were always so good at having a detached point of view. You'd get straight to the heart of whatever was causing confusion and sort things out. We could do with a bit of that talent of yours here."

"I'll come again. And although I'm going to leave you to it right now, just know that I'm thinking of you. Call if you want to, any time."

"Kath, I—"

The jarring ring of his desk phone filled the small room. She bent down to kiss the top of his head, then picked up her bag and with a wave left the room. She heard him answering the phone before the door shut behind her.

Karen had had no break at all since Christmas. She'd worked at least one day of every weekend. Bank holidays had never made much of a difference to her, but this time she knew she was exhausted. She missed the twins, and found herself resenting the fact that the constant demands of her job not only limited the time she planned to spend with them, but could often mean that she had to rush into work at the drop of a hat.

She'd also become aware of a niggling sense of conscience about how her job impacted her husband Gary, and their marriage. She was beginning to feel like an occasional visitor rather than a wife and mother. It was all a matter of priorities. For Karen, so decisive and managerial at work, it was an unsettling and unfamiliar experience to feel that she was definitely not in control at home.

In the end, she made a last-minute decision not to work at all over the four days of the Easter bank holiday weekend, and also to extend the break by booking off the Thursday before and the Tuesday after. The boys were thrilled. Gary made no comment. She knew he'd only believe she was sincere if they got to the end of her planned break without her having to take calls every hour or rushing back into work at a moment's notice.

The twins' school term had finished several days earlier, and they were in high spirits one minute and yelling at each other the next. Even though she had been looking forward to their time together so much, Karen was finding herself getting irritated by their constant demands, the tears, the toys thrown across the room, followed by the two of them acting as one to try and charm their way into getting whatever they wanted *right now*!

The greatest surprise, though, was that Gary seemed to be handling their tantrums much better than she was. Practice, she thought. He had been Max and Toby's main parent for so long now that whatever he might be lacking in housework skills, he was definitely making up for by being a terrific dad. He was firm when it was needed. He came up with lots of impromptu ideas when it was clear that boredom was beginning to set in because they had "absolutely nothing to do"! That was when Gary would bring out an Airfix kit for a helicopter that they could all build and paint together, or they'd go to the park to play frisbee, or they'd cuddle up to watch a Marvel film, usually with Gary falling asleep within minutes as he sat with one arm around each twin.

Watching how much time Gary invested in their young sons, Karen began to think, not for the first time, that it was unfair on her talented, artistic husband that his work life should be sacrificed in favour of hers. It was true she was the big earner. Without her wages, it would be impossible for them to have this roomy house with all the little luxuries that made it such a comfortable family home. But when she went into the box bedroom that they euphemistically called his office, she realized how cramped it was, and how difficult it must be for him to keep on top of the commissions he was asked to complete. She gently picked up one page after another from his work station. She knew these drawings all related to the huge Denison contract that was worrying him so much. The drawings weren't just unfinished. They were hardly started. Gary was struggling. He'd been trying to tell her that for months, but she'd been too busy, too exhausted, too absorbed with her own work challenges to listen.

She thought about all the times she'd arrived home after a long day hoping to find that everything was tidy and organized, with dinner in the oven and Toby and Max tucked up in bed waiting for her to read them a story. So often, what she actually walked into was total chaos, with the boys overtired and badly behaved, homework not done and no sign of dinner anywhere. She thought about how often she'd lost patience with Gary. Did she honestly think she could have done any better at juggling all the demands that Gary faced every day? How her patronizing expressions and acid comments must have hurt and belittled him!

On Good Friday evening, after a lovely day that ended with their first barbecue of the year in the back garden, the boys were sound asleep in bed at last. Gary was just walking in from the garden having cleaned the barbecue and put it away, when he looked up with surprise to see Karen was standing at the kitchen door with two glasses of wine.

"We need to talk," she said.

A moment of panic shot through him. What had he forgotten? Had he done something wrong? Had she somehow found out about his friendship with Claire? Or was it just the usual thing – she needed to go into work right now…

"Don't look so terrified," she laughed. "Come on, let's go and sit down."

Once they were settled, she took a while before she spoke, as if she was trying to work out exactly what to say.

"I owe you an apology."

"You do?"

"I've been very unfair to you. I've been so caught up in the demands of my own life, I've lost sight of why I'm working at all."

Wondering where this was heading, Gary said nothing.

"We made a decision, you and I, once the twins came along, that we needed as much money as we could earn to make sure they had the life we wanted for them. A nice house with everything we need in it, a new car, a family holiday abroad every year – that's what we wanted, and that's what we've got. But we've paid a high price for that. It's nearly cost you the career you love. It's cost me the relationship I really want to have with our children. And worst of all, it's costing us our marriage. We are so distant these days, and it's much more than just exhaustion. We never used to bicker, but that's what we do practically every day – when we're speaking at all. We've forgotten why we married, why we fell in love with each other in the first place."

Speechless, Gary laid down his wine glass and took her hand.

"Gary, you are a wonderful man and the most fantastic artist. That was what drew me to you right from the very start. Your pictures made me laugh. They made me think. They made me fall for you, and I've never stopped loving you from that moment on. But I've forgotten how to show it. I take you for granted. I moan at you and treat you as though you're an inefficient servant. I'm ashamed to think how awful I've been at times. I honestly can't imagine how you've put up with me."

"Well, I've probably not helped. I know how irritable I can be—"

"Of course you're irritable! You can't get on with your design work here, because looking after a house and a family with two lively boys takes every bit of your time and energy. I was looking at the drawings you're working on for Denison's…"

He looked embarrassed. "I wish you hadn't."

"Because you've hardly started them. I can see that. But you and I both know you could come up with exactly what they need in very little time, if you just had the chance."

He shrugged, moved by what she was saying, but most of all surprised that she had noticed any of this at all.

"You need to finish that work," she said decisively, "and I don't think you can do it here. I have some suggestions. The immediate one is that you ring Ken, and ask him if you can have a work station at his studio. He's been your friend for years. He doesn't use that studio much now he's retired, and it's just around the corner. That should give you the peace and quiet you need to persuade Denison's that they've chosen exactly the right man for this job."

"But what about the boys?"

"I need to work less. I am going to talk to them about working no more than thirty hours a week, some of which I can probably do at home."

Gary smiled. "It's hard working at home, you know."

"I'm beginning to understand that, but I also know that others at our place split their work between the office and home. Sometimes I have so many disturbances and distractions at work that it's possible I could actually get a lot more done here."

"Suppose the company won't play ball? It's obvious they need you there, or why would they keep demanding that you go back in?"

"Well, during the period of self-reflection that's led up to me saying all this to you, I can't help but wonder if it's *me* that doesn't want the company to get the idea they can manage without me."

Gary leaned forward so that their heads were touching. "It's us that need you," he said. "The twins and me."

"I know," she whispered. "I've been such a fool."

He kissed her then, a gentle kiss of promise and love and shared understanding.

"So," he said, his voice suddenly businesslike, "we need to sort out the logistics, but as soon as possible we want to be in a position where we both work for some of every week, and we both share the parenting. We both earn money – and what we can't afford, we'll do without."

She nodded. "All that matters is our family, this marriage, you and me…"

She could say no more. Taking her in his arms, Gary wouldn't let her.

Chapter 11

K ath wasn't the only one to heave a sigh of relief as she pulled back the curtains on Easter Monday morning. It was a glorious April day, with just a few light clouds scudding across the clear blue sky. There was still a slight chill in the air, but it looked as though the Hope Hall Centenary Fayre was going to take place on just the right day.

With the weather forecast looking good, an executive decision had been taken two days earlier that all the performance events would take place outside the hall in the school playground. The Rotary Club members had swung into action with gusto, arriving with staging, backdrops, seating, tables for the craft stalls, display boards, not to mention toolkits packed with drills, saws, screws and nails, superglue and a huge supply of white and magnolia emulsion, complete with paintbrushes in every possible size.

On Easter Saturday afternoon, all the various groups taking part in the displays turned up for a dress rehearsal inside the main hall. It was total chaos, with the occasional temperamental artiste having a hissy fit, but generally speaking the atmosphere was good-natured. As Maggie and Kath crossed paths at around six o'clock that evening when only two-thirds of the dress rehearsal had actually been completed, they stood watching for a while from the side of the hall wondering, not for the first time, why they had ever come up with the mad idea of this huge Easter event in the first place.

"Well," sighed Kath, "you know what they say. Bad rehearsal, great show."

Maggie chuckled. "Whoever said that obviously hadn't seen *this* rehearsal!"

"How have you got on today?"

"I think we're almost organized," Maggie replied. "Best of all, do you remember I put that notice up on the board asking people what meals and food favourites they remember most clearly from their childhood? Well, I've been amazed by the tremendous reaction and the ideas that have come pouring in. So many people have signed up saying they'd like to recreate those dishes themselves and bring them in on the day."

"It will be really interesting to see what turns up then."

"How about you? You've had such a lot to organize."

Kath grimaced. "I guess the main problem has been that there are just so many different groups involved, and they all think their contribution is the only one that counts. I could have done with a referee's whistle at times this afternoon during the dress rehearsal when the combination of panic and ruffled feathers became overwhelming."

"Well, we can't do any more now. It *will* be a great show on Monday. I just know it."

The memory of that conversation with Maggie came back to Kath as she arrived at the hall at nine o'clock on Easter Monday morning to find that several of the craft contributors were already unpacking their wares and beginning to set up their stalls. The Rotary sound engineer was soon at work laying cables and testing microphones, while his colleague hauled out of their lighting van a mountain of big sturdy boxes, on which he sat while he studied a drawing of where each set of lights should be positioned.

Della and her mother arrived a quarter of an hour later, heading for the old school hall, where they planned some last-minute practice for a couple of the dancing groups. Pianist Ronnie Andrews hurried up to the usual school classroom where members of the Can't Sing Singers were already gathered around the piano.

By mid-morning some of the Scout leaders had arrived in their own van, from which they unloaded all sorts of intriguing cases and packages, which were whisked away to wherever they needed to be in preparation for their display later in the afternoon.

From eleven o'clock onwards, there was a steady stream of people making for the kitchen, bringing covered bowls and plastic boxes that obviously contained home-made family favourites. Every time Kath passed the hatch, there were squeals of delight as the contents of various boxes were revealed, and plans were made about how to display all the contributions and stagger the supplies so that there was plenty on offer throughout the whole day.

The larger-than-life compère, Derek Simmons, arrived at twelve noon, shaking hands with everyone he met and smiling broadly, before spending some time with the sound engineer to test the microphone level before the afternoon's events began. He then disappeared into a huddle with Della, her mother Barbara, and Shirley, all of whom had been working together to shape the programme for the day.

By one o'clock the foyer and balcony area were packed with visitors who knew that Hope Hall was always the place to find a good lunch, and there was a lot of interest in the unusual menu that day. Among the wonderful selection of menu donations from people who had recreated old family favourites for the occasion were shepherd's pie, stew and dumplings, baked ham and pease pudding, jelly and blancmange, Black Forest gateau, coffee and walnut cakes, Victoria sponge, rich fruit cake, crumpets and jam tarts.

"Miss?" asked Kevin, pulling a face as he carried over a large oblong enamel pie dish. "The lady who brought this in said it reminded her of school dinners when she was in the infants. She said this strawberry jam had to go in with it. Is that right?"

Maggie looked down at the milky mixture that looked as if it was full of frogspawn. She burst out laughing as she recognized it as old-fashioned tapioca pudding.

"My gran used to make that every Sunday, but at school it

always came in a big enamel dish just like this, one for every table along with a pot of red jam sauce. It was great fun stirring the jam in so that the whole lot turned a sickly shade of pink."

"Yuck!" Kevin pulled a face at the thought.

"Put it out just as it is!" commanded Maggie. "That will go down a treat."

By twenty to two, all the seats surrounding the playground had been taken by the older and most needy visitors, with everyone else finding places to stand behind them. Kath was at the door of Hope Hall to welcome the mayor and his wife, a popular couple who spent the next quarter of an hour taking a good look at the extensive display of memorabilia that was on show in the main hall, along with dozens of others who exclaimed joyfully as they recognized items they recalled from their grandparents' homes, or which sparked memories of their own childhood.

At exactly two o'clock, Derek Simmons walked onto the stage that had been specially built at the far end of the school playground, and took the mic.

"Ladies and gentlemen, welcome to the Hope Hall Easter Monday Fayre – a very special occasion this year, because our beloved Hope Hall is celebrating its centenary! Over the last one hundred years, this hall has opened its doors to generations of local people who have come here to learn, to dance and sing, to play, to meet and eat, to be entertained and to celebrate together – and there are many opportunities for us to enjoy examples of every single one of those activities here today. The groups who regularly use Hope Hall right now have all been working together to present an afternoon of performances for our enjoyment.

"We begin with our brand new town band. These musicians, of all different ages, backgrounds and musical training, have been brought together by Don Walker, Head of the Music Department at the senior school. This is their very first performance after having a limited time to rehearse not just the music itself, but the skill of playing and marching at the same time, which they say is terrifying them all! So here they are with a piece of music that was written one hundred years ago, just as Hope Hall was opening its doors for the first time. Please can we have a great big cheer for our new town band!"

From the other end of the playground came a noise reminiscent of a pair of bagpipes tuning up, but within seconds the sound of several different brass instruments all starting to play at slightly different times and tempos began to take shape, and the audience gradually recognized the tune of "Alexander's Ragtime Band". After that, the crowd needed no encouragement to join in and sing, applauding and raising a cheer as the band marched into view.

Admittedly their footwork wasn't the best, but all the players looked splendid in their brand new, gold-braided jackets in a rich shade of poster blue. Most infectious of all was the fact that, although they were concentrating hard on the notes they were playing, there seemed to be a suggestion of a smile on every player's face as, with delight and relief, they acknowledged that their rehearsals had obviously paid off. The audience were leaving them in no doubt that they were enjoying every minute of the performance.

The band eventually took up a position right in the middle of the playground, and went on to play several other well-known songs from the 1920s. It was in the middle of their performance that Gary and Karen found a place for themselves halfway down the side of the playground, where they thought they would get the best view of the Scouts' display in which the Beavers were taking part.

"When are they due to be on?" asked Karen. "Hang on, I've got the programme here."

As she fumbled in her bag to dig out the printed programme, Gary glanced up to see Claire looking in his direction from where she was standing almost immediately opposite him. He saw that a tall man with glasses had his arm protectively around her shoulders, and realized with a jolt that it must be Nigel. Obviously things had improved between the two of them. Gary tried to analyse for a second what he was actually feeling as he watched Claire and Nigel together. His overwhelming reaction was surprise, because Claire had been so pessimistic about the hopelessness of their situation when they last spoke. Then, with relief, he also knew that he was genuinely pleased if Claire and her husband had managed to get over their differences and were heading for happier times.

"They're on next," announced Karen, pointing to the programme. "Oh, I'm so looking forward to seeing the boys. They've both been beside themselves with excitement."

Gary looked down at Karen, her face glowing with the thrill of just being there, and his heart lurched with love for her.

"I love you, Mrs Knights! It's not just the boys who are glad you're here today. I am too."

She reached up to put her arms around his neck and hugged him, not caring who might see them. They were married. They loved each other and their boys. Life didn't get better than this.

Watching from the other side of the playground, Claire was shocked to see the real affection between Gary and his wife. The twins had been so anxious that Karen wouldn't be able to come. It seemed to be a happy family outing for the four of them, and Claire was really glad to see that. She turned to look up at Nigel, who smiled down at her.

"Oh, there they are!" Nigel suddenly pointed over Claire's shoulder. She turned to see her mum and dad just walking in.

"Here we go then," she said, looking anxiously back towards him.

"The start of a new era – for all of us."

Touched by the determination in his reply, Claire reached up to plant a quick kiss on his cheek, then started waving enthusiastically to catch her parents' attention.

As the town band's last number came to a triumphant end, the audience burst into enthusiastic applause. The band members moved over to one corner of the playground, where stools and music stands were waiting for them. In the meantime, about a dozen young men dressed in Scout uniform rushed into the centre to erect wigwams, camp fires, flags and different tiers of staging as the master of ceremonies kept everyone entertained by introducing key people in the audience, as well as telling a cheeky joke about one of them, which had the crowd laughing out loud.

"And now, this is not just a special year for Hope Hall, but also an important year for the whole of the Scouting movement. To tell us all about it, and remind us of one hundred years of Jamboree, please welcome the combined forces of all our Scout and Guide clubs in the town!"

The town band struck up the introduction of a jaunty march that many in the audience immediately remembered as "We're Riding Along on the Crest of the Wave", which was always the big finale number for *The Gang Show*, devised by Scouting enthusiast Ralph Reader back in the 1930s. *The Gang Show* started with a performance in London's Scala Theatre, but was followed over many decades by similar shows featuring hundreds of Scouts in many other major concert halls and theatres, as well as countless local venues just like Hope Hall up and down the country. Singing the familiar words as they marched in from every corner of the playground, came lines of Scouts, Guides, Cubs, Brownies, Rainbows and finally the Beavers, all with beaming smiles, as a huge roar of appreciation went up from the crowd.

Eventually, all the young people marched into their positions around the ground, as one teenage Scout strode smartly up to the microphone, clutching his page of notes tightly, ready to speak once the song had come to an end.

"It was in August 1920 that the foundation stone was laid here to start the building of Hope Hall, and in exactly the same month the very first World Scout Jamboree was hosted in Britain at the Olympia Hall in Kensington, London. Symbolically, the Jamboree site bore the name of the birthplace of the Olympic Games. Eight thousand Scouts from thirty-four countries took part in the event, which was dedicated to the theme of world peace.

"That first Jamboree was an exhibition of Scouting around the world, showing the fellowship of Scouts everywhere, and the traditional skills that were learned by Scouts in preparation for life at home and in the great outdoors. One traditional Scouting activity is camping, and around the arena today you can see some examples of tents used in times gone by, as well as the modern facilities Scouts use in this area today.

"Over the years, Scouts have enjoyed singing songs around the camp fire, and we would like to demonstrate one of these to you now. It's called 'Dum, Dum, Da, Da' – and most of all, we would like you to join in with the actions!"

With another lively introduction from the band, all the groups around the playground launched into a song that had very little in the way of words, which made it fairly easy for the audience to join in:

Dum, dum, da, da,
Da-dum, dum, da, da,
Da-dum, dum, da, da, da, dum, da-dum, dum, dum
Dum, dum, da, da,
Da-dum, dum, da, da,
Da-dum, dum, da, da, da, dum.

The children led the audience through actions that had them patting their knees, touching their shoulders, crossing and uncrossing their arms, pointing to their elbows and snapping their fingers. The result was complete chaos, which had certain members of the audience almost crying with laughter either at the sight of some of the younger children as they struggled to remember the moves, or because they found it hilariously difficult themselves. When the song finally came to an end, there was general stamping and cheering as the band played another Scouting song while the children marched off the arena, waving to all as they left.

While the compère crossed the platform to take the mic again, some of the Scouts stayed on the stage to pick up some high-backed chairs and arrange them on the platform in three rows, with four chairs facing forward in each.

"Ladies and gentlemen, we bring you now a group of people who regularly come to Hope Hall because they want to have fun, enjoy some great music and stay fit and healthy too. I'm told the combined age of the twelve dancers about to come on stage is nearly eight hundred years! Please welcome Armchair Exercise!"

The crowd applauded as the group, all dressed in black trousers topped by floaty baby-blue chiffon blouses, made their slow way to the stage. In fact, the audience had to keep applauding for quite a while before the Armchair Exercise members had manoeuvred themselves into position, got their breath back and were ready to go. Pianist Ronnie struck a chord to get their attention before launching into the lovely old waltz melody "Alice Blue Gown", a song that was as old as Hope Hall itself. Ida, Flora and Betty were clearly visible in the second row back. Betty appeared to be counting out every beat and keeping a close eye on Doris, who was doing all the movements with great confidence in the front row. Flora was in her element, almost laughing as she swayed and sang along to the words. Ida looked stately and unsmiling, which may well have been the effect of stage-fright, although she would never admit to any sort of weakness like that.

Together, the group swung their arms and legs, and rolled their shoulders. They did side bends with first the left and then the right arm, then they got up and stood behind their chairs to bend their knees and stretch up onto their toes, all in time to the familiar lilting melody. They finished the dance sitting down again, with their hands linked along each line as they stretched rhythmically from side to side. When they all finished with their hands high in the air and cheers ringing in their ears, the group collapsed in giggles at the sheer triumph of all they'd achieved.

But then, without anything further from the compère, Ronnie started playing a new introduction with a completely different feel. What followed was a sing-along medley of American favourites that were all written in the 1920s. From each corner of the arena, dressed in a dazzling array of brightly coloured blouses and shirts conjuring up the magic of Caribbean islands, came lines of dancers, not one of them under the age of fifty, all doing a conga step as they held each other's waists and sang, "When the red, red robin comes bob, bob, bobbin' along." Once the lines had merged into a square in the middle of the playground, the music changed to "I'm Looking Over a Four Leafed Clover" as the dancers sang and moved into geometric patterns in the style of Busby Berkeley chorus line beauties, although admittedly not quite with the same precision or silhouette! Their arms swung and waved, their legs kicked, their heads turned in unison first one way and then the other. They twirled and twisted, encouraging the audience to join in and sing with them. When they finally formed themselves into the shape of a train that chuffed around the arena, with their arms linked and moving like engine wheels, their gleeful performance ended with a rousing chorus of "Bye Bye Blackbird".

Shouting to be heard over the rapturous reaction of the audience, the compère announced that the performance had come from the members of the Dance Sing-along exercise class at Hope

Hall. He then went on to explain that, just as music had entertained people down the years, so had comedy…

"Put your hands together, please, for a man who has a fund of funny stories, and he assures me every one of them is true. But knowing this chap as I do, I hope that today he's chosen a story that's *suitable* for your delicate ears! The irrepressible Percy Wilson!"

Percy looked splendid as he came on stage dressed a bit like Charlie Chaplin, complete with a little black moustache – except that where Charlie had been slim and petite, Percy was tall and big-boned, with a nicely rounded tummy. Unfortunately, he stopped short of the microphone stand, which meant that when he started talking, nobody could hear a word he was saying. The sound man immediately ran on to move Percy into the right position and adjust the mic to the correct angle and height.

"I'm dressed like this, because if my dad had still been alive, he would be celebrating his one hundredth birthday this year, just like Hope Hall. He was born in 1920, and at that time the most well-known entertainer and film star in the world was Charlie Chaplin, who was born the same year as my grandad, back in 1893.

"Now, because everybody loved Charlie Chaplin, this style of dress, especially the bowler hat, became very fashionable for quite a long time. My grandad worked in a factory that made machinery parts, where the workers used to have to clock in first thing every morning and clock out again every night when they'd finished. Grandad worked for many years with the same team, and they became great friends, but perhaps because the job was quite boring, they liked nothing better than playing practical jokes on each other.

"Grandad's friend Harry was always very dapper and loved dressing smartly, and he had noticed a gentlemen's outfitters' shop not far from the factory that was having a sale of bowler hats – and what's more, anyone who bought a hat that week could have their initials engraved for free in gold letters on the inside lining.

"Well, Harry rushed out to treat himself to a new bowler hat in his lunch break, and he couldn't wait to show all his friends what a bargain he'd found when he got back to work. He was especially proud when he walked out of the factory in the evening with his new hat firmly on his head.

"That night on the walk home, my grandad hatched a plan with a few of the other fellas. Next day, at lunchtime, Grandad nipped down to the shop himself, and he bought a hat that was two sizes larger than the one Harry had bought. Then he asked the shopkeeper to engrave the new hat with Harry's initials, just like the other one.

"When Grandad got back to the factory, his friends kept watch while he swapped the hats over, leaving the one that was two sizes too big hanging on Harry's hook.

"At home time, they all pretended not to notice – and definitely not laugh – as Harry put on the hat only to find that it slid down right over his ears and eyes so that he couldn't see a thing. He checked inside, and could see his initials. It definitely *was* his hat. Puzzled, and hoping no one else had noticed, he put the hat under his arm and walked quickly out of the factory. Grandad and all the rest of the lads waited until he was out of earshot before collapsing in helpless laughter.

"The next morning, Harry walked in wearing the hat – but he had stuffed newspaper inside the rim so that it fitted him again, even if it was rather wide on his head. He hung it up on his hook with care, and went off to work. While he was away, Grandad and his friends crept in, took the large hat off the hook, and pulled out the newspaper padding, which they then stuffed in exactly the same position into the original smaller hat.

"At home time, Harry put on his coat and popped on his hat. His face was a picture when he realized the hat didn't fit him at all, and all he could do was perch it on the very top of his head! Once again, confused and embarrassed, he hid the hat under his arm and hurried off home.

"The following day, when Harry didn't come into work, Grandad and the rest were longing to know why he'd stayed away, so they went round to his house after work and knocked on the door. His mother answered, and said that Harry was suffering from a terrible illness. He was down at the doctor's, because he was afflicted with a serious condition that was making his head expand one day and shrink most terribly the next."

By the time Percy got to this part of the story, the audience were in fits of laughter and there was a round of delighted applause – after which Percy added a postscript.

"But it was Harry who had the last laugh. He'd worked out when he got home the night before what had happened, so he was actually in the back room listening at the keyhole as his mother strung his friends along with the tragic story of how upset he was. Grandad and his friends got a real fit of conscience at the thought of Harry believing that he was dreadfully ill, so they went back that night with several bottles of beer and a box of sweets for him. He said that the looks on their faces when they realized he'd got his own back made it all worthwhile!

"It just goes to show, ladies and gentlemen, that as my dear old grandad used to say, there's naught so queer as folk! I thank you!" And with an exaggerated bow, Percy milked the applause for as long as possible before he finally left the stage.

"An invitation for us all now," announced the compère, "from the members of the Hope Hall pre-school playgroup, who are about to show us how children enjoyed singing and playing one hundred years ago. Here they are at the teddy bears' picnic!"

A huge sigh of affection rippled around the audience as, with a lot of gentle encouragement from Jen, Carol and the playgroup team, the under-five-year-olds all wandered onto the stage clutching their teddies in one arm and holding the hand of another little friend with the other. Ronnie was bashing out the melody of the famous old song, while a group of Cubs and Brownies stood at the side of the platform singing the words as loudly as they could in the hope that the little ones would join in with them. The children lined up along the front of the stage with various degrees of involvement. Some were singing loudly, hugging their teddies and nudging the child next to them when they forgot the moves. Some just stood staring out at the crowd, not sure why they were there at all. One at the far end was waving and calling out to his mum, who was waving back wildly from the side of the playground, and another little girl simply walked off the stage immediately, with her thumb in her mouth. The audience loved every moment and the applause was deafening as parents ran up to the stage to congratulate and collect their talented youngsters once the performance was over.

"And now for something completely different," announced the compère. "We've been remembering how children and grown-ups had fun in years gone by, but now we're coming bang up to date with a mind-blowing display from our very own street-dancing group, the Hip-hoppers!"

Electronic beeping and pulsing suddenly burst out at great volume from the sound speakers, as a group of teenagers, their faces painted like zombies, all dressed in black with rips strategically cut into their jeans and T-shirts, burst onto the stage, some running, some crawling, some twisting in the air, with the final boy and girl back-flipping straight into the central position. What followed was an amazing routine set to an ever-changing soundtrack that jumped from thumping rhythms to a single voice, then became a well-known piece of disco music before evolving into an electronic beeping that sounded as if it was coming from outer space.

It was clear that most of the young people were new to body popping, but they gave it a good go, thrusting themselves into unnaturally angular shapes that had the audience gasping with disbelief. The two stars centre stage went through an almost separate routine of lifts and drops that had Kath keeping her finger permanently on the button of her phone so that she could ring an ambulance on speed dial! On the ear-splitting final note, the dancers all dropped dramatically to the floor, only to rise again grinning and high-fiving each other as the audience clapped and cheered.

Eventually, the compère managed to clear the stage of excited teenagers and reclaim the microphone.

"Now, for the introduction to our next performance, I am going to hand over to the wife of Hope Hall's accountant, Trevor. Please welcome Mary Barrett!"

Obviously a little nervous, Mary walked slowly up to the microphone, followed by a group of Brownies and Cubs, who all arranged themselves in a line along the front of the stage.

"Today we're celebrating the way in which, down the years, people both made music and were entertained by it. I've been passing on a great way of making music to this new generation of young people – and, as you're about to see, they have enjoyed learning this lovely skill that my grandad taught me when I was their age. May I introduce the Hope Hall Spooners!"

From behind their backs, the Spooners each produced a pair of dessert spoons, while Ronnie launched into a breezy ragtime number. Holding the two spoons in just the right position so that they clicked loudly together, the youngsters went through a complicated routine of banging out the ragtime rhythm with the spoons tapping on their arms, legs – in fact, any part of the body that the spoons could reach! The expression of relief on their faces when they reached the end soon changed to thrilled excitement when they realized how well their playing had gone down with the audience.

"And now, ladies and gentlemen," declared the compère, "a demonstration of a traditional style of dance that has become really popular with the young people here at Hope Hall. Conjuring up the magic of Fred and Ginger, please welcome Della Lucas's tap-dancing team!"

Looking resplendent in their bright red, silver-sequinned taffeta jackets, with trilby hats lined with red ribbon, dancers from the age of about five to fifteen toe-heeled their way across the stage, following round in a circle as their tap shoes clicked out a series of rhythms on the hard platform. They shuffled and stamped. They shimmied and brush-stepped. They hopped and ball-changed, with their arms swinging and their hats twirling, while Ronnie played the old soft-shoe song "By the Light of the Silvery Moon", with a very definite tempo in order to keep all their feet tapping bang on time.

At the end of the number, as the audience burst into applause thinking that their display was over, Ronnie started the introduction to another well-known song, "Side by Side". As the younger dancers all stepped back to the rear of the platform, four new dancers – also dressed in bright red sequinned jackets and trilby hats – appeared at the side of the stage, entering with their arms stretched out to rest on the shoulder of the dancer in front of them. The line was led in stately style by Ida, followed by a beaming Doris, a very excited Flora and a rather nervous Betty, who seemed to be constantly checking what her feet were doing. The ladies turned towards the audience to perform their routine of basic tap steps in the style of the popular comedy duo Flanagan and Allen, as the audience clapped and joined in with the words of the song that all ages seemed to know. Finally, after the younger tap dancers had moved forward to join in with the quartet of senior ladies, the routine came to an end in true razzle-dazzle style.

The audience loved it. Ida accepted their applause as if she were a film star, Doris was enthusiastically blowing kisses out in every direction, Flora was waving to her fans, and Betty looked as if she could burst into tears of joy just knowing that she'd got through it all without tripping over.

When the applause at last died down, and the stage was cleared, the master of ceremonies went back to the microphone to make the final announcement of the Easter Monday Centenary Fayre.

"Hope Hall was built in 1920 as a memorial to all those who lost their lives, were wounded or whose peace of mind was wrecked forever as a result of the First World War. For our Grand Finale today, we look back to those years of the Great War with some of the music that kept our boys marching and their spirits up. Here, to lead the way, are a group of people who ask you not to expect too much of them, and you'll realize why when I tell you these are the Can't Sing Singers!"

Onto the stage walked Keith Turner, who took his place at the microphone. Forming a semi-circle around him were Pauline, the one who was known for always singing half a tone sharp of everyone else; eighty-year-old husband and wife Peter and Olive; the elderly sisters Mary and Elizabeth Brownlow, who had sung in St Mark's choir since their Sunday school days; operatically trained Sophia, and Bruce Edison, whose only experience of singing had been with a rock band forty years earlier.

Bruce brought a harmonica to his lips and gave Keith a note. Clear as a bell and with heart-stopping sweetness, Keith's beautiful tenor voice rang out, unaccompanied, singing the opening verse of "Keep the Home Fires Burning", written by Ivor Novello in 1914, and sung by troops in the trenches throughout the devastating years of the First World War. Silence fell across the gathered crowd as the tenderness of the melody, the sincerity in Keith's voice and the poignancy of the familiar words touched hearts and moistened eyes.

Then, as Keith continued to sing this deeply moving song, in ones and twos other members of the Can't Sing Singers started to join in, attempting to add backing harmony to the lines, with oohs and aahs that were not quite in time, and definitely not in tune. The audience held its collective breath, uncertain how to react. The song had started off with such deep emotion, and there was no doubting that all the backing singers were performing with real sincerity and commitment – but it sounded dreadful. It was so awful that before long people started giggling, but far from being offended, the choir seemed to be expecting and loving that reaction.

"They definitely chose the right name for themselves," laughed Trevor, who was standing at the side with Kath, Maggie and Mary. "They are *brilliantly* bad. It reminds me of Les Dawson playing the piano: all the right words and feel, but the notes are completely wrong."

When the singers reached the final excruciating note, the audience cheered more loudly than for anything else they'd seen that afternoon. Somehow this performance summed up what the day was all about: the community spirit, the endeavour, the wish to contribute even if the skill set still had a long way to go!

Then, before the cheering had started to fade, the central arena began to fill up with performers of every age – tap dancers, hip-hoppers, the armchair and sing-along dancers, Scouts and Guides – all of them providing enough volume to drown out the Can't Sing Singers for the last song. The audience didn't hesitate to join in too, enthusiastically singing "It's a Long Way to Tipperary", with its words that were as well known to the crowd gathered at Hope Hall in 2020 as the one that must have gathered in much the same way to lay the foundation stone one hundred years earlier.

It was almost as if time stood still for just a few magical moments when the old and the new, grandparents and toddlers, the past and the present of Hope Hall, merged into a timeless bond of shared humanity, experience and love. They all felt it – and knew they'd never forget that exquisite feeling, whatever the years ahead might bring to each and every one of them.

"They've got cakes!" yelled Josh, as Claire and Nigel, followed by Claire's parents, made their way through the crowd at the end of the concert. "You buy them here in the foyer. They've got red jam tarts and fairy cakes with wings sticking up out of the cream on top. Can I have one of each of those, Mummy, please? And they've got proper mugs for the tea, Daddy, so you'll be okay."

Nigel glanced at his father-in-law. "Shall we go and investigate, Bernard?"

"Definitely! I'm very partial to jam tarts."

Claire slipped her arm through her mum's as they watched the two men move off together. "It's been good today, hasn't it?"

"What a relief, Claire. I was worried that either Dad or Nigel might kick off an argument, but it's been wonderful – not just the programme, but us! We've all been great. It's been a lovely afternoon."

"What would you both like?" demanded a breathless Josh as he raced back towards them. "Daddy's gone to find a table, and Grandpa is keeping our place in the queue in case someone beats him to all the jam tarts and fairy cakes."

"Right," smiled Claire. "We're ready for cake too!"

They made their way inside the main front door of Hope Hall and into the foyer, where Nigel had managed to find seats for them all. Just as they reached their table, Josh shrieked like an excited puppy.

"Look over there, Mum! Toby and Max with their dad. I think that's their mum too. We could all sit together."

With her heart pounding in her chest, Claire hoped her face was calm as she smiled back at Josh. "There are too many of us to be on one table, Josh. Say hello to Toby and Max for me, and tell them we'll see them next time we're at Beavers."

Too late. At just that moment, Toby ran up dragging his mum by the hand, while Max was tugging at Gary's sleeve to bring him over to where Claire was standing.

"Hello," said Claire stiffly, hoping her face didn't reveal how flustered she felt as she looked at the newcomers. "I hope Josh isn't being a nuisance. Toby and Max are his favourite friends at Beavers."

"Claire," said Gary, "I don't think you've met my wife Karen."

Karen's smile was open and friendly as she acknowledged Claire, who covered her fluster by introducing her mother, who had just arrived at her side.

"Lovely to meet you, Karen. This is my mum Ruth – and my husband Nigel, who's doing a gallant job of keeping this table for us. My dad is in the queue drooling over all those gorgeous cakes."

Karen laughed. "We're on our way to join the queue now. Bang goes the waistline!"

With just the faintest acknowledgement, Gary nodded towards Claire. He understood. They both did.

Just as it was the boys who had brought the two families together, so it was the boys who dragged them apart again, as the twins hared off to speak to another group of friends.

"Sorry," said Karen. "It seems we have to go. Lovely to meet you, Claire. Have a wonderful tea, and perhaps I'll see you at Beavers before too long. I'm planning to be there more often from now on."

There was a flurry of goodbyes as the two families went their separate ways.

"They were nice lads," commented Nigel. "The boys seem to get on so well. Perhaps Josh should invite them round one day."

"Hmm," agreed Claire, as she busied herself settling her mother into a spare seat at the table.

On the other side of the foyer, Trevor and Mary were having a cup of tea with Ray.

"I used to be able to play spoons years ago," remembered Ray. "It was a grand idea of yours, Mary, to get the youngsters doing it today."

"They surprised me," replied Mary. "I really didn't know if it would appeal to them, but they loved it from the moment I showed them how to do it."

"It's all computers and technology for the kids now, isn't it?" mused Trevor. "They don't seem to use their own imaginations and *play*, like we used to."

"They're not allowed to climb trees or have conker matches, because it might be dangerous," sighed Mary.

"They can't ride their bikes without helmets, or roller-skate without kneepads," added Ray.

"They can't have secret dens or go out for the day with the kids next door, having no idea where they might go or what they'll end up doing."

Trevor chuckled. "I don't know how we all managed to get through our childhood in one piece. Do you? Nowadays, it would be considered a Health and Safety nightmare!"

"Shall I clear some of these plates away for you, to give you all a bit more room?"

They looked up to see Shirley heading their way carrying a tray that was already half loaded with empty crockery.

"Shirley!" squealed Mary. "You must be exhausted. You've been working non-stop for weeks to get everything ready for the show. It was a triumph!"

Shirley grinned with pleasure at the compliment. "It wasn't just me. There were lots of willing hands."

"Yes, but you pulled it all together."

"It's been a wonderful afternoon," agreed Trevor, "and we all know its success is largely due to you."

"Actually, Shirley," said Ray, rising from his seat, "I've been meaning to have a word with you. Have you a moment now?"

Shirley felt her stomach lurch at his suggestion. Was this it? Was he planning to tell her that now the fayre was over, and he was back to working at his former level of speed and efficiency, her services would no longer be required?

"Let me just put this tray down," she managed to say, "and I'll be right with you."

When she came out from the kitchen, she walked over to the corner where Ray was waiting, trying to gauge his expression. He wasn't smiling. In fact, he looked quite stern. Perhaps she'd done something wrong, overstepped the mark in some way? Her mouth went dry.

"Shirley, you know that some people were quite reluctant to take you on at the start. You had such definite opinions on everything that we worried you might find it difficult to fit in with the way we like things done here at Hope Hall. That was why we only agreed to employ you on a trial basis, until I was able to take up the reins of the job properly again."

Unusually for Shirley, she couldn't think of a thing to say.

"And now I'm back, and ready to resume every aspect of my role as caretaker here."

"Oh right. You won't be needing me any more then."

Suddenly, he smiled. "I think, my dear Shirley, that Hope Hall couldn't possibly do without you. You have worked miracles in so many different ways. You galvanize people into action. You give them a conscience if they don't care for the welfare of this hall as much as you do. You notice what's happening around you – who's in trouble, who's celebrating, who's unhappy or not feeling as well as they should. And you care – enough to anticipate people's needs before they know they need anything. I've experienced it personally. Your thoughtfulness towards Sara and me was so unexpected, but exactly what was required. No fuss, no demands – just kindness. You are a very special woman, Shirley Wells!"

Shirley stared at him with eyes that were rapidly filling up with tears. "But the job? You don't need me any more!"

"We took you on as a cleaner, but you've cleaned up so much more than dust and dirt! Kath, Trevor and I have had a talk about it, and we would like to offer you the role of Management Assistant. We thought that was a good way to describe how, whenever any of us need a helping hand, you'll manage to do it brilliantly."

Shirley threw her arms around Ray's neck and planted a great big kiss on his cheek.

"Hold on," he chuckled. "People will start talking!"

"Ah, but no one talks as loudly as me," she retorted with a belly laugh that could be heard all over the hall.

After the mad stampede for tea, cakes and other dishes had calmed down a little, and the crowds were beginning to leave for home, Maggie looked around the kitchen with a sense of achievement that everything had gone so well. Her team of helpers, including her talented and much trusted friend Liz, had been magnificent. Even newcomers like Kevin – who was bursting with a love of cooking and a burning ambition to learn, in spite of the difficulties of his home life – made her smile with affection and pride. There was so much in her life to warm and cheer her, so much she wanted to accomplish, so much to look forward to.

I've been concentrating too much on what I feel I'm losing, she thought, as she reached up absent-mindedly to put a row of glasses back in the cupboard. I couldn't imagine my life without Dave, but I have no wish to have that man in my life any more, after all that's happened. I didn't deserve to be treated like that, and I won't be again. She smiled as she thought of the letter that had arrived only two days earlier confirming that her offer on number 17 Linden Avenue had been accepted. It was so long since she'd bought a house that she had no idea how long it would take to process the purchase of the apartment, and how much more time would be needed to finalize the details of the divorce settlement. All she knew was that both were going through without any obvious problems. She just had a good feeling about it all. She'd been through so much upheaval and upset. What lay ahead was a new home that she already loved, and a new life that was hers, and hers alone.

She placed the last glass in the cupboard and shut the door with a decisive bang. Life was good – not brilliant, not settled – but good.

Kath was the last person to leave that evening. It was a measure of the kind-hearted people who used Hope Hall that so many of them stayed for quite a while to help with the clearing up. Ray and Shirley had done a general tidy, but they had arranged to come in first thing the next morning to complete the job and give Hope Hall a proper spring-clean.

As she walked through the empty hall with the light beginning to fade, she felt a wave of affection waft through her – a fondness for this old hall that had seen so much, known so many, kept their secrets, sheltered them from harm, nurtured the young, ached with the old. Year after year, within these walls local people had cried, laughed, worried, talked, hugged, mourned, and cared for one another.

Jack had come here and been too exhausted by the demands of his own work to understand the true glory of a place like Hope Hall. She knew she wasn't ready to give up on him. She also knew that she wasn't prepared to put her own life on hold in favour of his. That wouldn't be right for either of them.

Making her way towards the main door, she fancied that she heard a sigh of contentment, deep, warm and reassuring, from the heart of the hall itself. She listened again. Nothing. There was nothing to hear but the whine of the wind outside and the creaking of old joints within.

Smiling at her foolishness, she stepped out and pulled the main door of Hope Hall shut, turning the key in the lock before she walked away.

Who's Who at Hope Hall

Hope Hall staff and their families:

Kath Sutton – Manager of Hope Hall

Dr Jack Sawyer – Kath's former partner when they both worked in a London hospital, now based at a hospital in Southampton

Maggie Stapleton – Catering Manager at the Call-in Café

Dave Stapleton – Maggie's ex-husband

Mandy, Marlin and **Belle** – Dave's new partner and her children

Steph, Dale, and **Bobbie** (aged 2) – Maggie's daughter and her family

Darren and **Sonia** – Maggie's son and his girlfriend

Liz – Assistant Catering Manager at the Call-in Café

Ray and **Sara** – Hope Hall Caretaker and his wife who is ill with cancer

Shirley and **Mick Wells** – temporary assistant to Ray during his wife's illness and her husband

Trevor and **Mary Barrett** – Accountant at Hope Hall and his wife

Work experience pupils at the Call-in Café:

Jess

Gemma

Kevin Marley – wants to be the next Jamie Oliver; his family are **Deirdre** (Mum) and **Lily** (Nan)

Dance classes:

Della Lucas – recently back from working on cruise ships, and planning to start taking a variety of dance classes at Hope Hall

Barbara Lucas – Della's mother, recently retired as the dance schoolteacher in the town; sister of Shirley Wells

Ronnie Andrews – former variety professional pianist who plays both for Della's dancing classes and for the Can't Sing Singers

Grown-ups' Lunch Club members:

Percy Wilson – cheeky character, great storyteller

Connie – sits on Percy's table, leaving husband Eric at home in his beloved potting shed

John – widower on Percy's table

Robert – also on Percy's table, keen on indoor bowls

Ida – heads another table, bossy and organizing

Betty – sits on Ida's table, nervous about dancing

Doris – sits on Ida's table, married to Bert

Flora – sits on Ida's table, also in the Can't Sing Singers

Gerald – church member whose wife has recently gone into care, brought along to the Club by the vicar's wife, Ellie

Can't Sing Singers:

(all previous members of the St Marks' Church choir, thrown out when new musical director, Gregory Palmer, is appointed)

Pauline Owen – organizer

Peter and **Olive Spencer** – couple in their eighties

Mary and **Elizabeth Brownlow** – spinster sisters in choir since their Sunday school days

Bruce Edison – former rock group singer

Keith Turner – still in the St Mark's Church choir, but comes along to the Can't Sing Singers too

St Mark's Church:

James – vicar at the church for two years
Ellie – vicar's wife; knows Kath, Manager of Hope Hall, because they both run in the park
Gregory and **Fiona Palmer** – new Musical Director at the church and his wife

Playgroup:

Jen and **Rob** – organizer and her garage mechanic husband
Carol, **Phil** and **Little Joe** – senior helper and her husband and toddler; childhood friend of Jen

Beavers:

Andy – "Bear"
Gary, **Karen**, **Toby** and **Max Knights** – Toby and Max have just joined Beavers; Gary is their main caregiver in the day and works from home as a graphic designer
Claire, **Nigel**, son **Josh Hughes** – Josh attends Beavers. Claire's parents, Bernard and Ruth, don't get on with her husband, Nigel

Knit and Natter Club:

Elaine Clarke – organizer

Down Memory Lane Club:

Jean – dementia care therapist
Bill Cartwright, **Ruby** and **Celia** – members

Women's Institute:

Barbara Longstone – formidable Chair of the WI

PAM RHODES

Summer's out at Hope Hall

COMING APRIL 2021

Catch up with Kath and the rest of her Hope Hall
friends as summer comes to Hope Hall!